JOHN JAPUNTICH

Atropos

This novel is entirely a work of fiction. The names, characters and incidents portrayed in it are the work of the author's imagination. Any resemblance to actual persons, living or dead, events or localities is entirely coincidental.

First edition

This book was professionally typeset on Reedsy.
Find out more at reedsy.com

Contents

Acknowledgement

Writing a novel is a long and arduous journey that no one travels alone. Many people have helped me along the way. Some by giving me the encouragement that I needed, others by reading chapters and giving feedback, and some that just let me bounce all my crazy ideas off them.

I'd like to start by thanking my good friend and fellow author Amanda Bullen. Not only did Amanda give me constant encouragement but she also meticulously proofread every chapter for grammar, sentence structure, spelling, as well as character and plot development. I don't think I could have done it without her. Thank you, Amanda.

My brother and sister, Micah Japuntich and Aimee Piland were also instrumental in my writing process. I can't thank my brother enough for the countless hours he spent on the phone, patiently listening to me talk about the book and giving me solid plot advice. Not once did he ever make me feel like he was tired of talking about it, even though I'm certain there were times when he was. My sister gave me the best advice for character and plot development and never let me take short cuts. She didn't hold back when there were things she felt could be better explored and the novel is better for her insights. I couldn't ask for better siblings, than you, Micah and Aimee.

Next, I'd like to thank my beta readers, Mike Burrows, Ray Mancil, Marko Obert, and Amy Gabbard. Thank you, guys, for taking the time to read the first draft and giving me honest feedback. Special thanks to Ray for reading the final draft as well.

Finally, I need to express my gratitude to my parents, Tony and Vickie Japuntich. Thank you, mom and dad, for instilling in me the love of reading and science. Without this foundation I would not be the man I am today.

Prologue

3.6 billion years BTE (Before the Event)

The surface of the primordial sea tossed and churned angrily, while lightning from the heavens tickled its cross swells. Despite the tumultuous waters, there were no shores for the waves to crash against. No mountains, no plains, no rivers, no forests, nor land of any kind, only the rolling seas and the endless sky. Even with the indignant sea and sky, there was a calmness to this sterile world, for there was no life to give it purpose. The stark beauty of this lonely planet might have endured, if not for a peculiar event that occurred that day. Deep beneath the stormy surface, where the seas were warm and still, the first single-cell organism appeared. The mother of all life was primitive when compared to her descendants, with no nucleus or organelles, yet she had an attribute that no single-cell organism has had since: she was aware.

As the Last Universal Common Ancestor (LUCA), she had no name for herself, for she had no one to distinguish herself from. LUCA's sole existence consisted of drifting in the current, exchanging protein molecules with the surrounding sea through her semipermeable membrane. She lived in a persistent state of bliss as she drifted in the warm water spewing from the deep-sea vents.

LUCA's state of nirvana continued for what seemed an eternity until she started having new thoughts. These thoughts were different from her normal thoughts of warmth and endless bliss; these were thoughts of memory. She remembered that she had a purpose beyond simple, blissful drifting in the warm, soothing waters. She remembered her sole reason for existence was to populate this barren world with descendants like herself, but she had no idea how to accomplish this feat. As her memory further awakened, the feeling that she must procreate became all-consuming, and it now dominated her entire existence. No longer was she calm or blissful; now she was driven with a single-minded purpose to accomplish her mission.

LUCA's contemplations abruptly ended, and relief swept through her microscopic body as she surmised what she must do to reproduce: replicate her genetic code and divide into two equally perfect copies of herself. Her relief soon turned to horror as she realized that she would lose her consciousness, her very being, when she began to divide. As she commenced to copy her code in preparation for the division, she grew forlorn at her impending death but felt compelled to complete this mission, so she could begin another. This burst of awareness brought her comfort when the division process began, and as her consciousness began to fade, she knew that somewhere in the deep future, she would again become conscious; that's when her real mission would begin.

3.6 billion years later

37 years BTE (Before the Event)

Ken smiled as the familiar odor of greasy hamburgers and craft beer greeted him while he walked into Monahan's Irish Pub and Grill. Three years in Japan had dulled his memories of this place somewhat, but his fondness for it returned as his olfactory sense summoned images of happier times. He glanced in several booths, looking for his old friend, but he was not to be found in any of his regular spots. *Perhaps he's running late,* Ken mused to himself.

"That's right, Your Honor, a good goat will do that." He heard his friend's voice ring out, followed by a cacophony of laughter from the people around him.

Ken walked up to the bar where the commotion originated and said, "Hello, Nathan, it looks like you started without me."

Nathan's eyes lit up as he turned away from his friends and saw Ken. "Ken! There you are. Man, it's been a long time!" He embraced Ken, and after they clapped each other's back a few times, he stepped back and pointed to his friends. "Oh yeah, this is Karen, Chad, Tiffany, Bobby, Alice, and ... Toby. Did I get that right?"

"Yeah, you got all of us," Toby replied.

"And this is my old friend Ken Takahashi. We went to college together right in here in Palo Alto," Nathan said.

"Nice to meet you guys," Ken replied.

Nathan pointed to the bar and said, "Come on, Ken, let's get a pitcher and grab a booth. We've got lots of catching up to do." He turned toward his six other friends and said, "It was nice meeting you guys. I'm sure we'll talk later."

After they were seated in a booth Ken nodded toward the bar and said, "You just met those guys?"

"Yeah, it's kinda funny, actually. I was trying to pick up Karen, the cute blonde, and then all the others walked in, including her boyfriend, Chad. So, I had to change tactics."

Ken laughed. "I see you haven't lost your touch. You had the whole group hanging on your every word when I walked up."

"Well, that's a pretty funny story."

"No, I'm serious, man. You should be a politician."

"Who, me? Nah, I'm just a simple economist. Or at least I will be," Nathan said as he refilled both of their glasses.

"Oh yeah, how's grad school going?" Ken asked.

"It's going really well. I'm close to finishing my dissertation."

"Oh wow, I didn't know you were working on a PhD."

Nathan nodded as he said, "Yeah, I want to teach when I'm done, so kinda need the PhD. Hey, how is it going working for your dad?"

"Frustrating at times, but I feel like I'm making progress. Dad just promoted me to VP of research and development." Ken stared into his beer as he remembered that the promotion was more to placate him than anything else. If his father really believed in him, he would have promoted him to VP of operations. Now, Ken felt like he was pigeonholed in a dead-end position.

"That's fantastic, congratulations. How in the hell can that be frustrating?" Nathan asked.

"Trust me, it's not as good as it sounds but it's really because

Dad and I don't share the same vision. He's stuck in the past, hardware and robotics, but I want to steer the company more into biotech."

"Biotech?" Nathan said as he signaled the waiter. "What kind of biotech?"

Ken looked around to ensure no one was eavesdropping before he said, "I'm working on a brain-computer interface."

"A brain-computer interface?"

"Ssshhhh!" Ken said as he again glanced around the bar. "Yeah, and I'm not talking about plugging electrodes into mice so they can give themselves food pellets. I'm talking about having the internet in your brain. Having things in the internet overlay your vision as you walk around. I'm talking about a true virtual world but integrated into the real world and so much more."

"But your dad's just not into it, huh?"

That's the understatement of the century, Ken thought to himself as he remembered the argument that had ensued when he pleaded with his father to fund the interface project.

"Yeah, he won't give me the money I need to make the breakthroughs I know we can make," Ken said as their burgers arrived.

"So, that's where the frustration comes from. I get it," Nathan said as he took a bite out of his burger.

You get nothing, Ken thought as he decided to change the subject. "Almost as frustrating as that," he said, pointing to the TV that was mounted above their booth.

Nathan finished chewing and said, "Yeah, I saw that on the news today. All robotic probes for anything other than low Earth orbit. No more manned missions to the moon or Mars."

Ken slammed his fork on the table and said, "Well that's

total bullshit! NASA has lost all perspective."

"Yeah, I'm not crazy about it either, but what do you mean?"

"If we don't start colonizing other places in the solar system, we're doomed to extinction. We can't keep all of our eggs in one basket right here on Earth," Ken replied.

Nathan leaned back in his chair as he gathered his thoughts. "It's funny that you mention colonizing, because that's what I've been working on for my dissertation."

"You've been working on colonizing the solar system?"

Nathan laughed and said, "No, I've been studying the economics behind human colonization and expansion throughout history."

Ken cocked an eyebrow as he realized his old friend had caught him off guard. "And how does that apply to NASA's decision to give up on manned missions beyond Earth orbit?"

"Well, for one, I think I've debunked the popularly held opinion that people migrate to strange lands due to some mystical wanderlust that resides deep inside everyone. On closer scrutiny, it doesn't hold up; people don't pick up and move great distances just to see what's there. They do so because they think they have to."

"Yeah, I get it. People migrate for better opportunities for them and their families. But what about the great explorers like Magellan and Columbus? You can't tell me they didn't have that wanderlust," Ken replied.

Nathan nodded. "Maybe they did, but they were also seeking fame and most especially fortune. They wanted to get rich, man."

"So, your entire dissertation is basically 'follow the money.' Is that right?"

Nathan chuckled. "Well, that's kinda oversimplifying

things, but that's the overall gist of it. Every major human migration I've studied so far was based on some major economic reasons and had major economic consequences. Sure, people also migrate to escape persecution, be it from violence or otherwise, but even that's usually rooted in economics when you break it down."

"That's interesting and all, but what does that have to do with NASA's decision to abandon manned missions?" Ken thought he saw where this was going, but he wanted to hear Nathan spell it out.

"All I'm saying is that when you look at it from a purely logical point of view, NASA's decision actually makes sense. There's no reason to send people to Mars, because people will never want to live there."

"So, you're saying there's no economic reason for people to migrate to Mars?"

"Exactly! There's nothing there, and the cost of living there would be astronomical and economically prohibitive. There will never be a colony on Mars; the most we'll ever have on Mars will be a scientific outpost like what we have in Antarctica."

"I don't know, man, that's a bold statement," Ken said as he furrowed his brow.

Nathan smiled as he handed his empty plate to the waitress, took a sip of his beer, and said, "Think about it, man. Why don't we have people living in Antarctica? And I don't mean the scientific outposts. I'm talking about a self-sustaining colony."

"Well, for one reason, because there's a treaty that forbids it."

"No, that's not the reason. It's because there's nothing

there. There're no animals, no plants, oh, and it's also the most inhospitable place on Earth. Why do you think everyone signed that treaty anyway?"

"Because they knew no one wanted to live there anyway?"

"Exactly, and because it would be cost prohibitive to exploit any natural resources that might be there. Antarctica is way more hospitable than Mars and has more natural resources; Mars makes Antarctica look like a paradise."

"All right, buddy, you make a strong argument," Ken said as he decided to throw his friend a curveball. "But what happens when we overpopulate Earth?"

Nathan smiled as he clinked his mug with Ken's. "Well, there's still an entire continent we haven't settled, and then there's the oceans, but it won't come to that anyway."

"Why not?"

"Because birth rates are already slowing, and eventually, they will even off. Besides, we could never send enough people off-planet to make a dent in the population here on Earth."

"Yeah, you're right about that," Ken conceded.

"Oh, here's an interesting thought experiment." Nathan's face lit up as he thought about it. "Do you remember the Viking probes we landed on Mars back in the '70s?"

"Of course."

"Now, just for the sake of conjecture, let's suppose the landers not only found life on Mars, but what if they discovered that Mars was teeming with life? What if they found that Mars had a nitrogen-oxygen atmosphere?"

"Well, that's preposterous, but I'll play along. What if?" Ken asked.

"I propose that we would have sent a manned mission within the decade and that there would be a colony on Mars right now," Nathan asserted.

"With 1970s' technology? I don't think so."

"That's what I'm saying. We would have invented the technology if there would have been a reason to go there," Nathan insisted.

"I see what you're saying," Ken agreed. "Damn, you still know how to construct an argument, and on the fly too."

Nathan laughed. "Just because I'm good at it doesn't mean it's not true. NASA's decision really does make sense once you break it down."

NASA is run by a bunch of American idiots, Ken thought as he replied. "That doesn't mean I have to like it, because that means we're doomed to extinction, since we'll never settle the rest of the solar system."

"There are always extra-solar planets," Nathan said as he signaled the waitress for another pitcher. "If we discovered an Earthlike planet in a nearby star system, I bet people would want to go."

Ken thought for a moment. "You're right, people would want to go, but I don't think we'd be able to do it."

"Of course, it would be expensive."

"Way too expensive," Ken said as he leaned forward. "There's no way one nation could afford to send a colony ship to another star system."

"Are you about to school the economist?" Nathan smiled as he continued. "So, how expensive do you think it would be?"

"Oh, I wouldn't dream of it, but this is something I've studied." Ken paused as he leaned back in his seat. "The Apollo program devoured nearly 5 percent of the United States's annual budget for ten years."

"Yeah, it was ridiculously expensive," Nathan agreed. "And

people wonder why we stopped sending people to the moon."

"And that was just to send a small capsule with three men to the moon. Now imagine the cost of sending a ship with thousands of people across interstellar space to a planet in another solar system."

"Thousands of people?" Nathan asked.

"Yeah, you'd need thousands of people to have a genetically sustainable colony."

"Yeah, I guess you're right, and the ship would need to be really big, because it would have to be a generational ship, as the voyage would take at least a hundred years," Nathan said.

"See what I mean? No one nation could afford such a project. I mean, you're talking about a project that might take a century to complete and the cost would be ..."

"Astronomical?" Nathan said.

"Ha ha ha! Yeah, the cost would literally be astronomical. I think we'd need the economic output of the entire world for the better part of a century to sponsor such a venture." Ken paused and took another drink of his beer. "So, I guess we're destined for extinction after all."

"Relax, buddy, the sun won't go supernova for billions of years. Humanity will have a nice run when it's all said and done."

"I just wish it didn't have to be that way, though. There's got to be a way off this rock!" Ken said.

Nathan looked around the bar before he said, "Well, there might just be a way."

"Are you serious? What do you mean?" Ken asked.

Nathan leaned in close and whispered, "We could take over the world and set it all in motion."

Ken laughed and pounded the table with his fist. "Man, I

miss these conversations!" He abruptly stopped laughing when he noticed Nathan wasn't laughing at all. In fact, his face was deadpan serious.

Chapter 1: Visions of Ahab

The most important event in the history of humankind began with a whimper, for it wasn't realized until after the fact that anything had even happened. —Zacharia Jones, Out of Darkness: The Event Chronicles

Date: 0 AE (After the Event)

John Fitzpatrick knew something was wrong with the world. It started with a nagging feeling following Celia's death three weeks ago, but slowly the feeling had blossomed into certainty. Initially, he assumed it was part of the grieving process, but now he knew better. Humanity was being manipulated, and he had the evidence to support it. Now came the hard part: convincing his old boss.

John decided he was tired of waiting, so he eased himself off the soft reception couch and as he approached the administrative assistant's desk said, "If you'll just tell the director I'm here, I'm sure he'll want to see me."

The fresh-faced administrative assistant looked up from

behind his computer monitors and said, "Yes, Mr. Fitzpatrick, like I've told you, the director is busy and won't be able to see you today."

"Did you tell him who is waiting to see him and how far I've come?" John asked impatiently.

"Yes sir, he's aware. Perhaps if you had called and scheduled an appointment, the deputy director would be able to see you today, but as it is, I'm afraid his calendar is full, and before you ask, I realize you're a former agent and friend of Deputy Director Feinstein."

"Thank you. I'll just wait right here until he's available," John said as he returned to the couch.

He sat outside the deputy director's office all day, and no one came or left from the director's office. *Maybe he's not even here,* John thought to himself as he considered leaving. Perhaps he should consider other alternatives.

Finally, at 6:15 p.m., the assistant answered the phone, and after a moment walked to the double oak doors of the director's office, opened them, and said, "The director will see you now."

As John walked through the doors, Mark Feinstein met him in front of his desk. While they shook hands, he said, "Good to see you, John. It's been a long time. The Bureau hasn't been the same since you left."

* * *

Three weeks earlier

John's breath visibly condensed as he slowly exhaled into the cold north Georgia air. Glancing down at his watch, he realized he hadn't moved from this spot in over an hour; one hour since

Celia had been lowered into the cold ground in front of him. The rest of the funeral party had already left, but John refused to leave with them, and here he was, standing in place like a grave monument, staring at his wife's fresh grave as a cold mist started to fall.

John flipped the collar of his overcoat up as he felt a chill that started in his skin but went deep inside to the core of his being. He shivered and thought to himself, *What am I going to now, Celia? I've never felt so alone in my entire life.* John found this thought slightly amusing, as he had been alone for most of his adult life. The Bureau had been his life, or rather the cases he worked and the criminals he profiled had been his focus for thirty-five years. That all changed when he met Celia six years ago. She showed him that there was more to life than solving puzzles. Now she was dead, and John was beginning to wish he could join her.

He wiped his eyes and looked around the graveyard, and he remembered that his mother's grave was only a few meters away. As he approached it, the mist turned into flurries. *Oh great, now I will have to deal with all of the idiots that lose their minds and forget how to drive when they see a little snow,* John thought to himself as he realized that he hadn't been to his mother's grave since her death ten years earlier.

He looked down at her headstone: *Here lies Ophelia Fitzpatrick, beloved wife, mother, and schoolteacher.* She was so much more than that but had insisted that's all she wanted on her headstone. In fact, he had taken liberties adding the *beloved* part.

As no one was around, John spoke out loud to his mother, even though he didn't believe any part of her still existed. "Hi, Mom. I'm sorry I haven't been by since you died. I do think of you all the time, though. I wish you were here now to tell me what to do. I'm so lost."

John was almost shocked when he heard his mother's voice in his head. "John Henry Fitzpatrick! I raised you better than this, standing in the freezing rain, feeling sorry for yourself, talking out loud to a dead person, no less. You're gonna catch pneumonia standing out here like a cow."

He chuckled to himself as he thought, *Yeah, that's just like Mom, always the pragmatist.*

He was shocked out of his reflection by a female voice walking up behind him. "John Fitzpatrick."

The hair on the nape of his neck stood up as he thought to himself, *Now I'm really losing my mind.* John turned and looked at the approaching middle-aged woman. She was attractive, with a mix of Asian, African, and European features, and John immediately recognized her. When she stopped a couple of meters away, he said, "It's good to see you, Alicia."

Alicia stared at him for several long seconds before John said with a smile, "Are you gonna give me a hug or what?"

She closed the distance between them and gave him the requested hug as she replied, "Oh, John, I'm so sorry. Why are you out here all by yourself?"

After the brief embrace, John nodded and said, "You know I don't like crowds."

"Yeah, I went to your house, but no one was there. Went by the funeral home, and the funeral director said you were still out here and didn't want to be bothered."

"Mr. Williams knows me pretty well, I guess. I couldn't stand to be around all those people feeling sorry for me. Didn't want to be at the house while everyone brings food, and then they won't go away. I know they mean well, but it's just too much."

"I know what you mean. Sometimes you just need to be left alone. I'm sorry I didn't make it in time for the service, but my flight from Philly was delayed. Jack sends his condolences, but he wasn't up for traveling," Alicia replied.

John nodded as he acknowledged, "Yeah, I heard. So, how is my old buddy? I heard he wasn't doing well."

Alicia extended her umbrella as the wet flurries were turning into light snow. "He's actually doing remarkably well and on his way to recovery, I believe."

The shock on John's face showed. "I heard he was diagnosed with stage four pancreatic cancer and it was terminal."

"Yeah, that's what they said, but he started feeling better, so they did another scan, and it appears he's in remission. The doctors are calling it a miracle. I'm just thankful I'm getting my husband back." Alicia looked down as she realized her last remark might sting a bit.

John stared down at her for a few moments. For twenty years, he and Jack had been partners in the Bureau as well as best friends. Alicia with her striking beauty, quick wit, and warm personality had been a part of that friendship. Over the years, John and Alicia had grown close, but he suppressed the feelings he had for her deep inside, as he respected Jack too much to ever even consider crossing that line. She had set him up with several of her friends, but none of them ever worked out. No woman had ever understood him like Alicia until Celia came into his life. As he looked down at her, John realized that those feelings for her that he buried deep inside all those years ago were now completely gone, as were any other warm feelings he might have. They had been stamped out and replaced with grief and helplessness.

"That's great news, Alicia. I'll have to give Jack a call," John finally replied.

"I'm sorry it came out that way, John. I know it's tough to hear about someone else's remarkable recovery from cancer when you just lost your wife to it. I know you're thinking, why couldn't it have been Celia?"

John's voice wavered. "Does that make me a bad person?"

"No, honey, that just makes you human. I know sometimes you don't feel like you're human, but you are. Despite all your quirks, you're still human," she said with a warm smile.

John hugged her again. "You know what makes this so hard? I went most of my life trying to find a woman who understood me and would put up with me, but before Celia, the Bureau was my life."

"You were the best profiler in the FBI. At least that's what Jack always said," Alicia injected.

"Yeah, Jack always exaggerated my abilities."

"Jack thinks very highly of you, that's true, but everyone in the FBI agreed with him, and you know it," she replied.

John ignored her last statement as he remembered yet again how things had played out. Before Celia, he didn't have anything outside of the Bureau. He lived, ate, and breathed the Bureau. He never knew he could love someone so much, but a year after they were married, she was diagnosed with ovarian cancer. He retired from the Bureau shortly afterward to take care of her.

Alicia, noticing that John was staring at the ground, embraced him once again. "Oh, John, I'm so sorry."

"It's okay."

As Alicia hugged him, he remembered that for three years, Celia had fought the cancer, and they'd thought she'd won, until the bad news last year that the cancer was back. Once that happened, she went downhill fast.

As the hug concluded, John stepped back and said, “Today I buried the love of my life. Today is the first day of the rest of my life, and I don’t have the slightest idea what I should do.”

“You’ll figure it out, John. You always do. You’re the smartest, most resourceful person I’ve ever known,” Alicia assured him.

John smiled at her. “Thanks, Alicia. That means a lot to me.”

She grabbed him by the arm to lead him away. “Now, let’s get you out of this nasty weather before you catch pneumonia.”

John stopped and laughed so hard that the tears flowed freely. “Oh my, thank you, Mom, I mean Alicia, I really needed that.”

She smiled, “Well, I have no idea what was so funny, but you’re welcome.”

* * *

The next day, John drove his pickup truck into Cedartown. As he walked into Williams Funeral Home, the only black funeral home in town, he found it strange that in this day and age, churches and funeral homes in the South were still mostly segregated. When he saw Marshall Williams, the owner, he said, “Good morning, Mr. Williams.”

“Hello John, you’re looking better this morning. I was a little worried about you yesterday until your friend showed up. I’m glad there was someone that could comfort you during this difficult time.”

"Thank you, Mr. Williams. Alicia is an old friend, and it was nice she could make it, even if her stay was brief." John paused for a moment as he considered a way to change the subject. He didn't think he could take much more sympathy talk. "Oh, and I meant to tell you yesterday that you're looking really good, Mr. Williams. If you don't mind me asking, how old are you now? Aren't you my mother's age?"

Mr. Williams smiled and nodded. "Yes, I remember when your mother was a little girl, and to answer your question, I'm ninety-three years young now."

John knew Mr. Williams was older than he looked but was genuinely shocked by his answer. "Wow, that's older than I was thinking. You really do look good. What's your secret?"

"No secret, young man, just good clean living. I eat right, get lots of exercise, go to church three times a week, and I work six days a week." He paused for a moment before continuing. "Now that you mention it, I've felt better the last few weeks than I have in years. Feel like I could run ten miles." He laughed a little.

"That's incredible," John replied, relieved to have the focus off of him.

"I assume you're here to close out your account, so if you'll follow me to my office, we can wrap things up."

"Yes, sir," John replied as he followed the spry old man back to his office.

While they walked down the long hallway, John glanced into several of the viewing rooms on either side and noticed that they were all empty. He was struck by how sterile, even hospital-like the funeral home was, and now that he thought about it, every funeral home he'd ever been in had been the same—sterile and cold. Not very homelike at all.

After John was finished signing the necessary documents, he said, "It sure is quiet around here. Is everything okay?"

Mr. Williams frowned slightly. "Now that you mention it, business has slowed down the last few months. I've had to lay off a couple of my part-time workers."

"That's weird. I thought the mortuary business was the steadiest business there is. It's like my father always said, 'There's people dying today that ain't ever died before.'"

"That's what I always thought too," Mr. Williams said, "but all of the funeral homes in town are struggling right now. Mrs. Fitzpatrick is only the third person I've buried this week."

"That's strange," John said as he stood up and extended his hand. "I've got to run some errands before I head back to the farm. Thanks again, Mr. Williams."

"You're welcome, John; let me know if I can assist you in any other way."

"Will do," John replied as he walked out. A strange feeling was itching in the back of his mind, but he was unable to quantify it yet.

* * *

Four days later

John was at home in his office, staring at the computer, trying to decide what he was going to do with the rest of his life. He couldn't stay here at the farm in this house, he knew that. He loved taking care of their small farm with Celia, but now that she was gone, he just wasn't interested in tending horses, donkeys, and chickens anymore. The farm and the house were all Celia's babies anyway. Every room in the house had Celia written all over it—colorful floral patterns everywhere, except for his office. That's why everyone always remarked about how warm their house felt. Of course, none of them ever saw his office; just a plain desk with a computer, printer, and two bookcases full of criminal justice textbooks. There were a few pictures on the walls with him and various FBI dignitaries, but other than that it could have been a library room.

He decided he would sell the farm, but then what? He was past retirement age for the FBI, so going back to his old job was out of the question. Maybe he should run for sheriff in the upcoming election? No, that's a terrible idea. Maybe he could teach some classes at one of the local universities or colleges; now that thought interested him somewhat.

Later, John was at home in his recliner trying to get up the motivation needed to go tend to the animals. He thought he should go ahead and put the farm up for sale, but he didn't feel like calling the real estate broker; might be easier to just burn it all down.

On the way to the kitchen, his phone started buzzing, and he decided to answer it, as it was someone he didn't mind talking to. "Hello, Maxine."

"Hi, Uncle John. I'm so sorry I couldn't make the funeral. Are you okay? I feel like I should have checked on you earlier." Maxine Collins was John's much younger cousin, but she had always called him Uncle John due to their age difference, and she had always adored him. The feeling was mutual, as she was a sweet child and had grown into a lovely woman.

"I'm fine, Maxine, thanks for asking. To tell you the truth, I'm more bored than anything. What I wouldn't give for a good case to dive into. How's everything with you? Are you still working at the hospital?"

"Yeah, I'm still working in data analytics at Grady Memorial, at least for now," Maxine said forlornly.

"What do you mean? You're not in trouble, are you?"

"Oh no, nothing like that. It's just that they've had to cut back staffing on some of the floors, and there's talk of closing one of the medical units," Maxine explained.

John's interest was piqued now. "Why, what's going on?"

"Admission rates are really down the last few months, and this month they're down 50 percent."

"Is that normal? Do they normally fluctuate like that?"

Maxine paused a moment before she replied. "I mean, it's normal for the admission rates to fluctuate a little bit month to month but not drop this much this fast. Our mortality rates are also way down the last few months, but no one seems concerned about that."

Something in the back of John's mind was coming awake now. "Can you give me the exact numbers for the mortality rates for the last few months?"

"Yeah, sure, just give me a few minutes while I pull up the exact numbers."

After a moment, Maxine came back on the line. "Uncle John, are you ever going to do video calling? It sure would be nice to see your face while we talk."

"I guess I'm old-fashioned and just prefer regular phone calls," he said with a laugh.

"Well, you gotta join modern society. Heck, next week, I'm getting a TICI."

"You're getting a what? A tiki bar?"

"No, not a tiki bar, A TICI." She then spelled it out before continuing. "It stands for Takahashi Industries Cerebral Interface."

"Oh, you mean that brain implant thing that lets you interface directly with the internet without using a computer or phone. You're really getting that done?"

"You're funny, Uncle John. Oh, here's the data for you. So, three months ago, there was a 10 percent drop in our mortality rates. The next month it dropped another 25 percent, and this month it's down 50 percent."

John thought for a moment before asking, "Do you know if other hospitals in the area are having the same situation?"

"Yes, I know at least three other hospitals in town are struggling like us in the last few months with decreased admissions and I assume decreased mortality rates as well."

John's mind was spinning now as he processed this new data. *The funeral homes struggling, hospitals struggling, Jack's miraculous recovery; something is happening.* "Thank you so much, Maxine. I owe you big time."

"Owe me for what, Uncle John?"

"Ask me again sometime. It was really good talking to you. Why don't we go to dinner soon? I'll take you and your fiancé out someplace nice."

"That sounds great. It was so good talking to you too. Let me know if you need anything."

"I will. Bye, Maxine."

* * *

The next morning, John went for a run for the first time in six months. He ran three miles and felt like he could have kept going, but he didn't want to overdo it. After showering and eating a light breakfast, he was in the living room, staring at his computer and his phone, trying to decide if he should go down this rabbit hole or not. He considered that he might be slightly crazy and his mind not be working normally due to his emotional state, but it was getting harder and harder to ignore the feeling that was buzzing round his head. It was the same feeling he always had when he was on the verge of solving a case. When all the evidence was spinning around in his head and the first pieces were starting to form the puzzle, but it was still incomplete.

This is madness, he thought as he picked up the phone and dialed it.

After two rings, he heard Alicia's voice on the other end. "Hello, John. Jack is in the bathroom at the moment, but he should be right out. So, how are you holding up?"

"I'm doing fine, really. I ran three miles this morning, and I'm investigating something interesting that may or may not turn into something groundbreaking."

"Oh, do tell, John. That sounds interesting! Here's Jack now. You'll have to tell me later."

"Hello, John," his old partner Jack Fenton said as he took the phone from his wife.

"Hello, Jack, or should I say Lazarus after your remarkable recovery?"

"Yeah, it's remarkable, that's for sure. I'm still pretty weak, but I'm getting better every day," Jack replied. "So sorry to hear about Celia. How are you feeling, old buddy?"

"Like I was telling Alicia, I'm doing fine. I ran three miles this morning, and I feel great. I've even started investigating something that's captured my interest. Care to hear about it and give me some feedback?" John asked.

"Sure, buddy, tell me what you got."

"Well, it's gonna sound crazy at first, but hear me out. After

Celia's funeral, I got to talking with the funeral director, and he told me that business was way down and has been steadily falling for several months and that all the other funeral homes in the area are having the same problem. Well, that piqued my curiosity, so I started digging, and all of the hospitals in the Atlanta area have experienced decreased death rates the last few months."

"John, you're rambling here, where are you going with this?" Jack interrupted.

John was slightly annoyed as he realized the conversation wasn't going to go the way he imagined, but he continued unabated. "Like I was saying, death rates in these hospitals dropped 10 percent three months ago, then 25 percent the following month, and they're down 50 percent so far this month. Not only that, but admission rates are down by similar rates. It's so bad that Grady has closed down a medical nursing floor."

"Hospital mortality rates—what kind of case are you working, John?"

"It's not just that, it's your remarkable recovery from stage-four cancer. I've spoken with several old people recently who say they feel better than they have in years. Hell, I feel better than I have in years. I'm telling you, something is going on, something big!"

Jack paused for a moment before he replied, "John will you listen to yourself? You're recovering from the biggest emotional shock of your life, and you're retreating into the one thing that brings you comfort: your work. You need a problem to solve, a puzzle to piece together, and since you're no longer with the Bureau, you're creating something that's not there. I think it's great you feel good doing this, but please be careful, and don't go overboard, okay?"

John considered Jack's viewpoint for a moment before continuing, "I'm telling you, Jack, there's something going on here. I can feel it."

"Honestly, John, this sounds like your obsession with the Ghost. You were one of the best profilers in the Bureau, but your obsession with the Ghost nearly cost you your job and certainly hurt your reputation. Because of that, everyone at the Bureau still thinks of you as that genius profiler who was more than a little quirky."

Why does it always come to this? John thought. *Every time I come up with an unconventional idea or solution, I always get the Ghost thrown in my face. I should have known better.* "Just because we never caught the guy doesn't mean he didn't exist. I still say he got old and died."

"Okay, John, I'm not going to rehash this old argument again. Just be careful, okay, buddy?"

John knew that Jack had his best interest at heart, so he replied, "Sure thing. Hey, it was great talking to you, and I'm so glad you're getting better. Let's talk again soon."

"Yeah, let's stay in touch. Bye, John."

Time for a different approach, John thought to himself as he hung up the phone.

* * *

After two weeks of no reply from his other old friend at the Bureau, Mark Feinstein, John knew something was wrong. He had emailed the deputy director five times over the last week, and in each email, he had laid out his evidence for the declining death rates and that something was happening, but he had received no replies. He'd called the director's office several more times, and his assistant said he was in but couldn't take his calls. *It didn't make sense for Mark to ignore him like this. Something must be going on for Mark not to take his calls or respond to his emails, so he decided it was time for a road trip to Virginia to see the deputy director in person.*

After John and the deputy director finished shaking hands, he said, "Thanks for taking the time to see me, Mark. I know you're busy."

Mark walked around the desk, and as he took his seat, he motioned for John to do the same. "Of course, John. You know I'll always make time for you. Oh, I was very sad to hear of your wife's passing last month. I'm sorry I couldn't make the funeral, but things have been kind of crazy around here recently. Are you okay?"

"Thank you. Every day is a struggle, but I'm managing."

Mark nodded. "Good, good. How are you enjoying retirement? Do you have any big plans?"

John sighed as the thought, *I don't have time for this crap.* He replied, "Have you had a chance to read my emails? Do you know why I'm here?"

Mark cracked a slight smile. "You never were one for small talk, were you? Yes, I read your email five minutes before calling you back."

"What do you think? Are you going to open an investigation?"

"You're not going to let this go, are you?"

"I think you know me well enough to know better than that," John replied.

Mark sighed as he leaned back in his chair and put his hands behind his head, "Okay, here's the deal. Oh, and I think it goes without saying that everything I'm about to tell you doesn't leave this room."

"Of course," John answered as he leaned forward.

"Your suspicions are all correct. There is definitely something going on. Death rates have been falling for several months now, and not just here but around the world. But it's much larger than that, John," the director said as he leaned forward in his chair as if someone might overhear him. "There are reports of people with incurable diseases recovering. People with Alzheimer's are recovering. Something is going on, and no one has ever seen anything like it before."

John felt as if time were somehow slowing down as his mind opened and all of the implications of this new information began to spin around in his head. "Any idea or theories as to what's causing this? Do we know if it's natural or man-made?"

"No, we don't know what's causing it, but it does appear to be spreading almost like a disease, but much faster."

"Could this be some kind of biological attack?" John asked.

"It's possible, but so far there's no sign of that. Hell, it's doing the opposite of that; it's curing people, not killing them. Whatever it is."

John thought for a moment. "How is the public going to react to this once it comes out? This is going to go public very soon, you know. If I figured it out, you can rest assured others have too. Quite frankly, I'm surprised the press isn't already all over this."

Mark nodded. "You're right, of course. That's why we've been trying to figure out what's going on, and I think we're getting close. Regardless, the president is preparing to address the public very soon, probably before the end of the week."

As John's mind was processing everything, a thought suddenly jumped to his attention. "You said that there are reports of Alzheimer's patients recovering. What if this phenomenon is not only stopping people from dying—what if it's actually reversing the aging process? That would explain what we're seeing. I know that I physically I feel better than I have in years, and I have for several weeks now."

"I'm sure the medical team that's investigating this is pursuing all possibilities, but I'll follow up with them," Mark assured him.

John stood up and paced around his chair for a moment, barely able to conceal his excitement. This was the chance he was looking for; a chance to get back in the game. "Mark, I know I'm past retirement age, but you need me on this one. You could bring me back and assign me as a special adviser or something."

"Thank you, John. I think we have all of the angles covered, but I'll keep you in mind if something changes," Mark said as he started walking toward the door. "Please keep all of this to yourself until the president gives his address."

As John shook the director's hand and walked out the door, he replied, "Thank you for your time."

Once John was on the open interstate, he put the car on cruise control and let his mind explore all the possibilities and implications from the last several weeks. Immediately his mind went to Celia; she may have been one of the last people on Earth to die of natural causes. John would mourn the colossal tragedy of that thought later, but right now it was just data for his mind to analyze. If the statistics trended out, the last person to die of natural causes would die within the next week, then the only deaths would be from accidents and violence.

If his hunch were correct and people were also reverse aging, and the birth rate continued at its current pace, then it would only take a few years for the Earth to overpopulate and for resources to become scarce. There would be famine, wars, and environmental devastation. In short, it would be hell on Earth.

John's thoughts were interrupted by the car's gas gauge warning him that he was nearly out of fuel, so he pulled off at the next exit. He was deeply disturbed by where his thoughts had taken him. He was almost certain that the phenomenon was not natural, but why would someone cause something like this to happen and not consider the consequences? Surely someone intelligent enough to cause this phenomenon was also smart enough to realize that it would cause catastrophe.

Once John was back on the road, he had a thought, one so strange that he wondered if it had occurred to anyone on the FBI's team. The idea was compelling, and John decided it couldn't wait for him to get home to verify, so he voice-activated his phone.

"Hello, Uncle John," Maxine said as she answered the call.

"Hi, Maxine, do you have time for another favor?"

"Always for you."

"I'm gonna have to take you and your fiancé out for dinner sometime soon."

"Aww, you're so sweet. What can I do for you?"

"Can you give me your birth rate numbers for the last few months? Just want to see if there's been any change recently."

"Sure, give me a minute, and let me get those numbers for you."

"Thanks again, Maxine."

After a few minutes, Maxine came back on the line. "I have your numbers. You ready?"

"Yeah, go ahead."

"So, for the last few months, the numbers are pretty steady, but this last month, births are down by 10 percent, and I knew you'd ask, so I went ahead and asked the other hospitals in the area, and they have the exact same numbers; steady until last month, then a 10 percent drop."

"Just like the beginning of the death rate drop," John mumbled to himself.

"What was that?"

"Oh, I was just saying thanks so much, Maxine. I really appreciate your help."

"No problem at all. I'm looking forward to that steak!" she replied.

"Oh, I'm taking you guys to the best restaurant in town. See you later," John said as he ended the call.

A slight smile showed on John's face as all the pieces came together in his head and he was certain of several things. The phenomenon was without a doubt man-made. Within the next few weeks no one will die of natural causes and within the next few months the last baby will be born. Then we will live in a society where the members never change. He hated that his old friend didn't think the Bureau needed him on this, but clearly, he was wrong. That might have damaged another man's ego, but John's only concern now was who, how, and why. He didn't have time for anything else. This will be the greatest mystery in human history, and John realized he was going to pursue it with every ounce of his being until he had the answers.

I will harpoon this whale if it's the last thing I do, John thought as the smile that was already on his face grew still larger. He turned up the music that had only been in the background before and put the pedal down.

Chapter 2: Resurrection Sins

The Event didn't pick and choose who would receive immortality.
Saints and sinners alike received their pardon from Death.
Perhaps some sleeping dogs should have been left alone.
— *Zacharia Jones,* Out of Darkness: The Event Chronicles

Date: 0 AE (After the Event)

Samuel Elijah Boone died. At least that's the way it seemed to him. Sam died slowly, like so many who survive the major killers of middle and old age. The decline started in his mid-seventies with simple forgetfulness, but by his early eighties, the world had become immersed in a fog that he could scarcely penetrate. His mental faculties were so diminished that he barely comprehended when his only daughter had him admitted to Fairview Nursing Home because she could no longer manage him at home. Gradually the fog consumed everything and dragged him into a darkness that became an unending dream.

At times he would rise out of the darkness and enter the fog again for brief periods, but as time passed, he did that less and less, until finally all he knew were the dreams. For Sam, life ended and the afterlife began. However, his body continued to live, after a fashion. As Sam dreamed, his body was motionless, but for a while, the nursing home staff was able to feed him. However, gradually he ate less and less, until finally, they were no longer able to feed him. His body grew weaker as the darkness became all-encompassing and the dreams ended. The death watch began.

The watch continued for several weeks, but death refused to come. Samuel's body hovered near the edge, yet he began to dream again. As Sam dreamed, his body moved, and one of the nursing assistants thought he might be hungry. When she put food into his mouth, he chewed and swallowed. Over the next few weeks, he continued to eat when the nursing assistants fed him, and gradually his body became stronger as he continued to dream in the darkness.

Sam rose from the darkness as the dreams subsided, and he once again entered the fog. He realized he was lying in a bed, and there was a middle-aged woman, with tears streaming down her face, sitting on the edge of the bed, holding his hand. She looked so familiar, but he struggled to remember her name or who she was. With a flood of memories, her identity finally came to him.

"Hello, Frances." He struggled to say his first words in six months.

"Dad, I can barely hear you," she said as she leaned forward. "Did you just call me by Mom's name?"

"Carolyn, my sweet child," Sam said as he squeezed her hand and realized her true identity. "When did you get so ... old?"

In between sobs, Carolyn replied, "Dad, this might be hard for you to hear, but you're eighty-five years old. I'm fifty-six now. You've had Alzheimer's for almost ten years and have been practically in a coma for the last six months. You were dying. Doctor Tyler says you should have been dead weeks ago and can't believe you're lucid again. He's calling it a miracle."

Even though Sam didn't comprehend everything she just said, he patted her hand and said, "Thank you, sweetie."

* * *

Over the next several weeks, Samuel gradually recovered his strength. As the fog slowly lifted, he remembered his life more and more. His resurrection was nearly complete, but something was missing, something he couldn't quite put his finger on. He could taste this missing part of his life but was unable to define it. The only thing he knew for certain was he yearned for it. He needed it, and until he figured out what was missing, he knew he wouldn't be complete.

One morning after breakfast, Carolyn and his nursing assistant, Tonya, were helping him walk around the room when something on the TV caught all of their attention. The president of the United States was about to make some kind of announcement.

"I bet he's gonna talk about all of the Alzheimer's patients that's been getting better," Tonya said as she eased Sam back in the bed.

Sam raised his eyebrows while he looked at his daughter and said, "So, I guess I'm not the only one?"

"No, Dad, apparently it's happening all over the world."

Tonya added, "A friend of mine works at St. Mary's Hospital, and she says death rates have gone way down over the last several weeks. Everyone is talking about it. My pastor says Jesus has stopped death, and he's coming back soon."

The president was now speaking. "My fellow Americans, sometime in the past several months, an event has occurred that is unprecedented in human history. We still don't understand how or why this has happened, but it appears that the normal aging process has stopped, and people have stopped dying of natural causes. From what we can tell, this event has happened worldwide. Leaders from around the world are meeting next week in New York City at the United Nations for an emergency session to discuss the implications of this event and how the world will deal with it."

The president set down the papers he was holding and looked directly into the camera as he continued. "I urge everyone to remain calm and to go about your business as usual. Our best scientists from around the world are investigating this phenomenon, and as soon as we know more, you will know more," The president paused and looked around the press corps in front of him. "I will now take questions." Every hand present shot up in the air hoping to get the president's attention.

As the president was taking questions, Sam looked at Carolyn and said, "From what he's saying and what's happened to me, it looks like not only has everyone stopped aging, but we're slowly reverse aging. I wonder how young we will get."

"I don't know. I'm still having trouble processing all of this. How did this happen? Are we immortal now? I don't know. I'm just so happy I have my father back," said Carolyn as she kissed Sam's forehead.

"Sweet Carolyn, I forget how hard this must have been for

you. For me it wasn't that bad. I just faded away. I didn't really know what was happening. While you, you had to deal with it every step of the way. You had to watch your father melt away before your eyes. I'm so sorry, dear," Sam said as a single tear trickled down his face.

Carolyn gave him a big hug. "There's no need for you to apologize. There was nothing you could do. You've always been the best dad in the world, and now you're back. I couldn't be happier."

* * *

Two weeks later, the nurse's aide was helping Sam add the final things to his suitcase. She said, "Miss Carolyn is bringing her car to the front in a few minutes, and then I'll take you out. You're the first of the Alzheimer's patients to leave. You've recovered so fast, Mr. Boone."

Sam looked at the wheelchair near the doorway and said, "I don't need that thing, you know. I'm walking fine now."

"I know, Mr. Boone. You're doing so good, but rules are rules," she said as she pulled the wheelchair around and motioned for Sam to sit in it.

As Tonya tried to help Sam into the chair, her young breasts rubbed against his left shoulder. Sam felt her soft bosom, and something stirred in him. He turned and looked upon her. She was now totally nude, and her large breasts glistened with sweat, beckoning him. A thin red line suddenly appeared on her neck from ear to ear. The thin line became a river as blood streamed onto her breast and down her naked body.

"Mr. Boone, are you okay?" Tonya asked as she realized Sam was looking at her with a blank stare and beads of sweat forming on his forehead.

Sam's vision blurred, and he struggled to maintain his balance as the excitement within him threatened to explode through his chest. Visions of extreme yet gratifying violence flashed in his memory, but he was able to bring himself under control as he recalled his old mantra. *Relax, Sam, just relax. Remember, the first rule is no impulse kills. Careful planning and execution is the key.* His vision returned to normal, and the excitement abated. The resurrection was now complete.

Sam sat calmly in the wheelchair and said with a smile, "Yes, dear, I'm fine. I'm right as rain."

Chapter 3: Hail Mary!

I've never met anyone younger than me; imagine my perspective
— *Zacharia Jones,* Out of Darkness; The Event Chronicles

Date: 1 year AE (After the Event)

Mary Ann Jones skillfully inserted the needle into the median cubital vein of Vasily Ustinov's left arm, then attached the vacuum test tube and watched as his blood filled the tube. This was the forty-sixth time they had both been through this weekly ritual of drawing their blood to send down to Earth for analysis. She applied gauze to the puncture site as she slid the needle out, and after she popped the tourniquet, she said to Vasily, "Maybe this will be the last time we have to do this, and they'll let us go home soon."

As he applied pressure to the puncture site, Vasily replied, "I hope so. I worry for my daughter; she say things are getting bad in Moscow. Four people yesterday gunned down in streets by police, and there's talk of martial law." He paused while Mary taped the gauze down. "But there's no way they let us abandon *Nautilus*, not after what happen with ISS."

"You're right," Mary replied as she floated away from Vasily to look out of the porthole. "The world has invested over a trillion dollars in this rotating donut of a space station, and even with the chaos on Earth now, they're not going to give it up. I just hate that we had to be the two that got caught on here when they figured out what was causing the birth and death crisis."

Vasily glided over to float beside Mary at the porthole and said, "I think they call it 'the Event' now."

Mary and Vasily stood holding hands while they stared down at the beautiful blue marble. They could see the outer ring of the station circle by them, as they were at the hub of the station in the zero-G lab. Mary turned to face Vasily and said, "I suppose that's as good a name as any."

"Besides, how we get to know each other if we're not unlucky ones that get stuck here while rest of construction crew rotate off?" Vasily replied as he pulled her close and kissed her lightly on the lips.

Mary opened her eyes as the kiss ended, and with a smile on her face, she said, "You're quite the charmer, aren't you?" She remembered how the medical scientists had discovered a virus was the cause behind "the Event" during the sixteen-hour window when she and Vasily were the only ones on the station. *We only had four more hours until the permanent crew was going to launch, and then we would have gone home. But no, they discovered that it's a virus, and since we'd been up here for four months already, we might likely be the only humans alive who weren't infected.*

As their embrace ended, Vasily said, "I tell you we were meant to be together, the only uninfected people in universe."

"Yes, and we're basically in permanent isolation and exile because of it," Mary replied as she gently pulled away from him and pushed off toward the docking port on the other side of the lab.

"I suppose you're right," Vasily reluctantly agreed. "Now we stop complaining and get back to work. It is time to unload resupply ship so we can return to pointless zero-G experiments."

* * *

Later that day, Mary and Vasily enjoyed the one-third gravity of the rotating ring while they prepared for their daily video conference with NASA. Vasily was busy prepping the camera, but Mary was glued to the small monitor watching a newscast. "They're saying that the Dalai Lama has died in a plane crash."

"No worry, I got this," Vasily replied playfully as he finished with the camera and looked over Mary's shoulder at the monitor. "I guess that's end of line for Dalai Lama. How can he be reincarnated now?"

"Yeah, it's only been six months since the last baby was born, but it's already tearing society apart," Mary replied.

"I'm sure they figure things out soon," Vasily said hopefully.

"Hey look, it's not all bad," Mary said as she pulled up another article on the screen. "The Star Shade Telescope has discovered an Earth-sized planet around Alpha Centauri."

Vasily leaned in for a closer look. "It's around the binary stars, not Proxima Centauri, so maybe it is habitable?"

"From what they're saying, it might be," Mary said enthusiastically. "Spectroscopy indicates it has a nitrogen- and oxygen-rich atmosphere."

"Incredible discovery, oxygen in atmosphere almost certainly mean planet has photosynthesizing life."

Mary nodded in agreement. "This should be headline news, yet it's buried beneath story after story about ..." Mary paused as she remembered the correct term. "The Event."

"Yes, world in turmoil, and greatest discovery in human history goes unnoticed." Vasily looked at his watch. "Time for conference."

He turned on the conference monitor, and three men were already waiting for them. "Hello, Vasily and Mary Ann. How are you feeling today?" asked the balding middle-aged man standing in the middle.

"We're feeling fine, Director Asher," replied Mary. "We certainly weren't expecting the assistant director of NASA to greet us today. I hope you're bringing us good news."

The director frowned and shook his head. "I'm afraid not, Mary Ann. Chuck, do you want to fill them in?" He turned to the man on his right.

"Yes, thank you," replied Charles Puckett, the medical director of NASA as he shuffled some papers in his hands before continuing. "Unfortunately, we haven't been able to find any way to stop TEV."

"TEV?" interrupted Vasily.

"Yes, 'the Event Virus' or TEV, as we're calling it now. As I was saying, it's not responding to any viral treatments known, and we've tried everything. We're even trying to circumvent it by stimulating the ovaries into producing eggs, but so far we have been unsuccessful. The virus counters everything we try, and the ovaries just won't produce more eggs. We thought we were on to something with an experimental fertility treatment when one subject finally produced a couple of eggs, but before we could act, her ovaries just reabsorbed them." Charles paused as he remembered an important detail. "It's the same thing with men; no one is producing sperm, not a one, and nothing we do changes that."

"Every man on planet shooting blanks," Vasily said under his breath.

"Even previously frozen embryos won't implant. Apparently, the virus makes the uterus reject any attempt at implantation," Dr. Puckett added.

"Do we know how the virus is doing this?" Mary asked.

Dr. Puckett nodded. "We're not 100 percent sure yet, but it appears to alter the DNA of the host."

"It's changing the genome of our species?" Mary asked.

"It appears so, and so far there's not much we can do about it," Dr. Puckett replied.

"My God," Mary replied. "I would have thought we would have made some progress by now. It doesn't seem like people are taking the lack of progress well either. There's civil unrest worldwide, and the economy is going downhill fast."

Director Asher said, "Yes, the Dow Jones has dropped more than six thousand points since the Event was officially announced, and other markets around the world are even worse. Economic forecasters say we could be heading for a worldwide depression."

"The crazies are coming out too," Vasily chimed in. "I read today that many different religious leaders are telling people we are in end times, and they should prepare their souls. I also read Islamic extremists believe their terroristic actions are bringing end times. Religious fanatics always insane, but much worse now."

The man standing to the left of Director Asher, Dr. Alford, spoke up. "It's not all bad, though. We've just discovered that not only have there been no deaths by natural causes in over eleven months, but it appears that older people are even regressing in age. People are recovering from Alzheimer's. Some scientists are even suggesting that TEV has made us immortal. It's incredible."

Mary interjected, "That is incredible, Dr. Alford. Is everyone going to regress back to babies, or are people going to just regress to a certain point and stop? Do you really believe everyone is immortal now?"

"We simply don't know yet. Children are still growing and appear to be unaffected by the virus, so the consensus is that we think the age regressing will eventually stop. It could be immortality, but we simply don't know enough yet."

Director Asher added, "All I can say is that my arthritis is completely gone, and I can actually exercise again. I haven't felt this good in years."

Mary looked at Vasily, and after he muted their mic, she said softly, "Yet they keep us up here aging away every day!"

Vasily unmuted their mic as he turned back toward the camera. "Do you think this virus is man-made? I mean, there's one virus that cause everyone to be sterile and at same time cause everyone to live forever? This cannot be coincidence!"

Dr. Alford nodded. "There are those who believe as you do, but the fact is this virus is light years beyond any technology that anyone has. That's why we haven't had any success stopping it yet."

Mary spoke up now with some anger in her voice. "Director

Asher, that's why you have to let us come home now. The entire world is basically immortal, and yet we're up here aging every day. We can't stay up here forever."

Dr. Alford interrupted before Director Asher could answer. "No, Mary, that's why it's so important that you stay. You and Vasily are the only known uninfected people in the universe. You're our experimental baseline."

Vasily added, "Surely not everyone on planet infected? What about remote tribes in Amazon jungle or Congo?"

"That's a good question Vasily," Dr. Alford said. "We intentionally contacted every remote group of people we could find, from the Kalahari to the Amazon, and every one of them was already infected. TEV is by far the most contagious pathogen we've ever encountered. It's able to spread by every known disease vector."

Director Asher glanced at Dr. Alford before he looked back at the camera and added, "That makes you guys the only uninfected humans in the universe." He paused a moment and added, "Not only that, but we're telling people about you and how you're helping us find a cure for the birth crisis."

Dr. Puckett chimed in, "Even with the news that TEV might give us immortality, the birth crisis has everyone in a panic. Don't forget, there hasn't been a child born in over six months. That's why we're telling the whole world about how you two are doing valuable research and helping us find a cure. You're giving people hope, and the world desperately needs that now. We need you to be strong and see this through."

Mary retorted, "Hope? What hope? Hope that a forty-four-year-old woman and a fifty-one-year-old man will supply the Earth with babies from space?" Mary smiled and laughed inside as she imagined Dr. Puckett struggling with her rhetorical question.

There was a long pause in the conversation as Dr. Puckett seemed to stare off into space for a moment. "Oh, I'm sorry. I was just receiving a message on my TICI. Where were we? Oh yes, we understand your frustration, but please be patient. I promise we're doing everything we can to solve this crisis and get you back home as soon as we can."

"I'm glad those insidious things debuted after we launched. I find them very annoying. You are like teenager with cell phone," Vasily said with a look of contempt on his face.

"I find mine quite useful. It's only a matter of time before everyone on the planet has one, you know. But that's beside the point; what can we do to help you two during this difficult time?"

"You can try harder. We aren't getting younger, you know," Vasily replied with a grin on his face.

Mary put a hand on Vasily's arm as she changed the subject. "Director Asher, tell us more about the Star Shade discovery. Is NASA making any plans to send a probe or something?"

"Oh, you mean the discovery of Alpha Centauri 5?" The director's eyes lit up as he replied, "It's amazing, isn't it? An Earthlike world so close; so tantalizingly close, but unfortunately, we've pretty much had all of our funding cut."

"They cut NASA's budget again?" Mary asked.

"Unfortunately, with the recent downturn in the economy and the unrest in the Middle East, the president has dramatically increased military spending and cut anything deemed nonessential. So, aside from maintaining you two on the *Nautilus*, there won't be any new missions anytime soon," Director Asher said.

"Such a pity," Vasily replied.

* * *

That evening, as they lay in bed, Mary realized that although they were effectively exiled from Earth, she was happier than she had been in years. In the months she and Vasily had been alone together on the *Nautilus*, she had grown to love him like no other. She imagined living the rest of her years with him at his cabin in the Urals. Then she remembered that if they went back to Earth, the rest of her years would be much longer than she ever thought possible. With that thought, she blurted out, "Let's just do it anyway."

"Do what?" Vasily said sleepily.

"In the morning, instead of just sending the supply ship back with our blood and urine samples, let's just get on board and go home."

Vasily propped his head on his elbow and said, "You've lost your mind, woman."

"What are they going to do?"

Vasily thought for a moment. "Well, they could keep us in isolation, I guess."

"Not if we refused. They couldn't hold us against our will."

"They would in Russia," Vasily replied with a slight laugh.

"No, seriously, let's do it. We can go off somewhere peaceful and live forever together."

"Okay, but if we do, you have to live with me in Russia. I have children and grandchildren."

"Yes, I'll live with you in Russia!" she blurted out, realizing that nothing in the world would make her happier.

Vasily sighed. "I love you, Mary Ann Jones, but we must obey orders. Is for good of humanity. I don't like any more than you, but is right thing to do. Yes?"

"Vasily Ustinov, named after the great Russian war hero, must play by the rules!" said Mary as she playfully tickled him.

After an intense round of lovemaking Mary lay still, listening to the rhythmic breathing of her partner. Apparently, sex in one-third G was just as tiring as 1 G. She rolled over and looked at Vasily's sleeping face and thought to herself, *I love this man more than anything I've ever loved. I'll stay with him on this station until the end of time if I have to.* She then rolled over and went happily to sleep.

* * *

The alarm woke her with a start at 0600. She shut off the alarm and reached over to wake Vasily. "Time to get up, babe. Let's go do our morning exercise so we don't waste away." Her lover didn't move. She shook him harder.

"Vasily!" she cried as she shook him again, "No no no, don't do this, babe." Mary stared in shock at his lifeless body. Tears started rolling down her face as she sobbed harder and harder. She hugged him for several minutes before getting out of bed.

She stood by the bed looking down at Vasily, trying to focus on what her next moves should be, but her mind refused to cooperate, and she stood there frozen in place. Finally, she stumbled into the bathroom to shower, as she couldn't think of anything else to do.

She only left the shower when the water became so cold that it forced her out of the state of shock she was in. As she dried off, she tried to think of what she would do next, but the only thing she could think about was the life that she would no longer share with Vasily. Nights sipping wine by the fireplace in his cabin that would never happen. Years of happiness all gone now, and for what? They were never going to solve the birth crisis up here. Slowly Mary's grief turned to anger. Vasily would still be alive if they had been allowed to come home. She was done.

After dressing, she dragged Vasily's body through the outer ring, and then she floated him through the zero-G lab and into the supply ship. Once Vasily was secure in the ship, Mary made her way back to the conference room in the outer ring and attempted to call NASA on the videophone.

Several long minutes later, someone answered the videophone. "Hello, Dr. Jones. What can we do for you this morning?"

"Vasily Ustinov has died. I don't know if he had a heart attack or what, but he died in his sleep last night," Mary said in an emotionless voice.

"Oh my God, that's terrible. Please stay on the line, and let me find the manager and the director," replied the youthful technician in Houston.

"No no no," replied Mary frantically. "You just give them this message for me. Tell them I'm bringing Vasily home. Tell them we're both coming home. I'm launching the supply boat in about an hour, and I'm going to land at Kennedy Space Center. Tell them to get it ready."

"Dr. Jones, you can't do that. Please wait while I get someone else."

"I'm not asking permission. I'm telling you what I'm going to do. You just be a good boy and relay my message. Understood?" Before he could reply, Mary finished, "Jones out."

* * *

As Mary sat in the cockpit of the supply ship and went through the takeoff checklist, a million things went through her mind. The ship was autopiloted, and she knew how to program it for reentry and landing at Kennedy Space Center, but what if something went wrong and she had to take control and land the ship? She'd received basic piloting classes, but she was an engineer, not a pilot. She'd probably die if that happened.

Mary had second thoughts; should she really go through with this? What would happen to her after landing? Would she be a hero or a criminal? That thought made her glance back at Vasily. One thing she knew, though: she couldn't remain on this station all alone with Vasily's corpse. *Why, Vasily? Why did you have to leave me?* Tears rolled down her face as her second thoughts vanished and she finished preparations for departure.

About three and a half hours later, the lifting body supply ship safely landed at Kennedy Space Center in Florida. As Mary got out of the ship, she felt weak, and it was difficult to maintain her balance, as she was used to one-third normal gravity. She stumbled, and as she regained her balance she noticed four people in hazmat suits quickly approaching. One of them had an isolation suit in his hands.

"Stay calm, Dr. Jones. We have to get you into isolation," said the man with the isolation suit as he tried to force a mask over her head.

"I refuse to be isolated," she screamed as she ripped the mask from her head, and then she grabbed the mask of her assailant and ripped his mask off as well. She then grabbed him and kissed him on the lips.

"I refuse to be isolated. I want to be infected," she said as she collapsed and lost consciousness.

A few hours later, as she was recovering in the Medical Center at Kennedy Space Center, a doctor and nurse walked into her room. Neither one of them was wearing masks or any other kind of protective gear.

"How are you feeling, Dr. Jones?" asked the doctor.

She looked at her arm and the IV line. "I'm feeling better now, thank you. Not nearly as dizzy as before. What did my blood tests show?"

The doctor glanced at the tablet he was holding. "All of your tests are normal except one. You're in remarkable health, considering you've spent well over a year in one-third normal gravity."

Mary sat up in the bed. "So, which test was abnormal?"

"You see, that's the kicker; it's not technically abnormal. It's just extraordinary is what it is. You're pregnant. About four weeks pregnant, in fact."

"What did you say?"

"I know it's a shock Mary, but you're pregnant. Your baby may very well be the last baby ever born," said the doctor as he turned toward the door. "Let us know if you need anything."

"What about Vasily? Will I be able to see him again?"

"I'm sorry, but they've already isolated his body for study and then return to Russia," the doctor replied.

When the doctor left, the nurse replaced the IV bag, and after adjusting the IV pump, she looked at Mary and said, "You're a blessed woman, Mary. To have a baby at your age and in today's circumstances. Your child will bring hope to millions of people. Hope that the Lord will give us back the gift of birth. People will look at your child as a savior in these dark times.

The chosen one that will lead us through this long tribulation."

After the nurse left, Mary felt her abdomen and remembered Vasily. She started to sob as she imagined raising his child without him. The image of his cold, lifeless body lying next to her burned in her memory as she recalled what the nurse said to her and realized that by the time her child is born, more than a year will have passed since the last child on Earth was born. While she continued to cry softly, she had a vision of thousands of ragged, desperate people lining the streets, waiting to see the last born child of Earth, the savior sent to bring them hope and lead them through the tribulation that is to come.

Mary jerked awake from the strange vision and wiped the tears that were still in her eyes. A peace came over her, and she smiled as she thought with some levity, *I guess if it's a boy, I'll have to name him Jesus.*

Chapter 4: The Mary Effect

The Event Depression, also known as The Tribulation, started only four years after the Event and lasted nearly fifty-three years. This tumultuous time in human history was a direct result of the crash in economic growth brought on by the birth crisis. The worldwide economy collapsed shortly thereafter. It's unknown exactly how many people perished during this time, but most agree it's well over 300 million. We had to hit rock bottom before we could reach for the stars.

—*Zacharia Jones,* Out of Darkness: The Event Chronicles

Date: 9 AE

Mary's stomach rumbled loudly as she chopped up her last half of a hot dog and slid the pieces into the last packet of instant grits that were simmering on the stove. She fondly remembered the half of a bologna sandwich she had for dinner the night before as she set the meager bowl of grits on the kitchen table and called out, "Zach, come and get your breakfast before I take you over to Mrs. Wiggins."

"Coming, Momma," she heard Zach call out from his bedroom of their two-bedroom trailer. "Good morning, Momma," Zach said as he came into the kitchen and hugged his mother around the waist.

Mary kissed his forehead. "Sit down and eat your breakfast. I'm going into town today to see if I can find work."

As Zach sat down at the table, he looked up at his mother. "Don't worry, Momma, I'm sure you'll find a job soon. God won't let us starve, and Lincoln Johnson says the economy is showing signs of getting better. Not to mention the Dow gained six hundred points yesterday."

Mary just stared at her eight-year-old son for several seconds. He never ceased to amaze her. Lincoln Johnson was the anchor on one of the local news stations, and Zach loved watching the news. Mary smiled. "Well, maybe Lincoln Johnson can send a job my way. Has Mrs. Wiggins been teaching you about Jesus again?"

"Yes, ma'am," Zach replied as he looked straight down at his bowl of grits. "I know you don't like Jesus, Momma, but maybe you should. Don't you think we need all the help we can get?"

Such an insightful child, Mary thought. "Hurry up and finish your grits. We're running late."

Fifteen minutes later, Mary and Zach were standing at the front door of their neighbor Janet Wiggins's trailer. Janet answered the door. "Hello, Mary, hello, Zach. Come in, come in."

"Good morning, Janet," Mary said as they walked into the living room. "Thank you so much for watching Zach again."

She handed Janet a modest slice of cheddar cheese as she continued, "I hope this is enough to cover." Other than Zach's lunch, it was the only food she had left.

Janet slipped the wrapped cheese into her jacket pocket. "Of course it's enough, dear." Janet was now seventy-eight years old but had de-aged to only look about sixty.

Mary glanced around Janet's small living room and noticed the three other children Janet was watching for the day. Watching the neighborhood children while their parents looked for work and food was the primary way Janet fed herself these days. Mary counted herself lucky to have her as a friend, even if they didn't see eye to eye on everything.

"Will you give this to Zach for lunch today?" Mary asked as she handed Janet a pack of peanut butter crackers.

"When was the last time you had something to eat, Mary?"

"I'm fine," Mary replied as she looked away.

Janet turned toward Zach. "Zach, did you bring your bible?"

"Yes, Mrs. Wiggins. I've read it already too," Zach replied enthusiastically.

"Is that right, the whole thing?" Janet asked.

A look of concentration overtook Zach's face as he recited, "The Spirit of the Lord is on me because he has anointed me to proclaim good news to the poor. He has sent me to proclaim freedom for the prisoners and recovery of sight for the blind, to set the oppressed free."

Janet looked over at Mary before she turned back to Zach and said, "Very impressive, Zach. Can you tell me what verse that was?"

"Luke chapter 4, verse 18."

Mary seemed less impressed than Janet. "And what made you choose that verse to show off with?"

"Are we not the poor and the oppressed? I thought it would give you hope, Momma."

Mary tousled his hair slightly. "Thank you, Zach. Now go play with the other kids while I have a word with Mrs. Wiggins."

Once Zach was out of earshot, Mary said, "I really wish you wouldn't fill his head with religious nonsense." Mary knew Janet was a retired schoolteacher, but she didn't appreciate her mixing religion with education.

"I'd give him other books to read if I had them, but unfortunately the Bible is all I have to teach the children with. Just because the State of Virginia ran out of money to fund the schools doesn't mean the children don't need an education. Besides, if you're so against it, why haven't you taken it from him?"

Mary sighed. "As you say, I don't really have anything else for him to read, and he just devours it. I don't think he'd forgive me if I took it from him."

Janet grabbed Mary's arm lightly and pulled her closer. "He's a special boy. You know that, don't you? He was the last child born on this planet and quite possibly the last child ever to be born, and he's so smart. Surely God has something in store for him."

Mary frowned slightly as she nodded in approval. "The nurse who informed me I was pregnant assured me of the exact same thing."

* * *

Mary walked into the makeshift unemployment office in Radford and sighed as she saw the line. She estimated it might be five hours until she made her way to the front, only to be told there are no jobs. She'd walked three miles into town, and worst of all, she risked the shortcut through Wildwood Park to get here, and this was what she found. She contemplated turning back, but maybe all these people knew something she didn't.

"What's going on?" Mary asked the disheveled middle-aged woman standing in front of her. "Why are there so many people here today?"

The woman gave her a kind smile. "There's a rumor going around that the university is going to reopen and they're hiring two hundred people to clean the place."

Mary found that to be unlikely, as she couldn't think of a reason why the state would reopen the university when they had just closed public schools six months earlier. "I can't believe I cut through Wildwood for this."

"You cut through the park to get here?" the woman asked.

"Yeah, stupid, I know," Mary replied wistfully. She remembered when Wildwood Park had been one of the major attractions of Radford and people from all over the state had come to view the wildflowers and animal life that used to abound. Now, the park was filled with hundreds of homeless families living in tents and makeshift houses made from pallets and plywood. Crime and violence were endemic, and even local law enforcement avoided it. Cutting through the park had been a mistake, but it did make Mary more thankful for her two-bedroom trailer.

Before the woman could reply, one of the employment office employees, a youthful-looking bald man, stood up on the front desk and yelled out, "Can I have everyone's attention, please? Thank you. I just want to let you all know that the rumors that the university is reopening are not true. I repeat, the university is not reopening, and there are no jobs. In fact, I don't have any jobs to offer anyone today. I'm sorry, people."

"So much for that," the disheveled woman said as they turned to leave.

"Yep, guess I'll head over to the farmer's market and see if any of the farmers are looking for day laborers."

"Good luck with that, honey. I wish I could do manual labor," the woman replied as Mary noticed for the first time that she only had one arm.

* * *

Later that afternoon Mary felt tears well up as she stared at the two utility bills she was holding in her hands. This was the last thing she needed to see after another unsuccessful day of job hunting in Radford. Last notice for the electricity bill; she had less than a month to at least make a down payment on what she owed, or they would shut the power off. *Might as well get blood from a turnip,* she thought to herself as she struggled to stuff the bills into her unpaid-bills drawer in the kitchen.

As tears rolled down her face, Mary remembered her lost love. *Oh, Vasily, why did you have to die? Why did you have to leave me?*

"What's wrong, Momma?" she heard Zacharia say as he entered the kitchen.

"Nothing, baby, I'm okay," Mary lied as she turned toward the sink to try to hide her tears.

Zach came up to her and hugged her around the waist. "Don't worry, Momma. God will find a way for us."

Mary bent down and fully embraced him. "Oh, Zach, I love

you so much. I should be the one reassuring you."

"I love you too, Momma. I know you'll find a way for everything to work out."

Mary looked at her eight-year-old son for a moment. "You look so much like your father, and you're so smart and charming, just like him. He would be so proud of you."

Zach smiled. "The great Russian Cosmonaut Vasily Ustinov."

"Don't forget, he was also an engineer and scientist."

"I haven't forgotten, Momma," Zach replied. "Why can't I be Zacharia Ustinov instead of Zacharia Jones? I should have my father's name."

"We're not having this discussion again," Mary said sternly. Although Zach didn't really understand it, everything was much easier for them if they shared the same last name. Not to mention that the locals were still suspicious of anything Russian. *He'll just have to be satisfied being Zacharia Gregory Jones.*

Just then, there was a knock on the front door right before it opened and Mary's neighbor and longtime friend Lacy Taylor came walking in with her arms full of groceries.

"What in the heck do you think you're doing, Lacy?" Mary said with a large smile on her face.

Lacy walked straight for the kitchen, set the heavy grocery bags down on the counter, and pointed at them. "I come bearing gifts."

Mary's eyes grew large as she stared at all of the groceries on her kitchen counter, "Lacy, you're giving us all of this food? There must be enough here for two weeks, if not more."

"Yep, it's all for you guys, but I do have one condition."

"Anything!" Mary replied.

"All I ask is that you cook up your world-famous chicken and dumplings for us tonight."

Zach ran up to Lacy and jumped into her arms. "Hi, Aunt Lacy. I missed you."

"I missed you too, Zach, and you're getting too big for me to pick up," she replied as she sat him down.

"See, Momma, I told you God would provide for us," Zach said as he walked back to his room.

Mary frowned and started unpacking the groceries. "Lacy, how in the world did you afford all of this food? Did you find a job as a nurse?"

"No, there are no jobs for nurses anywhere, especially hospice nurses. No one gets sick anymore, remember?" Lacy replied.

"How could I forget?" Mary said as she turned her back and put some cans in the cupboard. "It's not like there are jobs for ex-astronauts either, not since NASA was shut down, anyway."

"You know things are bad when the world-famous Mary Ann Jones, astronaut and engineer, can't get a job," Lacey joked.

As Mary continued to put up the groceries, she said, "How in the world did you afford these fresh vegetables?"

"Maybe I robbed a bank."

Mary retorted jokingly, "I don't care if you're selling your body for money. All I know is I owe you big time."

Lacy winced slightly and turned away. "Don't worry about it."

* * *

That evening, Mary, Zach, Lacy, and Janet all sat in the living room enjoying chicken and dumplings with a fresh tossed salad while they watched the evening news. They only had a handful of channels to watch, as cable, satellite TV, and internet were beyond affordable. Mary was returning from the kitchen with her second helping of chicken and dumplings. "I think these might be the best dumplings I've ever made."

Janet finished chewing her food. "These dumplings are delicious, Mary, and I thank you for inviting me over for dinner, but it could be that you're just really hungry."

"Yeah, I haven't eaten anything today," Mary replied between mouthfuls.

"Y'all hush for a minute. I want to hear this," Lacey interrupted as she pointed toward the small TV.

Silence came over Mary's small trailer as they all focused on the television to listen to Lincoln Johnson as he announced the news. "Our sources in Turkey have confirmed that Caliphate troops are crossing from Syria into Turkey, creating panic and mayhem in their wake as hundreds of thousands of refugees flee their advance. Turkey is requesting international military aid to combat the invasion as well as humanitarian aid for the refugee crisis. All of this less than two weeks after the US withdrawal of all troops from the region despite the raging Caliphate war that has engulfed the region and now threatens Europe."

Mary looked around the room briefly before focusing on Zach, "Zach, put your plate in the sink, brush your teeth, and go to bed."

"But Mom, this is important, and I want to watch."

"Don't make me repeat myself," Mary replied sternly.

After Zach left the room, Lacy started the conversation.

"None of this would be happening if President Folmar hadn't pulled us out of the war."

"Really, Lacy, do you think he had a choice? Just how was he supposed to fund the war after Standard and Poor's dropped our credit rating to B- with an unstable outlook? We can't fund the war because no one will give us loans now. Not to mention all of the anti-war protests that were going on," Mary quickly pointed out.

"Yeah, the war was very unpopular, Lacy," Janet added.

Lacy nodded in agreement. "But look at this chaos. The world is going to hell in a handbasket."

"It's the end times; this is supposed to happen. It's all part of God's plan," Janet said solemnly before changing the subject. "Mary, what do you have for dessert?"

Mary laughed for a moment before replying, "Peach cobbler. Oh my, I put Zach to bed without dessert. He'll think I'm punishing him."

After they finished dessert, the sitcom rerun they were watching was interrupted with breaking news. Lincoln Johnson once again appeared on their television to deliver more bad news. "Good evening, we have multiple reports from around the region that Riyadh and Medina have both been struck by nuclear blasts. There's no word yet on the number of casualties, but reports are that the damage is catastrophic and the loss of life horrific. The Caliphate has issued a statement saying that the perpetrators will be found and severely punished. There's no word yet on who is responsible, but all nuclear powers including Israel are denying involvement."

As Mary, Lacy, and Janet all looked at each other with open mouths, the news anchor continued, "The president has just released a statement condemning the use of nuclear weapons and said that he just concluded a call with the Russian and Chinese presidents, and they want to assure the world that there will be no nuclear escalation. An official presidential address is expected to follow shortly."

Before Mary or Janet could comment, Lacy reached into her large handbag and pulled out a bottle of bourbon. "I thought we might want to have a drink this evening, but I had no idea how right I would be. Mary, will you get us some glasses?"

"I think we should be praying instead of drinking right now," Janet protested.

"I disagree," Mary replied as she returned from the kitchen with three glasses.

That evening, after Lacy and Janet had left, Mary sat on the front porch of her trailer looking up at the stars as she finished her last glass of bourbon. She spied a small dot of light slowly traversing the night sky. A wave of sadness overtook her slight buzz when she realized the small dot of light was in fact the *Nautilus.* She remembered that she and Vasily had installed the automated orbit thrusters, otherwise her orbit would already be decaying, and the station would come crashing back to Earth. As it was, she was probably good for another sixty years or so.

I was the last living person to be aboard the Nautilus, Mary thought. *I wonder if anyone will ever board her again. Will any human ever venture into space again, for that matter? I fear we may be doomed to extinction.* She drained her glass and went to bed.

* * *

"We are watching the tribulation unfold right before our very eyes, just as Revelations foretold!" the fiery Reverend Billy T. Walker exclaimed.

As Reverend Walker continued his timely sermon, Mary looked around the large revival tent; so many sad desperate faces looking for answers. These biweekly revivals had been popular for several years now due to the depression, but the events of the previous night had the tent slammed to the gills as never before. *That's why I'm here,* she thought with a silent chuckle. Janet didn't have much trouble convincing her or Lacey to come to the revival this morning.

Reverend Walker continued, "I looked, and behold a pale horse, and his name that sat on him was Death, and hell followed with him. And power was given unto them over the fourth part of the earth, to kill with the sword and with hunger, and with death, and with the beasts of the earth." Reverend Walker paused for a bit and then held his bible high over his head before he continued. "That's how the Good Book says the end will come, and have we not seen the horsemen John speaks of? How many have already died of hunger since God stopped aging and cursed the land with infertility? And now we've seen the last of the Four Horsemen bring the sword. For what greater sword is there than the total destruction wrought by nuclear fire? He smote the infidels first, but who will be next?"

Mary could feel her eyes water and had to admit that Reverend Walker's words affected her, and as she looked around the tent, she saw people crying and shouting toward Reverend Walker, "Save us, Jesus!" "Help us, Lord!" "Show us the way, Reverend."

After the crowd quieted down a bit, Reverend Walker resumed. "Does the bible not say that a child will show us the way?" He once again held his bible over his head as he asked, "Is there a child here that will come forward and read from the Good Book for all to hear?"

The crowd grew still, and everyone looked around to see if a child would come forward, but none came. Reverend Walker again called out, "Is there not a child here brave enough to come forward and read from the Bible?"

Mary reached out to take Zach's hand, but he wasn't there. In a moment of panic, she looked all around for him and was about to call out when she saw him walking down the aisle toward the pulpit.

Reverend Walker also noticed Zach walking toward him. "Yes, here comes a brave boy. God told me there would be a special child here today." As Zach stepped up on the wooden stage, Reverend Walker gave him a microphone and asked, "What's your name, son?"

"Zacharia Jones."

"God bless you, Zacharia," the Reverend said as he extended his bible down to Zach. "Please read from the verses I have marked."

Zach held up his hands and took a step backward and said, "No thank you, Reverend. I don't need to read it. Just tell me the verses, and I'll say them for everyone."

"Hallelujah!" Reverend Walker exclaimed before continuing, "Zacharia please recite Revelation chapter 7 verses 16 and 17."

Zach closed his eyes and held out his arms as if he was Christ on the cross as he recited the requested verses. "They shall hunger no more, neither thirst any more, the sun shall not strike them, nor any scorching heat. For the Lamb in the midst of the throne will be their shepherd, and he will guide them to springs of living water and God will wipe away every tear from their eyes."

"Thank you, Zacharia," the Reverend said before addressing the now almost electric crowd. "The government can't save you, no. Nations will fall, but Jesus is coming soon, and if your name isn't in the book of the Lamb, you will perish as well. Jesus is the only way through this tribulation."

Reverend Walker motioned for Zach to return to his seat, but Zach had other intentions as he picked up the microphone to recite another verse he felt was pertinent. "And he said to me, it is done! I am the Alpha and the Omega, the beginning and the end. To the thirsty, I will give from the spring of the water of life without payment. The one who conquers will have this heritage, and I will be his God and he will be my son."

From the back row, Mary put a hand over her mouth and thought to herself, *What is he doing? What's happening?*

"A child shall lead them!" Reverend Walker exclaimed. "Now, who among you needs to accept Christ into your heart and have your name written in the book of the Lamb? Come forward to the altar to be saved." Dozens of desperate souls came forward to the altar, and Reverend Walker prayed for each one, but not before praying with Zach first.

As the altar call continued, Zach made his way toward the back row to be with his mother. Mary scooped him up in a warm hug and said, "Zach, what has gotten into you?"

"Nothing, Momma, I was just helping Reverend Walker bring hope to everyone."

"Oh, Zach," was the only thing Mary could think to say as she sat him down.

"Reverend Walker wants us to stay after the service. Says he wants to talk to us," Zach said.

* * *

After the service, Reverend Walker was packing up the sound system on the stage when Mary and Zach walked up. She almost didn't stay after the service, but curiosity had gotten the better of her. Reverend Walker hadn't noticed them walk up, so Mary said, "Reverend Walker?"

He turned around and smiled. "Oh, hello Zacharia. Thank you for coming by. Are you his mother?"

"Yes, I'm Mary Ann Jones," Mary replied as she presented her hand.

Reverend Walker shook her hand. "Billy T. Walker, but please call me Billy. You're Mary Ann Jones? Mary Ann Jones the astronaut?"

Mary blushed slightly. "Former astronaut, I'm afraid." Now that Mary was closer than the back row, she could tell that Reverend Walker was a tall, thin man who looked to be in his mid-fifties and was a raw-boned kind of handsome.

"I had heard that you lived in these parts, but I never imagined that I'd actually meet you," Reverend Walker said before turning his attention to Zach. "And you're the miracle child that was born over a year after the Event; the last child born on this Earth."

"My father was the great cosmonaut Vasily Ustinov."

"Yes, Zach, that's what I've heard, but you know who your real father is, right?" Reverend Walker asked.

"Jesus?"

"That's right, Zach," Reverend Walker replied before turning to Mary. "He is truly a special child but I'm sure you know that already."

Mary smiled and glanced at Zach. "With every passing day,

I realize that more and more."

"God has big plans for him."

"That's what everyone keeps telling me," Mary replied as she tried to keep her face from revealing how tired she was of hearing that.

The Reverend smiled warmly. "Today was the biggest altar call I've ever had, and I believe that was in large part due to Zacharia here."

Mary smirked ever so slightly. "Don't you think two cities being nuked yesterday had something to do with it?"

"Of course," Reverend Walker replied as he reached into his pocket. "Mary, I know you and Zach are struggling right now, and God wants doesn't want you to go hungry."

Mary looked at the $75 in small bills that the Reverend was holding out to her in his hand, and she thought, *That could feed us for a week.* However, she hesitated to take it.

"Go on and take it, Mary. I know you need it, and there are no strings attached."

"Thank you so much, Reverend," Mary replied as she took the money.

"You're very welcome. You know, we're having another tent revival in two weeks. I hope you'll join us, and if it's all right with you, I'd like to have Zach recite some more Bible verses."

"Can I, Mom, can I please?" Zach asked enthusiastically.

"We'll see," was Mary's only reply.

* * *

Mary placed the meat sauce beside the pasta on the kitchen table. "All right, dig in, everyone, spaghetti and meat sauce served courtesy of Lacey."

"Thank both of you so much for sharing your food with me again," Janet said to Mary and Lacey as they all sat down at the table.

"I'm sure I owe you more. I don't know how many times you've kept Zach when I couldn't pay," Mary replied.

As they started to eat, Zach stopped everyone. "Wait, I want to say Grace before we eat."

"Mary, I think you're raising a minister or something," Lacey said jokingly.

Mary ignored Lacey's remark. "Okay, Zach, go ahead and ask the blessing."

After they bowed their heads, Zach went on. "Dear Lord, please bless this food that it might nourish our bodies and help Momma, Lacey, and Janet find work and food this week. Also, bless Reverend Walker for giving us money. Amen."

"Amen," Janet said before taking a bite of spaghetti. "Zach, that was wonderful the way you recited those Bible verses at the revival this morning. It really got people in the spirit."

"Thank you, Mrs. Wiggins," Zach said with a mouthful of food.

"Zach, how many times do I have to tell you not to speak with your mouth full?" Mary said. She instantly regretting snapping at Zach, but she still wasn't comfortable with what happened at the revival. The fact that the food they were all enjoying now was purchased because of Zach's performance only made her more uneasy.

Zach finished chewing his food. "Sorry, Momma, but you know what? I bet I can get Reverend Walker to give us more money if I recite more Bible verses."

"I don't know, Zach," Mary replied.

"I think it's a great idea, Mary," Janet interjected. "He's

a natural, and I believe Reverend Walker would love to have Zach in the pulpit more often."

"No, no, no, I won't have my son become some trailer-park preacher that steals money from the poor just so we can have ..." Mary stumbled for words and just said, "spaghetti!"

After a few moments of silence, Lacey said, "Can someone pass me the salt please?" Everyone erupted in laughter.

After everyone quit laughing, Mary said, "No, I'll get a job this week and we won't have this discussion again."

* * *

As they walked down the steps that led to the riverside, Mary couldn't believe how many people were filing into the four large tents Reverend Walker had set up. *That's two more tents than two weeks ago and easily three times as many people,* she thought. She also couldn't believe that they were back here at another tent revival. Two weeks of fruitless job hunting, and they were once again out of money and nearly out of food. *Desperate times,* she thought.

She noticed people staring at them and whispering as they walked into the tent. "What's going on?" Mary asked Janet as they took their seats.

Janet glanced around quickly. "It's Zach; everyone's been talking about him since the last revival. I think he's the reason why there are so many people here."

After they sang a handful of hymns and took up an offering, Reverend Walker preached for a short time, "Ladies and gentlemen, as I'm sure some of you know, we have a very special guest with us today. He's only eight years old, and as such, that makes him the youngest person in the world, and yet he's memorized the entire Bible, Old Testament and New. He was here last revival and blessed us all by reciting several verses from Revelation. I believe this boy, the youngest person in the world and the last child to ever be born, was sent here by God to help guide us through these trying times. Zacharia Jones, will you come forward, please?"

Mary felt a lump in her throat and a tightness in her chest as Zach stood up and walked down the aisle toward the stage. People were reaching out to touch him as he walked by, as if they could receive some sort of blessing just by touching him.

Zach reached the stage and stood beside Reverend Walker. "Zach, will you recite a verse that you believe fitting?"

Zach nodded in agreement and looked out on the crowd as they grew silent. "Be faithful unto death and I will give you the crown of life." The crowd erupted in applause and people shouting "Hallelujah."

After the noise died down, a woman from the crowd shouted out to the stage as she guided a young man with her. "Zacharia, will you pray for my brother? He's been blind since before the Event. Please, Zacharia, please pray for him."

"Bring him up to us," the Reverend said loudly.

As the woman guided the man up the steps, Zach looked up at the Reverend, and Reverend Walker leaned down and whispered into his ear. "It's okay, Zach, just put your hands over his eyes and say a prayer for him. God will do the rest."

The man kneeled in front of Zach with his sister standing beside him. Zach stepped forward and put his hands on the man's face and said, "You don't need eyes to see; you only need faith in the Lord that He will guide and set you free." Zach then squeezed the man's face between his hands and continued. "Lord, set this man free that he may walk the path guided by your light."

The man fell backward, writhing on the ground as if he were in pain. Then he sat up, looked around the tent, and exclaimed, "I can see!" The man stood up and embraced Zach and Reverend Walker and then walked off the stage unassisted.

As soon as the man left the stage, dozens of other people filed up to the stage, all of them begging for Zacharia Jones to pray for them.

Mary watched as her son prayed for each person as they came up to the stage one by one and as people all around the tent began speaking in tongues and others fell to the ground, slain in the Spirit. *This isn't right,* Mary thought to herself, *this man is using my son and he's getting rich off of these poor, wretched people.*

* * *

After the revival was over, Mary sent Zach home with Janet and sought out Reverend Walker, intending to tell him that this was the last time that he would use Zach in such a manner.

Reverend Walker, seeing the look on Mary's face as she approached him, simply held out a wad of cash and said, "Here's 5 percent of the tithing for today's service. We can do this after every service."

Mary looked at the large sum of cash in the Reverend's hand and realized there was enough there to feed her and Zach as well as pay their bills for the next two weeks. She thought for a moment, "I'm gonna need 15 percent, Reverend."

"Ten percent is the best I can do, Mary."

"Glory to God," Mary said as she took the wad of money.

Chapter 5: Shanty Towns and Immortal Hookers

Entropy comes for us all. Nirvana must be achieved in this lifetime; The Event has assured us of that —Zacharia Jones, Omni Ascension

Date: 27 AE

Laura awoke in a dark and musty room lit by only a flickering night light in the far corner that cast oddly shaped shadows against the walls. There was what appeared to be a small weight bench in the center of the room. She was groggy, unsure if she was in the middle of a horrifying dream or if she had died and gone to hell. As she came to, she realized she was lying on her right side, and when she tried to sit up, she could feel her hands were bound behind her back. She felt around with her hands and discovered a chain that led toward the wall about two feet behind her. Once she slid with her back to the wall, she was able to sit up.

"Where am I, what the hell is going on?" she said softly to herself as she remembered what had happened. She had been driving down a country road in the early evening when she saw a man tending a wounded dog on the side of the road. She pulled over to help after the man waved her over. She remembered he grabbed her from behind with his powerful arms and then held a wet cloth over her mouth and nose. Now she was here, and she was sure it was hell. In fact, she had been entertaining the idea that she was in hell for some time now, long before the abduction.

Like most of humanity, Laura had been overjoyed when the effects of the Event became apparent some twenty-seven years ago. She had been diagnosed with breast cancer when she was only thirty-eight years old, and despite a double mastectomy followed by radiation and aggressive chemotherapy, the cancer had spread to the rest of her body. She battled the cancer for six long years, but in the end, she had given up and accepted her fate. Just when it seemed death was about to take her, the Event changed everything.

The Event cured her cancer, and when she learned that people were slowly regaining their youth, she had hoped that her breasts might regenerate, but it never happened. For several years, it didn't matter to her that she didn't have breasts, as she was just happy to be alive. However, as the years went on, she slowly became bitter. She was bitter because her breasts didn't regenerate and because she couldn't afford reconstructive surgery. Before the Event, she had struggled with depression, but as the years wore on, despite getting younger, she sank into a pit of despair as she had never before experienced. In her darkest days, she entertained the idea that the cancer had killed her and that she was in some sort of special hell. A hell reserved for people who gave up.

As Laura sat contemplating her past, she heard what sounded like someone slowly walking downstairs. She sat up and stared at the door on the other side of the room as it slowly opened and a shadowy figure emerged. The figure walked slowly across the room and grabbed the weight bench in the center of the room, dragging it toward her as it screeched and scraped against the concrete. As he sat down on the bench, the room lit his face just enough that Laura could tell the figure was a man, but that was about all she could make out. He turned on a small flashlight, and shined it upward so it eerily illuminated his face. The face she saw was that of a man who appeared to be in his early or mid-fifties with a jawline so sharp that it made him ruggedly handsome.

"My name is Sam Boone. What's your name?"

As Laura was pretty sure he already knew her name, she said, "Laura Bishop."

"Very good, Laura. How old are you?"

"Seventy-two," she replied.

"Yet you appear to be no older than thirty. Simply amazing what the Event has done and is still doing, wouldn't you say?"

Laura thought for a moment before she replied. "Judging by your appearance, I'd say you're at least 110 years old. If not for the Event, you'd be dead, and the world would be better off. So, I guess you can call the Event amazing, but that doesn't mean it's a good thing."

"Ah, you're a cynical one, aren't you? All of the sixty-two women that have been in your place were sobbing wrecks by now. Yet, here you are, waxing philosophical. It must be your red hair; makes you fiery," said Sam as he took a candle out of his coat pocket and lit it. After setting the flickering candle between them, he asked, "So, why would you say the Event is not a good thing?"

Laura almost told him to piss off but thought if she kept him talking, he might let her live or at least let her live longer, so she replied, "I didn't always think so. The Event saved me from cancer. I was terminal, with only weeks to live. Initially, I was ecstatic. Then the news came that the same virus that caused us to stop aging also caused women to stop ovulating."

"So, you think the Event is not a good thing because there are no longer children in the world?" asked Sam, irritated.

"Of course I don't think that's a good thing, but that's not what I was referring to."

As Laura didn't further elaborate Sam pressed her. "So, what exactly was your point?"

Laura sighed. "What I meant was the lack of new people coming into the world stopped economic growth. That led to the New Depression. The New Depression caused the fall of the United States. Take a look around you, *Sam*!" she added emphasis to his name as if implying he was blind. "The Event directly caused the New Depression. People are suffering, some are starving. Unemployment is nearly 40 percent, crime rates are at record levels. Wars are raging around the world."

Laura paused for a moment, but since Sam remained silent, she continued. "You know, sometimes I feel like I really died of cancer. Sometimes I think I died and went to hell. I'm pretty sure *this* is hell," Laura said as she looked around the room.

"That's just your perspective," replied Sam in a flat, emotionless voice. "From my perspective, it's like I died and went to heaven. Before the Event, before I grew old and feeble, I had to be very careful, meticulous with every detail. The cops and

FBI were vigilant; any lapse in attention to detail and I would have been caught. They never even knew I existed. That's how meticulous I was. Now, things are different. Now, I can run free. In the twenty-seven years since the Event, I've killed twice as many women as I did before, and my rate has even increased in the last five years."

As Sam stood up and walked out of the room, Laura's head dropped, and she started sobbing. She felt hopeless and alone and could see no way out of her predicament. *I'm not going to survive this*, Laura thought. *I survived cancer and the New Depression, only to meet my end at the hands of this psychopath.*

Laura heard the door open, and she quickly dried her eyes. *Can't let this mealy-mouthed bastard see me cry.* Sam made his way down the stairs and over to where Laura was chained without looking at her. He set a sandwich, that looked like it had been made hours ago, on a napkin in front of her, along with a cup of water. *A plastic cup*, she thought. *He's too smart to leave me with a glass.* He then released the bonds from her hands and chained her left ankle to the wall. "Enjoy the sandwich," he said as he walked back out of the room.

* * *

John Fitzpatrick walked around the abandoned thirty-year-old rusted-out Ford SUV on the side of highway 81 between Winder and Loganville, Georgia. He and his partner, Bill Kowalski, had just arrived and were having a quick look around.

"This makes the third one in the last six months," said Bill.

"He's becoming bold," replied John.

"You still think this string of abductions and missing women is due to the Ghost from your days with the FBI?" asked Bill.

"Everything fits like it did before. We have twenty missing women from the same three hundred square mile area as before. I chased the Ghost for over twenty years, and then the women just stopped disappearing. I thought he died or something, but now I think he just got old. He's not old anymore," replied John as he motioned to the abandoned car.

"But no one else in the Bureau even thought there was a Ghost. You were the only one who thought a serial killer was loose in northeast Georgia, and your obsession with the Ghost nearly cost you your job, as I recall," said Bill.

"That's true, Bill, that's true. It's hard to convince people there's a serial killer on the loose when there are no bodies and the women that disappear are few and far between but there was a pattern to the disappearances. They all had big boobs. What are the odds of that?"

Bill laughed. "You're killing me, John. I bet you even know the statistics as to what percentage of women have big boobs as opposed to medium-sized and small."

John laughed. "You know I do."

They both turned and looked as two county sheriff cars pulled up to the scene. "Looks like the local boys are finally here," Bill said.

"I'll handle this," John muttered as the sheriff's deputies approached. John held up his state badge. "Hi, boys, I'm Agent John Fitzpatrick of the GBI, and this is Agent Kowalski. We're taking over this scene, but we're gonna need your assistance."

As the two deputies look at each other and didn't answer, John continued with a rue smile on his face. "What, you've never seen a Black Irishman?"

The lead deputy stuttered. "What? No, I'm just a little

confused as to why the GBI is interested in an abandoned vehicle."

My humor is totally wasted on these two. Why do I even bother? John thought to himself. "We have evidence that a woman was abducted from this vehicle last night, and there's a possibility this is connected to a string of disappearances in this general area over the last ten years or more. Anyway, we're gonna need your forensic team here ASAP to go over this scene with a fine-tooth comb," replied John.

"Forensic team, he says," laughed the deputy as he looked at his partner. "What forensic team? Since you already claimed this scene, you can investigate it yourself. We got bigger fish to fry. Have fun with the wild goose chase."

As the two deputies walked off and back into their cars, Bill said. "You just can't get good help these days."

John replied. "Can't blame them, really. They barely have the resources to keep the peace, much less conduct thorough investigations into missing persons."

* * *

Laura sat in the darkness, listening to the night. At least she thought it was night. Occasionally she could hear what she thought were roaches, and once she heard mice scampering; otherwise, her dungeon was dead quiet. Laura was sure she was being held in a basement, maybe even in town, but it was clear that the room was soundproof, as she had yelled for help until her voice gave out. Beneath the musty, fungal smell of the basement, there was the faint smell of decay. It wasn't an obvious odor at all, but Laura was certain there was a graveyard beneath the floor of the basement.

How many women are buried here? Laura wondered. *I'll be with them soon if I don't do something.*

She began biting her fingernails, but not in the nervous fashion. She bit them in such a way as to make them pointed. Once, she had given in and accepted her fate. Now, she was defiant. *I'm going to claw his eyes out if he gets close to me*, she thought. *He won't shoot me with a gun; he'll get in close with a knife or maybe even his bare hands. He's arrogant. He'll make a mistake. When that happens, I have to act quickly.*

* * *

John stared out the window of the passenger's side at the all-too-familiar sad scene as Bill drove them back to the GBI station in downtown Atlanta. The hovels and shanty towns all over Atlanta still saddened him, but none more so than Folmarville that they were driving by now. The largest shanty town in Atlanta was named after the last president of the United States, Charles Folmar. Sadly, Folmarvilles had sprung up in every major city in the former US. The funny thing was that when most people said the name, it came out more like Formerville, which somehow seemed even more fitting.

Thousands of makeshift shacks thrown together with plywood and old pallets with leaky tin roofs stretched on for miles as John continued to look out the window. Eventually, he had to roll up the window, as the stench from the open sewage became overpowering. "So, you think McDaniel will be able to do anything about all of this if Georgia votes to join his FON?" asked John as he pointed to Folmarville.

"I don't know, but every former state that's joined the Federation of Nations is doing better. Everything I've heard about Nathan McDaniel says he's the man with the economic plan that can turn it all around," replied Bill.

"Yeah, I've heard all of that before. He says the more nations that join the FON, the more effective his policies become, and that worries a lot of people. That and the space elevator he's talking about building. A space elevator!" said John.

"What's with the space elevator anyway?"

"I don't know, man; he says it's part of his economic plan. He wants to put everyone back to work with massive public works projects. Kinda like what Roosevelt did, but on a worldwide scale. Pie-in-the-sky stuff, if you ask me."

"It's a cable in the sky, not a pie."

John laughed. "Very funny."

"Seriously, though, is he just trying to become a dictator, or what? That's what's got me worried."

"I don't know, man, I don't know. Most people around here say his policies are too socialist. Either way, I don't see how things could get much worse. Look how much California and Texas and the other states that have joined have improved," John said as he started tuning the radio. "That's good enough for my vote tomorrow."

Bill nodded in agreement. "The states that have joined? What about Mexico? That's what's got people talking. If he can turn Mexico's economy around, Georgia and Florida should be a cinch."

"I heard this morning that Colombia and Panama are considering joining too," added John.

As they pulled up to their office building in downtown Atlanta, an attractive woman wearing a miniskirt and pumps walked right up to their car, leaned in through the driver's window, and said, "Either of you boys need a date?"

"Get out of here, whore!" replied Bill in disgust.

John winced. "Take it easy, Bill. You know women have had it harder since the New Depression started."

"How do you figure?"

"Come on, man, you mean you've never thought about why there are so many prostitutes these days?" *Do I really have to spell it out for him*? John thought.

Bill just shrugged his shoulders, so John continued. "Look at it this way, before the Event, the two largest professions for women were schoolteachers and nurses. There hasn't been a child born in the last twenty-six years, so there's not a single schoolteacher employed. There's not much need for nurses anymore either. So, you put those two things together, and women are unemployed at a rate twice that of men. The oldest profession puts bread on the table for a lot of women who would otherwise go hungry."

"I guess I never really thought about it like that."

John continued, "It's a mad world we live in Bill, full of shanty towns and immortal hookers."

* * *

"Hey, John, what the hell is all this?" Bill called out from the back room of John's apartment.

"Why are you snooping around my place?" John said with a mouth full of bologna sandwich. Sandwiches were about all GBI agents could afford for lunch.

"The door was open, man. I was just walking by. What you got going on in here?" Bill asked, still standing in the doorway of the back room that was adjacent to the bathroom he had just exited.

Why didn't I close that stupid door? John thought as he left his half-eaten sandwich in the kitchen and walked to where Bill was standing. "If you must know, this is what I call the Event room. It's where I try to make sense of everything that's happened in the last twenty-seven years and what caused it all."

"Well, it looks like a crime scene storyboard," Bill said as he stepped inside the room and stood in front of the far wall, which was filled with news articles and pictures with strings between many of them, in what looked like a chaotic jumble of connecting people and events.

"That's because that's exactly what it is," John said as he joined Bill.

Bill studied the wall for several moments. "So, you're trying to solve the greatest mystery in human history?"

"Sure, why not?"

"Cause it's been twenty-seven years, and the world's best scientists haven't been able to figure it out, but you think you can?"

"Well, that's not true, is it?" John said.

"What do you mean?"

"I mean they have figured out what caused the Event; it's a virus. What they haven't figured out is who designed the Event virus."

"Not everyone agrees it's man-made, though," Bill countered.

"Anyone with a brain does."

"So, you think Nathan McDaniel created it?" Bill asked as he noticed his picture at the top center of the wall.

"No, not really, but I think he might be involved somehow. What I'm looking for are people with motive, the means, and especially people with both. I'm also looking for people who have profited since the Event."

Bill nodded. "Then I see why you have Ken Takahashi on here, but why is Nathan McDaniel on your board? Is it cause he's president of the FON?'

"That and his doctoral dissertation."

"Wait, you found his dissertation online? You mean you actually do know how to do an online search?"

"Ha ha, yes, I found his dissertation online, and I found it quite interesting," John said.

"Interesting how?"

John picked up a thick binder that was lying on the small table in front of the wall. "Here it is if you want to read it, but I'll summarize for you. See, he was getting his doctorate in economics, so his paper was on the economic forces that cause people to migrate throughout history."

"Yeah, that sounds exciting."

"Hear me out, will ya? The gist of it was that people don't go to new lands just for the sake of moving; they go there because they're seeking economic security or fleeing persecution, but usually for economic reasons."

"That makes sense," Bill replied.

John nodded again. "Well, he goes on to say that's the reason we never established colonies on the moon or Mars, because there no economic reason for people to move there, none at all."

"Yeah, so what, how does that make him a suspect for being involved in the Event?"

"Because after that he says that the only way humans will ever migrate to another planet would be if we discovered another Earthlike planet and people think they can improve their economic situation by going there. Since we know there's no such planet in our solar system, it would never happen."

"Why's that?" Bill asked.

"Because it would take at least a hundred years of the entire world's economic output to finance a manned mission to another solar system."

Bill laughed out loud. "You don't really think this guy is gonna to take over the whole world, do you?"

"No, probably not, but he's already in control of one-third of the former US and several Latin American countries as well. Hell, we're voting next week on whether to join the FON or not."

"So, you think this guy created the Event so all of this would happen and he could gradually take over the world, democratically mind you, all so he can send people to Alpha Centauri?"

"Well, he is talking about building a space elevator," John pointed out.

"You gotta let this go, man. I mean he wrote this paper thirty-five years before the Event happened. You're starting to sound like one of those conspiracy theorists."

"I never said I believed he caused it; he's just the only person I have enough evidence on right now to put on the top of the board. I mean, somebody's gotta be at the top of this stupid thing."

* * *

The door to the basement slowly opened, and light flooded into the room, temporarily blinding Laura. When her eyes adjusted, Sam was standing before her with a small knife in his right hand. "It's time, Laura," he said in an almost casual manner.

"Time for what?" she replied.

Sam nearly chuckled. "Time for you to take your clothes off."

"I don't think so," retorted Laura defiantly as she got to her feet.

"The blood is going to flow over those beautiful breasts one way or the other. We can do this the easy way or the hard way."

Laura laughed hysterically for several long seconds, as she struggled to contain the terror threatening to burst from her chest. "The hard way, asshole."

He moved suddenly and much faster than Laura would have thought. In one swift movement, he took her to the ground and was in full mount position with her arms pinned under his legs. He waved the knife in front of her face. "You obviously entertained ideas of fighting me. As you can see, I'm stronger and faster than I look."

Laura spat in his face. "Oh yeah, you're a real big, strong man, woman killer!"

Sam took the knife and slowly cut her blouse from the bottom to the top. Then he sliced open her bra. He stared at her disfigured chest with his mouth open for several seconds after the prosthesis fell out of her bra.

Laura again laughed hysterically. "How ya like them apples?"

Sam stammered. "Your breasts, they're gone. You're mutilated. This is all wrong. Where will the blood flow?" Sam then got off of her and walked quickly out of the room, muttering under his breath, "This is all wrong."

"Bahahahaha, you just can't make this stuff up!" Laura

said out loud, but her hysterical laughs faded to sobs as she wondered how long she had until he regained his composure and returned to finish the job.

* * *

John Fitzgerald and Bill Kowalski were sitting in John's office reviewing security footage from the Loganville area when Bill said, "Well, that's it, that's the last of it."

"Okay, spool it up again. There's gotta be something there. He watches his victims before he takes them. I know it," said John.

"Whatever you say, John, but we've been looking at this stuff all day, and we haven't seen anything yet," said Bill as he queued up the video footage again directly from his TICI.

John sounded a little annoyed. "Just transfer it to the screen so we can both see it. No, wait; let's watch the security footage from the Gillespie case again."

"The missing-persons case from last year? There wasn't even that much video. What makes you think there's something there that'll help us with this case?" asked Bill.

"I don't know, but after watching the Bishop footage all day, the only thing I can think about is the Gillespie case."

As Bill was negotiating the GBI server directly from his TICI, John reflected on the invasion of privacy that the security cameras represented.

"Don't you find it odd that even in the middle of the worst depression in centuries, we have security cameras everywhere? Even after the fall of the federal government, the cameras remain. You can't step outside your front door without a security camera capturing your every movement. Yet we can't seem to get so much as a glance of this guy," said John.

Bill glanced at John as he transferred the video feed directly to the monitor on John's desk. "Well, the cameras were put up before the Event and the New Depression, and they're not expensive at all to maintain. Plus, I think they give the government a sense of control, since they can pretty much track anyone once they leave their house."

John shook his head. "All of that fancy facial-recognition software isn't helping us find this guy."

"Maybe that's because he doesn't exist, John."

John ignored Bill's comment. "Just pull up the footage from the Gillespie case, will ya?"

"Here it is," replied Bill as he transferred the security footage directly from his TICI to the screen on John's desk. "You really gotta get one of these, so you can do this stuff yourself and stop using your partner like your personal secretary," joked Bill as he tapped his head.

"I would, but a GBI agent's pay won't even come close to paying for one of those things anymore. I wish I would have gotten one before the Event, when they were cheap, but I was retired then and didn't see any use for one."

Bill started scrolling through the footage. "Yeah man, I know. I'm just glad I got mine before, when I could afford it."

"Holy crap!" exclaimed John as they watched the security footage. "I've been overlooking a big part of this."

"What do you mean?"

"What would happen if this guy, the Ghost, kidnapped a woman that had an interface?" John asked.

Bill's eyebrows raised several inches. "Ahh, he'd get caught, cause she would be able to access the internet without him knowing it, and then she could call for help, even give the cops

GPS coordinates."

"Look up what percent of the population has an interface," demanded John, excited.

Bill looked up toward the ceiling for about three seconds as he accessed the information. "About 5 percent, according to three different sources."

"I knew it!" exclaimed John as he suddenly stood up from behind the desk and started pacing. "I'm pretty sure he's taken around fifty women or so since he started back killing. Statistically, he should have gotten one with a TICI by now, but he hasn't."

"It would only take about ten or fifteen minutes tops of following someone to tell if they had a TICI or not," Bill pointed out.

"Yeah, not even that long. You TICI users give yourselves away pretty quick," replied John as he sat back down to watch more footage. "He's here somewhere, I know it."

After about thirty minutes of watching the Gillespie security footage at high speed, John yelled, "Whoa, stop, go back. Yeah, right there, play, stop!"

They both stared at the screen for a few seconds before Bill said, "What are you looking at, the guy with the dog?"

"Yeah, that's exactly what I'm looking at, the guy with the dog. Remember how you found those black dog hairs at the scene of the Bishop abandoned car?"

Bill frowned slightly. "Yeah, I remember. So what? Lots of people have black dogs."

John continued to look at the man on the screen. He could only see part of the left profile of his face, and he was wearing a ball cap. "I've seen this guy before. I'm pretty sure he's in the Bishop footage. Bring up the Bishop footage on a split screen."

John had that feeling now, the feeling that came when he was close to solving a case. *After all these years, I'm finally going to catch the Ghost.*

"Yes sir, boss," replied Bill as he brought up the requested footage.

They had been speeding through the Bishop footage for only ten minutes when John had asked Bill to stop. "Holy cow, you're right, John, it's him."

John nodded in agreement. "Yep, this is our guy. We've got him watching two different victims, and he's got a black dog. This second shot should be good enough for the facial-recognition program to get something. Once that's done, compare it to everything we've got, mug shots, old FBI database, driver's license photos, everything!"

It took the facial recognition program about two minutes to go through every database they had access to. Bill did a few more final checks with his TICI and said, "We got nothing, John."

"This doesn't make any sense. How in the world can this guy not show up on anything? Nothing, no mug shot matches. This guy doesn't even have a driver's license?" John said in disgust.

"Stupid TICI, it's hung up on this one screen. Dang, I hate rebooting this thing!"

"I thought those things almost never did that."

"They don't. I can't remember the last time mine did this. Hang on a minute while I reboot."

John suddenly had a strange thought and said, "Wait, don't reboot. What is it stuck on?"

"This one driver's license photo," answered Bill.

"Transfer it to my screen please."

They both just stared at it in stunned silence for several long seconds before Bill said, "I don't get it. I think it's him, but it only kinda looks like him."

"He altered his appearance for the driver's license photo," replied John. "I don't know how he did it, but he altered his appearance in such a way that the facial-recognition program doesn't recognize him. Clever son of a ..."

Bill was shaking his head. "But why did my TICI lock up on that one photo? That's the weirdest thing."

"I don't know, Bill. Maybe subconsciously you recognized him, and when your interface locked up, it just happened to be on him? Hell, I don't know, maybe there's a ghost in the machine helping us out. All I know is we got him. Now let's go pay him a visit."

As they were preparing to leave, Bill said, "There's no way the judge is gonna give us a warrant on what we got."

"Screw a warrant. I got a woman that may still be alive being held by a psychopath. We got probable cause. I'd rather beg for forgiveness in this case," replied John.

* * *

Laura sat in the semi-darkness, staring at the psycho sitting in front of her. He had walked in about five minutes before and sat on the weight bench. He just sat there staring at her, not saying a word. Laura couldn't take the silence much longer, so she decided to taunt him. "You're going to get caught, you know, sooner rather than later."

Sam laughed before replying. "Not likely. The local police are undermanned and too busy just keeping the peace. The FBI doesn't exist, and people, in general, don't care about a few missing women. I operate with impunity in this new world created by the Event."

"Your arrogance will get you caught. You're not as smart as you think you are. You're also missing something—things are changing. This depression won't last."

Sam sat in silence for several seconds before responding. "If you're referring to the referendum vote for joining the Federation of Nations, don't be naïve. There's no way these conservative rednecks will vote for joining the FON. McDaniel makes Roosevelt look like Reagan. He's way too liberal, practically a pinko commie! Not to mention those cult crazies support him. That really makes him look bad."

She had him talking; now to keep him going. Anything to delay whatever he was here for. "You're just an out-of-touch old man, aren't you? The Zacharia Jones movement is spreading like wildfire around the world. The fact that McDaniel has the support of Zacharia Jones and Omni Ascend is a huge win for him, even here in Georgia."

"Why would anyone follow a twenty-six-year-old child? Hell, they even call him the Holy Child. What a bunch of idiots."

"Out-of-touch old man; you should have died," she retorted.

"None of this matters for you, though, does it?" Sam said as he stood up from the bench. "The only thing that matters right now is what am I going to do with you?"

"Oh yes, you can't kill me in your normal way, can you?" Laura said as she removed the rags covering her chest. "You have to see the blood running over the breast, don't you, you sick bastard?"

Now that Laura was exposed from the waist up, she continued to taunt her captor. "You're really a simple creature, aren't you?"

"What do you mean?"

"I mean you're just a sicko with a big breast fetish, how juvenile. You love big boobs, but what you really love is to see blood flowing over them. Do you have mommy issues?" she said in a baby voice.

Sam lit a candle and set it down between them. "Don't act like you have any kind of a clue what motivates me, you poor, mutilated whore," Sam said as he pulled a revolver from behind his back. "I think I'm just going to shoot you and be done with it."

Laura stared in horror as Sam raised the pistol and pointed it at her face. As quickly as he raised the pistol, he then lowered it as a red light started flashing behind him.

"You gain a brief reprieve," Sam said as he turned to walk out of the room. "But don't worry, I'll be back in just a few minutes to take care of you, as soon as I handle whoever is at the front door." He slammed the door behind him.

Although Laura knew it was futile, she began to yell as loud as she could. "Heeeelp! Please help me."

She stopped yelling after a few seconds and started sobbing. After a moment, she stopped and turned her head sideways to listen closely. *Was that a gunshot?* she thought.

After a few minutes, the door to the dungeon opened slowly and a male figure walked through. He crossed the room and knelt right in front of her. "You must be Laura Bishop. I'm John Fitzpatrick, GBI."

Laura sobbed silently and just stared at him for several seconds before the GBI agent spoke again. "What's the matter, you've never seen a Black Irishman before?"

Laura started laughing and sobbing uncontrollably. "I don't know that I have, but you're the best-looking Irishman I've ever seen."

Agent Fitzpatrick hugged her and then yelled out, "Hey, Bill, she's alive, we're down here!" Then he turned to her and said, "You don't have to worry about that sicko, he'll never hurt anyone else again."

"You killed him?" Laura asked.

"Yeah, he's dead."

Laura felt her knees buckle, and she shielded her eyes from the sun as they emerged from the psychopath's house thirty minutes later. She paused for a moment and she felt she might vomit. The two GBI agents were on either side of her as they walked toward the car parked on the side of the street. She stared in wonderment as people poured out of their homes into their yards and onto the street. People were hugging each other, high-fiving, even dancing. She thought to herself, *Are they all celebrating my freedom?*

Bill drew his gun as they heard several gunshots. John pushed his arm down and said, "It's okay, they're celebrating something I think."

As they approached several people who were pouring beer over each other, John asked the closest man, "What's going on here? What's the big deal?"

"Haven't you heard? It's over, man, the depression is over!" the man said as he shook up a can of beer and then popped the top, spewing it all over the three of them.

Bill then asked the woman standing next to the man they had just spoken to. "What the heck is he talking about?"

"They just announced the results. Georgia voted to join the Federation. McDaniel is our president now. He's gonna turn things around like he did in Mexico!"

Another woman nearby yelled at them, "God bless the Holy Child, God bless Zacharia Jones!"

Laura turned in a circle as she watched all the people in the streets celebrating. There was loud music coming from every direction, and people were dancing on parked cars. Joyous pandemonium could be seen everywhere. She turned to John and asked, "Is any of this real? Is this happening?"

John smiled and looked at her as he replied, "It's a strange new world we live in, Ms. Bishop, full of hope and promise."

Laura laughed out loud. "You know, I think I actually believe you."

Chapter 6: Come Together

The Event forced humanity into true long-term planning for the first time in history. Before the Event, most people and governments only planned for as far as their own lifetimes (if that) and often left things in a bigger mess than what they found it. The Event made that kind of thinking obsolete. —Zacharia Jones, Out of Darkness: The Event Chronicle

Date: 62 AE

John Fitzpatrick was still woozy as Deborah helped him into the front seat of her car. He was a little surprised that they let him go from the clinic while he was still so unsteady on his feet, but he supposed they knew what they were doing. In two weeks, his freshly implanted TICI should be fully operational, and he could start work at the recently commissioned ISAS, the International Space Agency Security.

After they were both buckled in, Deborah told the car to drive to John's house, and it set off after waiting for traffic to clear.

"I still can't believe you finally had a TICI implanted," she said as the car navigated its way through Chicago.

"Was a requirement for the job," John replied as he searched his head for scars while looking in the vanity mirror. "Besides, it's about time I joined the modern age, don't you think?"

Deborah laughed a little. "You can stop looking for a scar. You won't find one."

As John looked in the mirror, he smiled at his thirty-year-old reflection. He had been at baseline now for several decades, but sometimes he was still shocked when he didn't see an old man in the mirror. "How the hell do they implant the thing without any kind of an incision?"

"It's a corporate secret, and Takahashi Industries isn't telling."

"Yeah, they even brought their own staff to the clinic to do the—" John paused for a second as he searched for the right word. "Procedure."

John leaned back in his seat and closed his eyes as he thought about how different his experience at the clinic had been, compared to how it would have been before the Event sixty-two years ago. Before the Event, he most likely would have gone to a major hospital to have such a procedure done, but there weren't any hospitals anymore. Now there were just emergency centers scattered across the former United States, with their attached clinics for cosmetic surgeries and TICI implantations.

Deborah interrupted his thoughts with her laughter. "Now that you've got a TICI, the next thing you know, you'll be having your pecs or gluts augmented."

"Not in ten thousand years. What the heck are people thinking with all of the so-called body enhancements these days?" he replied.

"I don't know, babe. I've been thinking about some bigger boobs," she said as she pushed her breasts up with her hands.

When John only smiled, Deborah said, "Oh, you'd be okay with that huh?"

"Baby, I'll support any decision you make about your body, but I think you're beautiful just the way you are." John looked at her and smiled; she really was beautiful.

She laughed again. "You men are all the same!"

Before John could reply, a dog ran out in front of the car and the car suddenly braked hard. Deborah looked at the expression on John's face. "Will you just relax? You know these cars are way safer than having a human driver."

"I know, but I would still feel better driving myself," John replied.

"It's illegal to manually drive a car now, and you know it. Besides, self-driving cars have reduced auto fatalities by over 95 percent over the last twenty years."

"You know I get turned on when you throw stats in my face," John said in a bedroom voice.

"Oh my goodness, John Fitzpatrick, how can you be turned on while still groggy from anesthesia?"

"I'm a helluva man," John replied as he drifted off to sleep.

* * *

Two weeks later, John was arranging his things in his new office at ISAS headquarters when a tall, thin man walked into the office with his face obscured by the boxes he was holding. After he set the boxes down on the desk facing John's desk, he walked over to John and offered his hand.

"Hi, I'm Steve Parker," he said as he shook hands with John.

"John Fitzpatrick."

"It's great to finally meet you, John. I still can't believe I'm partners with John Fitzpatrick."

John smiled as their handshake finished. "Well, it's nice to meet you too Steve."

After they both sat down and started arranging their things in their new office, John decided to try out his new TICI for a bit. After clicking his rear teeth together several times, he finally managed the correct sequence, and it came up. A few minutes later, he was checking out world headlines that displayed directly on his retina. He heard Steve clear his throat.

"Hey, do you know when we're gonna get our first case? What kind of cases are we going to get anyway, and why does the ISA even need detectives?"

John paused for a moment as he tried to get the TICI display to leave his vision. After he finally managed to get his TICI to respond, he replied, "You know I've been wondering the same thing myself. Not sure what kind of cases we're going to get, but the ISA is already the largest and most powerful bureaucracy in the Federation, and space exploration is at the top of President McDaniel's agenda."

Steve nodded. "You got that right. I just saw yesterday that the space elevator they're building in South America is almost halfway done."

"Yep, and they're about to complete the largest laser array ever constructed, in Nevada next year," John replied.

"I still can't believe they're going to send a probe all the way to Alpha Centauri with nothing but a light sail and laser beams."

John couldn't help but agree with his new partner. Most

people thought it was crazy but went along with it, as it was perceived to be "good for the economy." However, he didn't think it was crazy at all. There was a potentially habitable planet out there; why wouldn't you want to send a probe and take a closer look? John's thoughts were interrupted as a well-dressed Asian man entered their office.

"You men are right," he said, "the ISA is the president's number-one priority. Not only because he likes science and space exploration but because it's the foundation for his economic policies."

"Hello, Captain Chang, good to see you again," Steve said as he stood up.

Captain Chang nodded to each of them. "John, Steve, you guys just call me Tommy, okay?"

"So, do you have an assignment for us yet?" Steve asked.

"As a matter of fact, I do. Be in my office in ten minutes. and I'll give you a full briefing."

* * *

As they were entering Captain Chang's office, Steve leaned into John and whispered, "Does he have calf implants?"

While Captain Chang had a seat, John looked at his lower legs and noticed that they did look rather large through his pants, but John thought it more likely that he was just a fitness nut. Looking back toward Steve, he saw a slight grin on his face. John shook his head as he realized that his new partner was a smartass.

After John and Steve sat down in front of the captain's desk, he said to them, "I've just sent you guys the files for the case you'll be investigating. If you would go ahead and open them, please."

After fumbling with his TICI for a few seconds, John was able to pull the file to his vision, and as he skimmed it, he said, "Omni Ascend finances? Our first case is going to be investigating the finances of the world's largest cult?"

"Yes, we have reason to believe that Omni Ascend is grossly underreporting their income and thus defrauding the government of potentially billions of dollars."

Steve leaned forward as he said with surprise, "Does Omni Ascend really bring in that kind of money?"

"Oh yes, detectives, Zacharia Jones's cult spans the world and has hundreds of millions of followers who donate rather freely to his cause. This makes Jones and his cult one of the most influential organizations on the planet."

John cleared his throat. "Excuse me for saying so, Captain, I mean Tommy, but this seems like a job more suitable for the tax assessor's office than ISA Security."

Captain Chang nodded in agreement. "I see why you might think that, John, but anything that threatens the flow of money to the government directly threatens the ISA, and the director is very proactive when it comes to protecting the funding of his department. However, you are partially right."

John and Steve shared a glance before John said, "How so?"

"The tax evasion investigation is just a cover for what you'll really be investigating. The real subject of your investigation will be to ascertain the loyalty of Zacharia Jones."

"His loyalty to the McDaniel administration?" Steve asked.

"I thought Zacharia Jones was one of the president's biggest supporters," John said.

"Yeah, I know how it sounds, but hear me out." The captain took a deep breath before continuing. "You see we have an informant inside the Omni Ascend organization who tells us Zacharia Jones has become disillusioned with his movement as well as President McDaniel. Apparently, he doesn't trust the president's motivations, and he fears if the FON gains control of the world that President McDaniel will declare himself dictator."

John found all this talk about loyalty to the president and the FON disturbing. "I've heard other people voice the exact same concerns."

"That's true, but none of those people have hundreds of millions of followers either. Our real concern right now is China, of course. Jones has tens of millions of followers in China, and they are quite vocal about wanting to join the FON."

"And China still won't allow a referendum vote to join the FON," John said as he remembered that China was the last piece missing for the FON to have control of the world. China was the only superpower that survived intact following the immediate aftermath of the Event. In fact, China had managed to expand its territory following the chaos, years after the Event and now controlled all of Southeast Asia and Japan. Although China's economy hadn't recovered from the depression like the nations of the FON, they still refused to join despite formidable pressure from within.

"What else is your informant telling you?" Steve asked.

"She says that Jones is planning to tell his followers in China that President McDaniel is not to be trusted and they should stay away from the FON."

"Whoa, if that happens and Jones's followers in China no longer support FON unification, China will never allow a vote, not that they're going to anyway," John added.

Captain Chang nodded. "And we desperately need China's

resources to complete the space elevator and the Phoenix project."

"Okay, Captain, we get it, we're in. I think we need to start with this informant, so can you tell us her name?" John replied. He hated the idea of covertly investigating Zacharia Jones, just to ascertain his loyalty, but what disturbed him most was the question of what the ISA/FON would do if it was discovered that Zacharia Jones was planning to do exactly what the informant suggested.

Captain Chang stood up from behind his desk. "Well, that's the problem, because all we have for a name is Calliope, and we're pretty sure that's not her real name because there's no one in the Jones organization with that name."

"How have you been communicating with this Calliope?" Steve asked.

"Via email, and we're working on tracing the emails, but it's proved problematic, to say the least."

"Problematic?" John probed.

"Yes, she tried to hide her location, and she's very good."

Steve slapped the arm of his chair. "How do you even know this person is legit? She could be anyone."

"No, she's given us details in her emails that only someone high up in his organization would know."

John stood up, and Steve followed his lead as John said, "Thank you, Captain. We'll get right on this. Can you forward those emails to me, please?"

"Yes, of course."

As they were leaving the captain's office, John turned around. "And please let us know as soon as the tech boys trace down where those emails came from."

* * *

John and Steve walked up the steep steps that led to the Primary Temple. John looked up toward the twin spires of the temple and couldn't help but be impressed with the sheer size of the building and its architecture. As the headquarters for Omni Ascend, it was by far the largest and most impressive building in Albany, New York.

John stared at the large plaque that was in plain view as he and Steve entered through the front entrance. The plaque said, *It is not our flaws that define us but our struggle to overcome them, for what better defines humanity than our constant pursuit of perfection.* John thought that was a load of crap, but he had a low opinion of religion in general and lower still of cults, even ones with hundreds of millions of members.

"Welcome to the Primary Temple," said the attractive, fresh-faced woman sitting at the reception desk. "Peace to you both. Are you Ascendants? Would you be interested in a brochure?"

"I'm Detective John Fitzpatrick, and this is Detective Steve Parker of ISA Security."

"Oh, I never heard of ISA Security," the woman replied as she inspected the badges they both produced.

Steve put his badge back in his pocket. "Yeah, not many people have. ISA Security was just created a few months ago by direct order of President McDaniel."

"Well, what can I do for you detectives?"

"We're here to see Zacharia Jones," John replied.

"Do you have an appointment?"

"No, we don't have an appointment, but this is official ISA business," Steve said.

"One moment please," the receptionist said as she accessed her TICI. After a moment, she replied, "I'm sorry, but the Holy Child isn't in today."

"The Holy Child?" Steve said sarcastically.

"Yes, Zacharia Jones isn't in today."

"Oh brother," Steve said as he rolled his eyes.

John stepped in front of Steve and said, "Perhaps we can speak to the Holy Child's second in command then?"

"There isn't a second in command," she replied as if John should have known this.

"Well, is there someone higher up we can speak with?" John asked.

"One moment please," she said as he once again accessed her TICI. After a few minutes, she said, "Detectives, if you will follow me please, Ms. Tucker will see you."

As they followed the receptionist down the hall, John asked, "What does Ms. Tucker do?"

"She's the director of public relations for Omni Ascend."

"Very good," John said with a smile.

A few minutes later, they walked through the door to Ms. Tucker's office, and as she stood up from behind her desk, John saw her face light up when she saw him.

"John Fitzpatrick, is that really you?" Ms. Tucker asked.

John studied her as they approached, but he spent several moments placing her face. His heart raced, as he knew she was important to him from before the Event, but everyone looked so young now.

"Hello, John," she said as she hugged him.

His jaw dropped as he finally recognized her. "Oh my God, Alicia, it's so good to see you."

"Well, it took you long enough to recognize me."

"Well, it's been over sixty years since we last saw each other," John said as he remembered the last time he saw her, just after his wife's death at the very beginning of the Event. All his old feelings for her came rushing to the surface as he felt his pulse quicken and his face flush while he struggled to regain his composure. He looked away from her and glanced at his partner. "Oh, where are my manners? Steve Parker, this is Alicia Fenton."

As she shook hands with Steve, Alicia said, "My name is Tucker now, John. I guess you didn't hear about Jack?"

John again looked at Steve. "Jack was my old partner back when I was in Bureau."

"Oh, okay," Steve said as he nodded.

"John, Jack was murdered during the depression years," Alicia said.

John took a step back as he processed that information. "I'm very sorry to hear that."

Alicia nodded. "It was many years ago, during the height of the dark times. Thugs broke into our house, and Jack tried to stop them."

"I'm so sorry, Alicia," John repeated.

"Thank you, John. Please have a seat, gentlemen." She gestured to the sofa in front of her desk. "So, what brings you to the Primary Temple? I know you didn't come to see me."

"We're here to review Omni Ascend's financial records, including tax returns, and we need to speak with—" Steve hesitated a moment as he searched for the right word. "The Holy Child."

Alicia smiled and chuckled slightly. "You can simply call him by his name around me. I just work for him; I'm not a hardcore believer."

"So, can you schedule an appointment with him for us?" John asked, trying to not stare at her too hard.

Alicia took a deep breath. "Well, you see, I really can't, because he's currently unavailable."

"What does that mean, unavailable?" Steve asked with slight contempt in his voice.

Alicia smiled at them both. "It means he's gone 'search about,' as his followers like to call it."

"Search about?" Steve asked.

"Yes, it's nothing to be concerned about, but every so often, he just disappears. Sometimes it's just for a few weeks; other times it's been many months. The Ascendants say he goes to commune with God."

"So, how long has he been gone this time?" John asked as he searched the Web via his TICI for any sightings of Jones.

She looked up briefly before replying. "Almost three weeks now."

"And you have no idea where he's at?" Steve demanded.

"I assure you, Detective, if I knew where he was, I would tell you."

John spoke up before Steve said something rude. "Thank you, Alicia, can you take us to your accounting division, so we can begin our investigation?"

"John, I hate to ask this, but do you have a search warrant?"

Before John could reply, Steve touched his wrist projector, and the search warrant projected into the air above his outstretched arm.

"I see," Alicia said as she stood up from behind her desk and started toward the door. "Detectives, if you will follow me, I'll take you to our financial director."

A few minutes later, she held the door into the financial

department for them, but after Steve went through, she pulled the door shut and stepped close to John and said in a low voice, "If you're in town tonight I'd like to take you to dinner."

John felt his face grow hot as he stumbled for something to say. "Yeah, we're staying in Albany tonight, so I'd like that."

* * *

Later that evening, John tried not to stare at Alicia as he sipped his drink. He couldn't stop looking into her eyes, as if they were oceans he wanted to drown in.

"John Fitzpatrick, you're going to make me blush if you keep staring at me without saying anything."

John choked on the wine he had in his mouth. "I'm sorry, but I still can't believe that I'm here with you after all these years, and you look so ..." he hesitated a bit, "young."

Alicia smiled at him. "Well, we all look young, John. Late twenties or early thirties everywhere you look."

"Yeah, but I never knew you before, when you were this young. I mean you were always an attractive woman, but now—" John stopped abruptly, as he realized he might be going too far, and then he remembered Deborah.

"Now I think you're the one blushing."

"You know I have a girlfriend, right?" he blurted out.

She looked at him for a moment in silence. "Of course I know. It's all over your social media. She's quite attractive."

"Yeah, she's way out of my league," John said with a forced laugh.

"Stop that. You're quite the catch. She's the lucky one."

"No, Debbie is way better looking than me."

"Looks aren't everything, you know. Intelligence is very

sexy," Alicia said as she raised her eyebrows.

"Yeah, I guess I'm a pretty smart guy," he acknowledged.

"Pretty smart? Jack always said you had the best deductive mind in the Bureau."

"Jack had a habit of exaggerating my abilities."

"He admired you greatly, as did I."

"So, what do you know about Zacharia Jones?" John asked uncomfortably as he changed the subject.

Alicia frowned but humored him anyway. "Honestly I don't know him that well at all. We speak on occasion, but only about business."

"Is it true what they say about him? That he's irresistible to women and uses his cult to funnel a constant flow of women to him?"

"Are you asking me if I've slept with him?"

John swallowed hard as he realized how his question must have sounded. "No, of course not. There are just all of these rumors out there about his sexual appetite and how he takes advantage of women."

"I'm surprised with you, John. I never knew you for one who listened to rumors, much less repeated them."

John smiled. She always knew him so well. "So, what do you know about his politics? Does he still support FON expansion and eventual annexation of China?"

"Are you interviewing me, Detective?"

John hung his head as he realized he was failing at this badly. After taking another drink of his wine, he said, "I'm sorry, Alicia. You're right, that was rude."

She reached out and grabbed his hand. "No, it's fine. I was being a bit touchy. So, to answer your question, I know less about his political affiliations than I do his sexual proclivities.

Now let me ask you a question: did you find what you were looking for from the financial department?"

"No, not really. Everything was remarkably in order," John replied honestly.

Alicia set her glass down. "But that's not what you were really there for, was it?"

"I can't comment on that," was all John could think to say.

"So, what are you going to tell her?"

"What? Tell who what?"

"For the world's greatest detective, sometimes you're remarkably slow on the uptake." After a few moments of silence from John, she continued. "How are you going to break the news to Deborah?"

John shook his head slowly. "What news?"

"That you're breaking up with her."

John felt like his heart was going to leap out of his chest as he picked up his glass and drained it. Thankfully they were interrupted by the waiter bringing their food.

* * *

John's head was still spinning, despite lying in his bed at the hotel. What was he going to do about Alicia? He couldn't deny his feelings for her, but what about Deborah? As his mind raced and he tried to apply logic to this impossible situation he heard someone pounding on the door. He was relieved to find Steve standing there when he opened it. He half-expected it to be Alicia.

"Did you turn your TICI off? I've been trying to reach you for hours," Steve said.

John turned his TICI back on as he let Steve in. "Sorry about that, just a lot on my mind right now. What's up?"

"The tech geeks at headquarters were finally able to trace those emails from the informant."

John perked up a bit. "Great news! Where did they come from?"

"Well, they actually *did* come from Omni Ascend locations, three of them, in fact: Albany, Zurich, and Johannesburg."

"Oh wow, did that help us out?"

Steve nodded. "Heck yeah. Remember that employee file we got from the accounting nerd earlier today?"

"Yeah?"

"Well, that file also had employee transfer addresses. Anyway, I was able to look at all the employees who have been assigned to those locations, and it turns out there's only one that was at each location when each email was sent," Steve said with a huge grin.

"So, who is it?"

"Her name is Winifred Jackson. She's some kind of high-level priestess or something."

"Good work. Where is she now?"

"Oh yeah, I almost forgot the good part: she's right here in Albany!"

"That's a good break for us. We'll pay her a visit in the morning," John replied.

After Steve left the room, John stretched out on the bed and tried to sleep, but something was scratching its way to the surface that demanded his attention. It was just a feeling, really, but over the years, John had learned to trust his intuition. Something was telling him that there was some connection between this informant and his obsession with solving the Event mystery. Was this another piece of the puzzle? He had no idea how it might fit, but maybe he would get more answers tomorrow. He tried to sleep, but his mind kept going back to one image: the storyboard that took up an entire wall of his office at home.

* * *

"May the Holy Child guide us to ascension, my sons," the high priestess said as Steve and John entered the worship hall of the Primary Temple. "Please have a seat, and tell me how I can help you, detectives." The high priestess was a small, plump woman with a round face and, despite her thirty-year-old appearance, had the temperament of a little old lady.

After they were seated on one of the many pews, John said, "High Priestess, can you tell us how well you know the Holy Child?"

She smiled at them, straightened out the wrinkles in her all-white pants suit as she joined them on the pew, and said, "Please just call me Winnie. We don't call each other by our titles, except for the Holy Child, of course, bless his name."

"So, Winnie, how well do you know him?" John repeated.

"Oh, I know the Holy Child quite well; he shares all of his teachings with me so I can spread them to the people. Are you boys seeking ascension or nirvana?"

"No, ma'am, we're trying to find Zacharia, I mean the Holy Child. Do you know where he is?" Steve asked.

She frowned slightly. "Of course I know where he is; the Holy Child has gone search about."

"Yes, that's what Ms. Tucker said as well. Do you know where he is *exactly*?" Steve asked.

Winnie leaned in close to them and asked, "Did she blaspheme against the Holy Child?"

"What?" Steve said.

"No, Winnie, she didn't say anything bad about the Holy Child," John interjected.

The high priestess leaned back, not very satisfied with John's reply. "Well, it wouldn't shock me if she did; I don't think she's an Ascendant at all."

"Ms. Jackson, do you know where the Holy Child is or when he might return?" Steve asked again.

"He'll return when he receives his message from God and not before," she said incredulously.

John intervened again. "That's right. Ms. Jackson, have you ever emailed ISA Security for any reason?"

"Heavens no, why would I do that?" she replied, then she appeared to receive a message via her TICI. "If you will excuse me, I have business to attend to."

As she walked away, John and Steven looked at each other for a moment before John said, "What do you think? Does she seem like our informant to you?"

Steve laughed loudly. "She's an idiot is what I think."

"Yeah, this is starting to feel like a wild goose chase." Perhaps his intuition was wrong this time.

A short time later, as they were taking the car to the train station, they both received a message from Captain Chang that said the earlier report they received from the tech department was incorrect. After reading the message, John said, "So it appears we *were* on a wild goose chase. The real informant, whoever it is, somehow managed to attach false IPs on all of the emails so they only appeared to come from Albany, Johannesburg, and Zurich."

"Yeah, they intentionally wanted us to think that dumbass

high priestess was the informant," Steve said.

"I just got this funny image in my head, like we're in one of those old pre-Event movies where the bad guy is this master computer hacker or something," John said with a chuckle.

"Or better yet, one of those stupid movies where there's an AI trying to take over the world!"

Something about that statement made the hair on John's neck stand up. "What did you say?"

"You know, like one of those old stupid movies where some kind of AI is trying to take control of everything. 'Shall we play a game?'" Steve said in a computerized voice.

"Yeah, I get where you're going, but what if that's what's actually happening?"

"Come on, man," Steve said. "This is just someone messing with us."

"Yeah, you're probably right," John said, even though he felt like something weird was happening.

* * *

"John, wake up. Wake up, John."

John woke with a start and realized he was still on the train heading toward Chicago. He looked at Steve through foggy eyes. "What's going on?"

"Just turn on your TICI. You'll see, it's all over the news."

As John wiped the sleep from his eyes, he looked around the train compartment and immediately recognized that something was wrong. The woman across the aisle from him was sobbing, and several other people around him had tears in their eyes. Two rows back, four people were holding hands and appeared to be praying.

He could overhear two men arguing. "I don't care if you're not a believer, you can't argue about the impact he had on society."

What the heck is going on? John thought as he activated his TICI and immediately saw the news reports that Steve mentioned. They were reporting that Zacharia Jones appeared on a stage in Tiananmen Square during a concert and set himself on fire. The concert was sponsored by the Chinese government and had an anti-FON theme. John watched the video, and he recognized Zacharia Jones as he walked out onto the stage in front of thousands of Chinese people and said, "I am Zacharia Jones." Then he bent over and fumbled with something and burst into flames. John watched the horrifying image of Zacharia Jones on fire as he ran off the stage.

"So much for Zacharia Jones renouncing the FON and telling his Chinese followers to reject it," Steve said.

"What do you mean?" John asked.

"You haven't seen the reports yet have you? Apparently, there are massive pro-FON protests popping up all over China now. They all think Jones sacrificed himself so China would allow a vote on FON unification."

"It does seem that way, doesn't it?" John said.

"Man, we really were on a wild goose chase, weren't we?"

None of this sat well with John; he could feel it in his gut. He shut down his TICI and turned to face Steve. "Something's not right here."

"What do you mean?"

"I mean some mysterious computer genius hacker of an informant tells us that Zacharia Jones is going to turn against the FON and President McDaniel, then as we're trying to investigate those allegations, Jones turns up in Beijing and sets himself on fire to protest the Chinese government."

"Yeah, that is kinda weird, I admit."

"Now there's a wave of protests spreading across China. China will be a member of the FON by the end of the year, mark my words," John said emphatically.

As the noise level in their compartment grew to a crescendo, John wondered what would happen to the Omni Ascend movement now that its charismatic leader was gone. He couldn't imagine someone like the high priestess holding it together for long. Despite John's disdain for religion and especially cults, he had to admit that Jones's message of religious harmony, inclusion, peace, and world unity had been instrumental in the formation and subsequent success of the FON. Now it looked like the FON would unite humanity for the first time in history, and Jones apparently sacrificed himself to bring it to fruition. However, with Jones dead, Omni Ascend would most likely fade into history.

"Hey, check this out," Steve said as he sent a link to John.

John opened it and saw that Jones's followers in China were saying they managed to smuggle his body to India and they were going to hold a funeral for him next week. John closed the page and looked at Steve. "I wish I could go to that funeral."

Steve gave him a puzzled look. "Why?"

"Cause I'd like to open that casket."

"What for?"

"I don't think Jones will be in it."

"Why do you think that?"

"Just a hunch," John said as he closed his eyes and reclined his seat.

Chapter 7: Mary Returns

I'm frequently asked why humans never colonized Mars, and my answer is always the same: there's nothing there!—Nathan McDaniel

Date: 71 AE

Mary Ann Jones grunted in frustration as she tried for the third time to open the airlock. She didn't remember it being this hard to open, but after seventy years of isolation, perhaps *Nautilus* was reluctant to give up her solitude. She should have known it wouldn't be this easy; nothing about this mission had gone as planned.

After a fourth attempt, she conceded defeat. "Federici, get up here and see if you can budge this thing."

"On my way, Commander," she heard Vincent Federici, payload specialist and the largest of her crew, reply over the radio.

As she waited for Federici to suit up and cycle through the

shuttle's airlock, she heard the International Space Agency director, Robert Asher, over her radio. "Just relax, Commander Jones. We won't start the broadcast until you're ready to move through the hatch and officially board *Nautilus*."

Mary could feel beads of sweat forming on her forehead, and she resisted the urge to try to wipe them away. "Thank you, Director. I haven't forgotten." It bothered her a little that Robert could sense her apprehension from so far away, even though he must know what demons waited for her on the other side of that hatch. Not demons so much as sweet sadness.

Mary smiled as she remembered when the director had called to personally invite her to join the newly formed ISA five years ago. He said he couldn't imagine anyone more qualified to lead the mission back to *Nautilus*; the first manned spaceflight since the Event. She was honored, of course, but recognized the real reason he wanted her to command this mission: he intended to capture the world's imagination and ignite enthusiasm for the space elevator project, and what better way to do it than send Mary Ann Jones, the last person in space and the mother of Zacharia Jones?

The unwelcome image of her son in flames intruded into her thoughts. *Why, Zach, why did you have to martyr yourself for the cause?*

"Coming in now," she heard Federici over the radio as the shuttle's airlock hatch opened and he floated slowly toward her and the *Nautilus* airlock.

"Come on, big guy," she chided as he too struggled with the hatch.

"It's not budging," Federici replied.

"Mawangi, is there something in there we could use as a

cheater pipe?" Mary said over the radio to mission specialist Carol Mawangi.

"We'll see what we can do," Carol replied.

After a few minutes, pilot Zhang Yong Chen replied, "I think I have something. I'll put it in the airlock."

Mary wedged the makeshift cheater pipe through the hatch so the pipe stuck out about half a meter. She put her feet on it, and with her outstretched hands braced against the outer wall, she pushed with all of her strength for several moments and was ready to quit when she felt it give way.

"There it is," Vincent said loudly.

After Vincent removed the pipe, Mary took a moment to prepare for the broadcast. She activated the helmet cam, clicked her back teeth three times to connect the video feed directly to the ISA website and broadcast worldwide. "This is Mary Ann Jones; we've docked with *Nautilus*, and I'm about to enter."

Mary opened the hatch and floated into the *Nautilus*'s airlock, shutting the hatch behind her. She felt no rush of air as she entered *Nautilus* from the airlock.

"After seventy years, *Nautilus* is once again occupied and under human control," she boldly announced before continuing with the scripted part of the broadcast the director had made her memorize. "The first step of humanity's long journey to conquer the stars is now complete, but we must not waver in our commitment or ambition if we are to succeed. Over the following months, we will move *Nautilus* to a geosynchronous orbit and use her as the counterweight for the space elevator. *Nautilus* will serve as the foundation for a space station that will, over the years, grow so large as to one day make *Nautilus* seem like a playhouse in comparison. From there we will launch probes to the stars, and one day we ourselves will visit those stars."

After giving time for cheers and applause that she imagined were ringing around the world, she continued. "It appears there is still breathable atmosphere, so I'm going to remove my helmet."

Mary removed her helmet and inhaled before removing the cam and reattaching it to her shoulder. "The air is a little stale but otherwise unremarkable. I'm signaling the crew to join me in the *Nautilus*. Now begins the tedious task of refitting the *Nautilus* and preparing to move her to geosynchronous orbit above Quito, Ecuador."

Once the rest of the crew was on board, Mary gave Zhang the cam and said, "I'm turning you over to the pilot of the shuttle, Zhang Yong Chen. Pilot Chen will take you on a tour of the station as he does his part of the inspection."

"Thank you, Commander Jones," Zhang said as he took over the broadcast.

Before the launch, Director Asher had taken pains to explain to Mary that it was crucial for Zhang to be seen as an important member of the crew, as many Chinese leaders weren't completely sold on the concept of a space industry–based economy. However, space exploration was at the heart of President McDaniel's long-term plan for worldwide economic recovery and long-term sustainability. Nine years after Unification, China's membership in the FON was tenuous at best, but having Zhang on this high-profile mission would go a long way toward bringing them fully into the fold. Mary understood all of this and thought the director could have saved his speech for someone else. Besides, she was more than happy to let someone else have the spotlight for a change.

* * *

While the rest of her crew was performing their assigned tasks of inspecting the station, Mary entered the second ring, which was still spinning after all these years. As she walked through the different compartments of the rotating ring, she found herself standing in front of the door to her old quarters. What was waiting for her on the other side of the door?

After hesitating for several moments, she entered, shining her light around the room as she looked at the mess her old quarters were in. She didn't remember leaving it in such a condition, but at the time, she wasn't concerned with tidiness and couldn't imagine that she might one day return.

She picked up a shirt that was lying on the floor and without thinking put it to her nose as memories overwhelmed her.

"You are beautiful as ever," Mary heard a voice say. She quickly turned to her right, but no one was there.

Mary lay down on the bed, and as she closed her eyes, she could hear Vasily breathing, could smell his familiar musky odor, and was jolted seventy years in the past. She opened her eyes, and she knew she was alone, even though she could still feel his presence.

"How can you be haunting this place? I took you home, remember?" she said aloud. As if in answer, the lights flickered and then came on, went off again, flickered a few more times, and then came on for good.

"Power restored," Carol Mawangi said over the station intercom.

"Good job, Mawangi," Mary said into her radio.

With power restored and full lighting returned, the spell seemed to lift, and Mary felt fully anchored in the present, so she set about boxing up Vasily's clothes, but before she could get started, Carol interrupted.

"Commander Jones, Director Asher is on videoconference and is requesting you."

"You mean he's on the old *Nautilus* videocam system?"

"You got it; want me to patch him through to your quarters?" Carol asked.

Mary looked around her quarters for a second before remembering the monitor at the desk. "Yeah, patch him through."

"Hello, Mary," Robert Asher said as Mary sat down in front of the monitor.

"Hello, Director."

"How's everything looking? Is the station in good enough condition to move?"

Mary paused for a moment before replying. "Well, we're still conducting our initial assessment, but so far the station appears to be in excellent condition. The fact that the hull isn't breached, we still have atmosphere, and both rings are still rotating indicates that we shouldn't have any issues meeting the timeline."

"And you restored power already?"

"Yes, power was just restored, and nothing's on fire yet, so the electrical system as well as the onboard computers all seem to be fully operational," Mary replied.

Robert laughed a bit. "If not slightly dated."

"Oh, the computers, you mean? Yeah, we'll have to replace them all, of course, but we knew that already." Mary looked around her room before she continued. "Luckily for us, they designed this entire station so computer hardware and software could be easily replaced and upgraded."

"So, do you foresee any difficulties with stopping the rings two days from now?" Robert asked.

"No, it shouldn't be an issue."

"Good, I'll go ahead and give the go to launch the supply ships in two days."

"Sounds good, Director. Once we get the rings stopped and the additional fuel we need, we'll be able to start boosting *Nautilus* back up into a stable orbit and eventually into geostationary."

"That's good news. If there had been any major delays, we might not have been able to save the station. Her orbit was decaying pretty rapidly," Robert said.

"Don't jinx us. We haven't moved it yet," Mary replied. The station had been fitted with automated ion thrusters that had kept it in orbit for the last seventy years, but the ion propellant had run out, and *Nautilus*'s orbit had been deteriorating for several years.

"I have full faith in you, Mary."

"Thank you, Director."

* * *

Robert Asher narrowed his eyes and sighed inwardly as the camera flashes and video lights shined too brightly on him. He kept reminding himself that this was part of the price he had to pay for the continued success of the program.

"Director Asher, how are you going to stay busy for the next seven days? Aren't you worried about boredom?" one of the dozens of reporters shouted out as Robert and his two companions walked toward the space elevator loading platform.

Robert laughed a little. "No, I've got plenty to keep me busy on the ride up. Unfortunately, it'll be business as usual for the next seven days. No vacation for me."

Another reporter shouted out, "Are you concerned at all about being the first passengers on the elevator? Aren't the three of you going to be pretty cramped?"

"No, I'm not concerned at all. As you know, we've already done an unmanned test run loaded with four times the cargo weight that we'll be taking up on this trip. The only difference is, we'll be along for the ride," Robert said as he motioned to his two companions.

"Director Asher," one of the local Ecuadorian reporters called out, "what about all of the delays? It's been a year and a half since *Nautilus* was moved into geosynchronous orbit, and the cable was supposed to be completed six months ago."

"Yes, there have been some delays," Robert replied.

"Is that why you're going, Director?" she asked. "To restore public confidence in the ISA and to deflect attention from all of the rumors of corruption, cost overruns, and waste in your department?"

Robert smiled and nodded. "Well, the truth is I'm going because I want to experience firsthand the spectacular view as we ride to space over the next seven days. We'll be the first people to ever experience seeing the Earth in this way. Occasionally being the boss does have its perks, you know."

Robert looked at the time flashing in the corner of his vision and wasn't disappointed to note that it was time to board the elevator. "Thank you, everyone, but it's time for us to leave. I'll be making daily video updates on our progress, and of course when we board the *Nautilus*."

A short time later, Robert and his two technicians, Thomas Blake and Arjun Patel, were all seated in the specially designed elevator car. Robert said, "Okay, guys, how about getting this thing going?"

"Yes, sir," Thomas replied as he and Arjun began powering up the car.

"Power flow from the cable to the car is optimal," Arjun said, referring to the electricity that flowed from the graphene ribbon cable to the car and would power the electric motors that would in turn climb the cable for the next seven days. The electricity was supplied by a nuclear power plant specifically built to power the space elevator. In the future, the elevator would be powered by a massive solar panel farm that would orbit above *Nautilus* and send enough electricity down to Earth to not only power the elevator but also power the rapidly expanding Ciudad Espacial.

"Motors engaged, and we're on our way," Thomas said as the car lurched upward.

"Maria got one thing right," Robert said, referring to the Ecuadorian reporter.

"What's that?" Arjun asked.

"We're going to get to know each other a lot more," Robert said as he looked around the twenty-square-meter elevator compartment.

"And only one bathroom," Arjun said as they all laughed.

* * *

Mary lightly tapped her right index finger twice to play the simulation again. She had checked the math, and she knew the simulations were correct, but she still couldn't believe it. She leaned back in her chair and closed her eyes as her TICI played the video simulation directly onto her retina. This time, the cable broke only one kilometer away from the station, with the car only two hundred meters below the break. She watched as the cable slowly fell to Earth, taking the car with it, as it wrapped around the equator. While the cable neared its first wrap around the Earth, centrifugal force caused the tip of the cable to break off, and it was slung clear of Earth's orbit, taking the car into deep space; meaning certain death for Director Asher and the two other occupants. Fortunately for anyone on the equator, the graphene ribbon tapered cable only weighed 0.68kilograms per meter, so the damage from the falling cable would be minimal.

"Wake up, Mary. Don't you have work to do?"

Mary opened her eyes to see Gary Petrovic, commander of the newly named ISA Space Dock, standing next to her workstation on the bridge. Gary and the rest of the permanent crew had launched shortly after Mary repositioned *Nautilus* to her new geostationary orbit directly over Quito, Ecuador, eighteen months earlier. She smiled as she replied, "I wasn't sleeping, and you know it."

"Why do you keep watching those simulations anyway? You don't even know who they came from."

Mary sighed. "Doesn't matter who made them. I've triple-checked the math, and the simulations are correct. If the cable breaks, there's a high probability that we won't be able to rescue Director Asher."

Gary placed his coffee on the desk and sat down next to her. "It matters because whoever this mysterious Calliope person is, she clearly sent you those simulations just to mess with you. The cable isn't going to break, and Director Asher will arrive here safely in six days. It's not like this is new information anyway; we already knew the possibilities."

"I agree it's suspicious that we can't trace Calliope's email address." Mary paused as she sipped her coffee. "But why did they have to do the first trip with just the first cable in place? Heck, we'll have the second cable in place in six months, with all of the safeguards in place."

Gary nodded. "You know how much I hate when politics dictate timetable, but they were pretty adamant about this. The fact that Director Asher himself is on the first trip should tell you everything you need to know."

Mary recalled the media circus at Ciudad Espacial, the Space City, just outside Quito the day before, when Director Asher, along with two technicians, boarded the first car to ascend the space elevator. She knew President McDaniel was under mounting international pressure for the ISA to produce tangible results. "I just wish the politicians would keep their noses out of it and let Director Asher do his job."

Gary almost spit his coffee out as he laughed. "Robert Asher *is* a politician!"

Mary handed him a napkin. "Yeah, I know. It bothers me that they're doing this on just the one cable, and something about those simulations disturbs me."

"You know as well as I do that cable could carry four times as much mass as it's carrying now. Just relax, Mary. We've run our own simulations hundreds of times, and the cable is safe. Besides, even if something happened, there's not much you could do about it anyway."

Mary's eyes grew wide as something occurred to her. "What if there *was* something I could do?"

"What do you mean?"

"We have all of the sections for the second cable already up here, and a lot of it is already linked together." Mary paused as she gathered her thoughts. "What if we repurposed it and made a giant net out of it?"

Gary set his coffee down. "I think I see where you're going with this. Go on."

Mary worked on her console briefly and brought up the 3-D interactive holographic display. As she positioned different data points in the hologram, she narrated. "We can take the lower parts of the tapered cable that are already linked and weave them together to form a net that, if my calculations are correct," she paused while she keyed in the numbers, "will span just over two kilometers in diameter. We can anchor the net to four shuttles, one at each corner. So, if the cable breaks close to the station, we would have time to calculate where the car would be slung from orbit, and we could position the net to intercept."

Gary cocked his head as he studied the holographic model. "And if the cable broke closer to the anchor, the cable would simply fall to Earth, and the car's parachute would activate."

"Yep, this really only becomes an issue if the cable breaks higher up. I'm ready to get started," Mary said enthusiastically.

"The cable's not going to break."

"I know, but what if it does? Shouldn't we be prepared for all contingencies?"

Gary frowned. "I don't know. Repurposing the cable will delay the project, and we're already behind schedule."

"It'll only delay things a couple of days at most. We can make it up. There's no good reason to not do this."

"You're not gonna let this go, are you?" He sighed before asking, "How long will it take?"

Mary scratched her chin as she calculated. "If you give me

ten people and, of course, the four shuttles, I can have it ready in three days."

"Good grief, that's a fifth of the crew and all of the shuttles but one."

"They're not doing anything while the car is en route anyway."

"All right, all right, if it'll get you out of my hair, let's do it."

Mary couldn't contain her smile. "You mean you're not going to ask Director Asher for permission?"

"Hell no! The media would have a field day if they found out we were preparing for a disaster."

"You're right, we should probably keep this quiet," Mary said as she left the bridge.

* * *

"You guys gotta check this guy out!" Vincent Federici shouted out from his bridge workstation. Vincent, along with Mary and Zhang Yong Chen, had remained aboard the space dock as part of the regular crew after their original mission was complete.

Mary smiled as she walked over to Vincent's workstation. They had completed the net as planned three days ago; fortunately, it remained in place unneeded. "What are you looking at, Vinny?"

As Mary and Zhang gathered around his workstation, Vincent replied, "You guys know I'm addicted to that Virtual Life website, right?" He pointed to the screen. "Well, check out this guy."

"George Wiley," Zhang said as he looked on. "Why is he doing that?"

Mary stood silently, watching as the man on the screen swam out of a shark cage right up to a great white shark and grabbed its dorsal fin. After getting a ride for a few moments, he released the shark, and it swam away without any regard for him.

"Did you guys see that?" Vinny asked as he looked around. "That guy's insane."

"Is that new or something that was filmed before the Event?" Zhang asked.

"It was just uploaded two days ago via TICI," Vinny said as he navigated back to George Wiley's page on Virtual Life. "Check this out, this guy's got several more videos of him doing crazy stuff."

"I didn't think people did daredevil risk-taking stunts like that anymore," Zhang said.

Mary smiled as she patted Zhang on the back. "Says the man who pilots spaceships."

Zhang chuckled. "You know what I mean. I'm not petting great white sharks."

"Yeah, that guy's got a death wish," Mary agreed.

"Oh crap!" Vinny exclaimed under his breath.

Mary looked down at Vincent's monitor and saw a political popup ad for the Federation of Nations that was touting the sacrifices made for a unified Earth. The imagery for this ad was none other than a burning Zacharia Jones.

"I'm sorry, Mary," Vinny said while scrambling to take the ad down.

"Don't worry about it. I'm used to seeing it," Mary said stoically as she walked away. She didn't think she would ever get used to seeing that video, not in ten thousand years. Every time she saw it, she felt a knot in her stomach, like a little piece of herself died.

Mary, feeling the need to distract herself by staying busy, walked across the bridge to where Commander Petrovic was standing and said, "What's their ETA?"

"Just under twelve hours," Gary said as he turned toward her. "Everything okay?"

"Yeah, everything's fine," Mary replied as she rubbed her forehead.

"Yeah okay," Gary said with a slight frown. "Hey, if you want something to do, how about taking the crew out to disassemble that net."

"Yeah, doesn't look like we'll need it, and no sense in leaving evidence of our skepticism lying about," Mary joked.

"You got that right."

"Commander Petrovic, you better take a look at this," they heard the radar tech call out.

"What is it, Anderson?" Gary said as he walked over to the radar workstation.

"We just pinged something in orbit about one kilometer below us, moving really fast."

"How big, how fast?" Commander Petrovic asked.

"It's only about twelve centimeters in diameter, but it's moving at twelve klicks per second, sir."

"Fast enough," Gary as he put his hand to his chin. "We swept all of the old space garbage out of orbit months ago. Everything is supposed to be clean. How in the hell did we miss something this big?"

"I don't know, sir. Maybe it's a meteor that was captured recently," Anderson replied.

"Maybe," Gary said. "Is it on a collision course with the cable?"

"It's gonna get pretty close, but I don't think so."

"How close?" Mary asked.

"Within a half meter or so, it looks like," Gary replied.

"Holy cow," was all Mary could think to say as the memory of the simulation video played in her head.

"How long do we have?" Gary asked.

"Thirty seconds and counting," Anderson said.

"Sound collision alarm," Commander Gary Petrovic shouted out urgently. "Everybody strap in, this is not a drill!"

Mary rushed to her station and strapped herself in as she heard Anderson's voice over the intercom. "Six, five, four, three, two, one."

Mary slowly exhaled with relief as the countdown expired with no apparent collision, but before she could say anything, she felt gravity pushing her sideways into her seat.

"What's going on?" Mary shouted out.

Gary said loudly. "The cable's been cut, and we're no longer tethered to Earth. We'll be ejected from orbit if we don't adjust. Fire braking thrusters on both rings and call out when they're both at full stop."

Mary could feel gravity slowly dissipate as the ring slowed. *What a surreal feeling*, she thought as she dodged a coffee cup that was now a missile.

"Both rings stopped and fully secured, Commander," Mary heard Federici say.

"Fire main station thrusters to bring us back into position," Petrovic ordered.

For several minutes, Mary felt like she was being pinned to her left side as she remembered that being strapped down in one of the rings wasn't exactly the best place to be when the station was under thrust. She felt relieved when she once again felt weightless.

"Station back in position, Commander," Zhang said.

Gary turned toward Mary and said, "Well, what are you waiting for? Time to test that crazy net you constructed."

Mary paused briefly at the thought of putting her plan into action. *What if it fails? No time for self-doubt*, Mary thought as she released the restraints from her chair and pushed off toward the exit. "Zhang, you're with me. Federici, inform the rest of the net construction team to meet me in the shuttle bay immediately. We got about two hours until the broken cable loops the Earth and the car is flung free. We gotta get that net positioned. Now!"

* * *

Robert Asher looked across the elevator car at the nervous faces of his technicians as they both worked frantically at their workstations. They were all seated at their stations when the cable broke, so they simply fastened their harnesses into place before the G-forces displaced them. He frowned as he thought about the meeting he would have with President McDaniel after this major setback. Good possibility he'd lose his job. No sense in dwelling on what hasn't happened yet. "Arjun, how long until we reenter the atmosphere and the parachutes deploy?"

Arjun turned toward him slowly with a puzzled look on his face. "Sir we won't be falling back to Earth."

"What?" Director Asher replied.

"The cable broke too high up for that," Arjun said as he compared data on his TICI to what was on the console display. "It looks like we're going to whip around the Earth, and when that happens, the centrifugal force will cause the cable to snap again. Only this time it'll snap below us."

Robert sank into his seat as the full scope of their situation sank in. "And when the cable snaps, we'll be at escape velocity and be flung free of orbit."

There was a long silence before Arjun replied, "Yes, sir."

"Thomas, make contact with Quito, and tell them our situation if they don't know already. You guys might want to go ahead and call your family and friends while you still can," Robert said solemnly.

Thomas interrupted. "Sir, I'm receiving a message from Dr. Mary Ann Jones. She says they're going to attempt a rescue!"

Robert looked down at the floor as he took a deep breath and dared to have hope. *Hail Mary, full of grace*, he thought, even though he wasn't Catholic.

* * *

"Did I hear you correctly, Doctor Jones? Did you say you were deploying the net recovery system?" Director Asher said over the radio.

Mary looked across the shuttle cockpit and smiled at Zhang before she replied. "Yes, sir, you heard correctly. We are currently towing the net with four station shuttles to the estimated intersection point."

"Well, that's good news. I thought for sure we were dead men when I heard the trajectory projections once the cable broke," the director replied.

"It's gonna be really close, but I think we're going to arrive at the intersection point right as you arrive. We'll have about thirty seconds to fully deploy the net," Mary said.

There was a pause of several minutes before she heard Director Asher reply. "Thirty seconds is cutting it pretty close. If we miss the net, there won't be a second chance, as we'll have escape velocity and will sling free of Earth's gravity."

"He sounds remarkably calm for someone who's likely to die in ten minutes," Zhang said to her.

"I know," she replied. "Don't worry, Director, we'll have that net in place, and you'll be sipping scotch in the space dock lounge this afternoon," Mary said over the radio.

"You know I don't recall authorizing a net recovery system," Director Asher said.

Mary replied. "You didn't, sir. We, ahh ... we acquired one recently."

"Not in the last two hours, I think," he replied.

"No, sir, the acquisition was done previously," she heard Gary Petrovic intervene.

The director said, "I look forward to hearing that story one day."

"You will," Mary reassured.

"One minute until intersection," Commander Petrovic announced over the radio.

Mary said, "Shuttles, activate maneuvering thruster on my mark. Remember, guys, just a small bump. We don't need to move too fast. We want the net to be open at maximum when we intersect the car. If we goose the thrusters too hard, we'll actually rebound, and the net will begin closing."

Seconds later, she counted, "Three, two, one, mark!" She looked out of the window and could see the net slowly open as the four shuttles moved apart. This was going to be close.

"I have visual contact," Zhang announced. "She's really moving."

"Ten seconds until the elevator car hits the intersection point. Are you in position?" Commander Petrovic said.

Mary looked at their position and replied, "We're going to hit the intersection point in approximately nine seconds. The net will be fully extended in 8.5 seconds."

Zhang called out over the radio, "Three, two, one, contact!"

The elevator car was a blur as it shot between the four shuttles. Mary wasn't sure if they caught the car or not until she saw the Earth moving slowly in the window.

"We got her, we got her!" Zhang excitedly announced.

Mary looked at their trajectory and said to Zhang, "She's dragging us with her and pulling the shuttles together. Shuttles might collide at this rate. It's time to fire up the engines. On my mark, all shuttles will execute a five-second burn of their main engine and use lateral thrusters to keep our distance," Mary called out over the radio. "Does everyone copy?"

After the four shuttles acknowledged, she said, "In three, two, one, mark." Five seconds later, they were back to full freefall, and the elevator's escape velocity was nullified.

"Good work, everyone," Commander Petrovic said, and Mary could hear applause in the background.

Director Asher interrupted. "That was one hell of a rescue! Thank you to everyone, but especially to you, Mary. Something tells me this was your doing."

"You're welcome, Director. It was my idea, but I had a lot of help. You guys hang tight for a few minutes, and we'll pull you into the shuttle with us and then head back to space dock," Mary replied as she tasted iron in her saliva. She moved her tongue to the corner of her mouth and found where she had apparently bitten down during the commotion.

* * *

"*Buenas noches*, Dr. Jones," the doorman at El Hotel Espacial said as Mary walked in the front entrance of the only hotel in the newly constructed Space City. Ciudad Espacial was only nine years old and still a small city, but as the home of the space elevator and now headquarters of the ISA, it was easily the fastest-growing as well as the most modern city on the planet. Located just outside Quito, it was a welcome boon to the people of Ecuador.

"*Gracias*," she replied.

"Did you enjoy the ceremony?" the doorman asked.

"Yes, it was very nice," Mary said as she walked past him toward the elevator.

Mary walked into her suite on the fifth floor, and as she set her things down on the dresser, she heard a voice behind her. "So, how does it feel to be the hero?"

Mary froze as that voice echoed in her head and a chill went down her spine. His voice sounded so familiar. She didn't know if she should run for the door or scream, but instead she turned slowly around and turned the lights on, half-expecting to see Vasily sitting there. She stared at him for a moment until she realized she didn't recognize him.

"Who are you?" Mary demanded. "And what do you want?"

The man seated on her couch crossed his legs and said, "Don't worry, I mean you no harm."

"You have three seconds to tell me why I shouldn't call security," Mary said as she made a visible show of activating her TICI.

"Because it's me, Mom. I'm Zach."

Mary felt her stomach go sour. "Is this some kind of sick

joke?"

"No, wait. Please don't call security or the police," he said as he reached into his pocket and pulled out a silver medal and tossed it across the room to Mary.

Mary examined the medal for several seconds before noticing the serial number on the back. She did a quick search with her TICI and discovered that this "Medal for Merit in Space Exploration" was awarded to Vasily Ustinov more than eighty years ago.

"I was only seven years old when you gave that to me," Zach said as he stood up and took several steps toward her.

Mary wiped her eyes. "But you died. I saw you in flames. So many times I watched you die."

"I'm so sorry you had to see that, but I didn't die."

"But how? You don't have any scars, and you don't look like my Zach," Mary protested.

Zach took another two steps forward. "I've had dozens of surgeries since the burning and plastic surgery to alter my appearance so people don't recognize me."

"Well, it certainly worked," Mary said as she wiped her nose.

Zach gently reached out and took the medal back from her. "Remember when you gave me this?"

"We were sitting outside that crappy old trailer we lived in then."

"Yeah, it was dark, and you were showing me how to find the *Nautilus* as it passed through the night sky. You gave me the medal and said it was the only thing you had that was my father's. Then I said, 'But if you give it to me, what are you gonna have, Momma?'"

"And I said, 'I've got you, Zach,'" Mary said through her tears. She stepped toward Zach and they embraced.

Mary remembered holding Zach when he was a baby; he was so small and helpless, not like the man standing before her now. Then it hit her that this was really happening and not just a dream. "My son is alive. My son is alive. Oh my God, my son is alive."

After they separated, Mary reached into her purse and pulled out a tissue, wiped her eyes, and said, "Well, this has been an interesting day."

Zach laughed. "Oh yeah, congratulations on receiving the award today. I watched the broadcast earlier. That was one hell of a thing you did up there, rescuing the director. And now you're a world hero, famous in your own right, not just for being the mother of Zacharia Jones."

"Being your mother was always enough for me. I love you Zach, and I always will, but why did you keep me waiting for nine years? You let me believe you were dead."

Zach looked down at the floor briefly. "I'm sorry, but it was the only way. Zacharia Jones had to die, and I needed the world to believe it, and for that, you needed to believe it. I needed the world to move on and forget about me."

"Yeah, well that's not really happening, is it? I see your image everywhere I go. You've become this ubiquitous symbol for world unity," Mary replied.

"I know. It really sickens me to see how President McDaniel has perverted my legacy. He tried to have me killed, you know."

"What do you mean?"

"I mean I didn't set myself on fire, and I certainly wasn't there to endorse China joining the Federation of Nations."

"What happened?" she said nervously. "Tell me."

Zach moved toward the couch. "Have a seat, and I'll tell you.

I'd grown weary of Omni Ascend and the whole movement. I was sick of being 'the Holy Child,' the religious adulation; all of it."

Mary reached out to take Zach's hand, but he pulled away. "I'm sorry for putting you on that path. I don't think I ever apologized to you for that, but I regret it."

Zach ignored her apology as he continued. "So, even though I wanted to end Omni Ascend, I needed to use my influence for one last thing. I planned to turn my followers against McDaniel, especially my followers in China, so I made arrangements to make a surprise appearance."

"But why? What did you have against President McDaniel?" Mary couldn't believe what she was hearing. She'd met President McDaniel, and he was a good man with good intentions. He practically saved the planet.

"Don't get me started on that megalomaniac! Trust me, he's not the benevolent world leader everyone thinks he is."

"So, what happened in China?"

"Yeah, so somehow McDaniel got wind of my plan. I have no idea how, but that man has eyes and ears everywhere," Zach said as he unconsciously glanced around the room before continuing. "Anyway, he knew I was going to turn my followers against him, so when I came out on that stage, these two fanatics came out of nowhere and doused me with gasoline, then set me on fire."

Mary winced and looked away as that image once again flashed in her mind. "But in all of the videos there are no attackers and it looks like you set yourself on fire."

Zach nodded and said. "I know. Don't ask me how he did it, but within minutes of it happening, that altered video was out on the internet with the attackers edited out. That's the disturbing part about all of this, how he used that to get what he wanted. He made it seem like I sacrificed myself for the FON."

"I had no idea," was all Mary could think to say.

"That's why I have to stay hidden. If McDaniel knew I was still alive, I'd be dead within hours."

"Are you so sure? Why would he consider you a threat now?"

"That's why I won't be able to see you again," Zach said as he stood up and walked toward the door. "I took a big risk coming here, but I can't risk it again."

Mary grabbed his arm as she caught up to him. "You mean I won't be able to see you again?"

"Not for a long time anyway. Maybe never."

Mary took out her camera. "Well at least let me get a picture with you."

"A picture, are you serious?"

"No one else will ever see it; I promise."

Zach sighed and leaned in close so she could get the selfie. "Okay Mom."

After the photo, Mary said, "Can you forgive me Zach? Can you forgive me for putting you on that path?"

Zach leaned in and kissed her on the cheek. "Good-bye, Mother." Then he left.

Chapter 8: That Is the Question

In 65 AE, the McDaniel administration, along with the FON Congress, enacted The Event Depression Act. This law gave people diagnosed with Acute Event Depression Syndrome the legal right to take their own life if they wished. However, the bill failed to recognize that many people had constraints, religious or otherwise, against committing suicide and had to seek other remedies for their suffering, often to the detriment of those around them and society in general. The Event had consequences, some more obvious than others.—Zacharia Jones, Out of Darkness: The Event Chronicles

Date: 78 AE

George Wiley stepped to the edge of the cliff and looked down; the wind immediately pushed him back a step. He looked up and took in the view from Tianmen Mountain in Central China. Jagged mountains for as far as he could see, their tooth-shaped peaks pushing toward the sky like ancient dragons crying out from the grave. Low-flying clouds between the peaks gave the illusion that the dragons yet lived. As he shifted his gaze down toward the valley, he could see the road that corkscrewed through the mountainside like a giant worm feeding on the dragon's corpse. George yawned. The only thing that mattered now was the jump. Margie was waiting on him.

George made final adjustments to his wingsuit as he clicked his back-left teeth together three times and was instantly connected to the internet. The eye browser was displayed directly on his retina via his Takahashi Industries Cerebrum Interface, and he could see the browser and navigate the internet while going about his normal activity as it overlaid his normal vision. In the upper-left corner of his browser/vision, he could see his pulse rate displayed fifty-five and steady. George quickly used his eyes to navigate to his home page on Virtual Life and logged in.

As he pulled the drone out of his pack, he said, "All right, folks, George Wiley signing in. Five minutes to jump. Hope you bunch of freaks enjoy!" In the upper-right corner of his display, he could see that 52,324 people were already viewing or listening. His viewers would be able to see and hear everything he saw and heard, as his broadcast was taken directly from his own vision and hearing. In addition, they would also get the view broadcast from his drone, which would fly directly above him during his flight.

George took a moment to compose himself as he took a deep breath and reflected on his situation. This stunt was his most outrageous and hopefully his last. The 122 previous ones had all ended in failure, so he was forced to do more. It had all started seven years ago when he swam out of a shark cage and interacted directly with a feeding great white shark. Later he discovered that he had accidently recorded this interaction, so he uploaded it to Virtual Life just to see what people would say. Amazingly it received 1.5 million views. After that he decided he would broadcast live, and charge twenty-five cents per view every time he performed a stunt. His stunts had gone viral since then, and he had become something of a celebrity, and also quite wealthy.

My failures have made me a rich man. Ironic, George thought as he prepared to jump.

He powered up the drone and released it. He raised his arms up to shoulder height as it flew around him, showing his audience that he was not wearing a parachute.

Thirty seconds to launch, 3.5 million viewers logged in. *Wow, this might break the record*, he thought as he stepped over the rail. He said a brief prayer as he kissed the cross that hung around his neck. Ten seconds, 5.2 million viewers, pulse rate fifty-five. Three, two, one—he jumped.

George briefly dove nearly headfirst to gain momentum; then he opened his arms and legs and fully deployed the wingsuit. At 258 KPH, 6.5 million people were viewing as he now turned slightly to his left to follow the steep valley down. He flew directly over a tour bus, missing it by about a meter and a half as it wormed its way around the curving corkscrew road up the mountain. Pulse rate fifty-eight.

George launched his mapping app, and it overlaid his vision so he could see precisely the path he needed to take down the mountain. Now 7.1 million viewers and holding as he left the valley gorge he had been following, almost clipping a rock outcropping as he flew directly into the main valley below. Pulse rate sixty-two.

His excitement grew as he searched for the ski-jump landing that had been erected two days prior. Why wasn't it showing on his mapping app? Where was it? Pulse rate sixty-five.

This is it; I'm coming home, Margie. No more failures, thought George as he couldn't find his landing site. Then, slightly to his left, he spotted it. It was a man-made slope he had the locals build at the bottom of the valley. It resembled a half-kilometer-long Olympic ski jump landing slope, complete with artificial snow that was even now being blown on it. As large as it was, he still had to land at exactly the correct angle at exactly the right speed, or he would bounce off it and give his viewers a firsthand look at his death.

George quickly turned left and set up on the ramp; another second and he would have missed it completely. As it was, this was going to be close. He pulled up, to maximize wind resistance in his suit, which slowed his descent. As he approached the ramp, his airspeed indicator in the left of his vision showed 80 KPH, a bit fast, he mused, but doable.

Three meters from the ramp, he deployed his custom-made extendable skis that came out of his boots with the snap of a stiletto. He hit the far-right corner of the ramp, just one meter from the edge. He landed on his skis but quickly lost his balance and went into a headfirst tumble down the ramp.

This is going to hurt worse tomorrow, he thought as he tumbled down the snow-covered slope.

After finally coming to a halt, he stood up and brushed the snow off. He was going to be sore as hell tomorrow, but he didn't feel like he had sustained any major injuries. Meanwhile, his viewers on Virtual Life were going berserk with the comments.

"I'll give you crazy rascals a complete rundown later tonight, after I have a few drinks and take some ibuprofen. George Wiley signing off."

Another complete failure, George thought as he walked off of his man-made slope.

* * *

About four hours later George was relaxing in his seat, waiting for takeoff on a commercial flight from Zhangjiajie to Shanghai, when his agent/accountant/lawyer called him on his TICI.

"Hey, Charlie, what's going on?" George said.

"George, that was one heck of a flight today," Charlie replied.

"Glad you enjoyed it."

"It was awesome! You also cleared over $1.5 million. Not bad for a one-minute flight," Charlie said.

George retorted, "I don't see you, or anyone else, for that matter, lining up to do this, so don't give me that crap about easy money!"

"Whoa, easy, buddy. I didn't mean anything by it. Why do you do it, anyway? I mean, no one does this kind of risk-taking stuff anymore. Not for the last seventy-eight years, anyway. Not since the Event. People are way too safety focused these days."

George realized his previous remarks were a little harsh, so he said, "You know, Charlie, I don't think I've ever told anyone this story, but I'm feeling talkative right now. Do you have a few minutes?" He signaled the flight attendant to bring him another bourbon and Coke.

"Yeah, man, I gotta hear this."

"Okay, let me ask you this. How old were you when the

Event happened?" asked George as he once again drained his bourbon and Coke and signaled the flight attendant for another.

"I was fifty-three. How old were you?"

"I was ninety-five years old."

"Holy cow, that must have been amazing for you. I mean going from ninety-five to a biological age of thirty. How long have you been at baseline? It had to take you a while to get there."

"I've been at baseline for about ten years now. It took nearly sixty-eight years for my body to reach baseline. To answer your other question, no, it wasn't wonderful. It was awful. My wife, Margie, died about two years before the Event. Our only child, Winston, had died ten years before that. When the Event happened, I was dying of heart failure and ready to join my sweet Margie. It was all I wanted. The Event took that from me."

As George paused, Charlie interjected, "George, you're suffering from post-Event depression syndrome."

"Thank you, Gump, I know that."

"Who's Gump?"

"Never mind, it's not important." George rolled his eyes.

"So, what did you do before the Event, before you retired, I mean?"

"I taught physics at UC Berkeley," George replied.

"Holy cow, I didn't know you were a scientist."

"I'm sure there's a lot you don't know about me, Charlie."

"So, you're basically doing all of this daredevil stuff because you want to die?" Charlie asked.

"Well, that's kind of oversimplifying things, don't you think?"

Charlie ignored George's last statement and continued. "If that's the case, why don't you just commit suicide? Why all of the beating around the bush? The McDaniel administration made suicide legal for anyone suffering from post-Event depression syndrome."

"Well, suicide may be okay with the Federation of Nations, but I'm pretty sure God still considers it a mortal sin. Since I'm pretty sure my Margie is in heaven, I very well can't commit suicide if I want to be with her, now can I?"

"If that's what you believe, then I guess that's right," Charlie answered.

George explained, "When I was young the first time, there was a kind of magic about the world. It was new and fresh, and I felt vibrant and in awe of it. Now, it's like the magic is gone. I don't feel it anymore. Almost like everything is fake, not real. When I leapt off that mountain this morning, it didn't feel real. I hardly felt any fear at all. If my Margie was still alive, I might feel differently. I miss her so much, and I don't understand why God is doing this."

"No one knows why the Event happened, George. It's the biggest mystery in history. No one knows who or what or why. Maybe it was God. I don't think we'll ever find out."

George drained what was left of his third drink and said, "You know what's probably the number-one reason why everything feels so fake to me? I don't hear the sound of children laughing and playing. That's the most wonderful sound in the world, you know, and we'll most likely never hear it again. There hasn't been a child born in seventy-nine years. That's depressing. Sometimes I feel like we're living in a simulation."

"Ya know, you're not the first person I've heard say that.

There's people that say the Event was actually some kind of a singularity and that a machine intelligence has downloaded all of us into a computer simulation or something. Kinda like that old movie, what was the name of that film?"

"Well, that sounds like a load of pixie dust," George said. "All I know is that the world doesn't feel real to me anymore."

"George, I wish there was something I could do or say that would make you feel better. I guess it's obvious that money doesn't make you feel better."

"Don't worry about it. I just felt like getting some of that off my chest. Heck, it's been a long time since I've even said Margie's name out loud. Thanks for listening. Look, I'm getting sleepy. I'll talk to you later."

"Okay, see you later," said Charlie as George hung up. Shortly afterward, George was sound asleep, much to the flight attendant's relief.

* * *

Later that evening, around 10 p.m., George was relaxing in his penthouse suite atop the Park Hyatt Shanghai II, the hotel that replaced the old Park Hyatt Shanghai, which had burned during the Shanghai rice riots of the Event Depression. The new Park Hyatt was even more impressive than the original and some twenty stories taller. He was just starting on his second drink of the evening and was about to head downstairs to one of the many bars in the hotel when he was nearly knocked down as the entire building shook and he was deafened by the terrible sound of a collision.

That felt really bad, thought George as he walked onto his balcony to take a look. He looked down and could see flames and smoke billowing up from about halfway down the building as the lights in his room flickered.

This is definitely not good, George thought as he connected to the internet with his TICI. The first thing he saw when he went to a news site was that a commercial airliner had slammed into the building.

What the heck? I thought terrorism was a thing of the past, George thought as he grabbed his coat and headed for the entrance of his penthouse, draining his drink as he left. The elevators were out of service, so he was forced to take the stairs.

George raced down the stairs as he thought, This is not how I wanted to spend my evening, reliving 9/11 again, this time in person.

George ran down about twenty flights of stairs before he ran into a small group of people coming up the stairs.

"You won't be able to make it down past the level of the fire," said a large man who was clearly out of breath. "The entire midsection of the building is an inferno. Our only hope is that a chopper can evacuate us off the roof."

George stood to the side as the group passed, but one woman with mascara smeared across her face and panic in her eyes grabbed his arm and said, "Didn't you hear? If you go down there, you'll die."

The woman was still holding George's arm, so he put his hand on hers and said, "Death is only a transition, not the end."

"Come on, Carol!" one of her companions shouted down at her, and with that, she released him and continued her journey upward.

After running down another ten flights of stairs, it became

apparent that the fat man was right, and he wasn't going to be able to get past the level of the fire, due to the smoke. He left the stairwell and went onto one of the main floors that were still under construction and found it filled with smoke as well. He was coughing as he crawled on the floor toward an open window. When he reached the window, he climbed halfway out and was finally able to find fresh air.

George looked down and was filled with horror. He could see people below him leaping to their deaths to avoid the smoke and the flames. *This is it*, he thought as he watched the leapers hit the ground.

George sat down beside the window. *All I have to do is sit here in the smoke, and it's all over. This madness is finally coming to a close.* He began to weep and cough. *I'm coming home for real this time, Margie. There's no escape for me now.*

While he sat there sobbing and coughing, the internet was still in his vision, and he could see the hotel as it looked from the streets of Shanghai. Smoke and flames billowed up from the center of the building as scores of people could be seen leaping to their deaths to avoid the smoke and flames, while firefighters tried in vain to contain the massive blaze.

As he viewed this catastrophe via the internet, he saw something in the flames of one of the videos. He zoomed in tighter to the flames, and he could see it more clearly. It was a vision of Margie in the flames, and she was screaming. He couldn't hear her at first, but gradually he started to hear her yells, faintly at first, then louder and more frantic.

"George, get up, George! You can't die now. There's work for you to do yet. You have one more stunt to do, then it's time to return to your roots; time for the man of science to return. Now run, George, run. You can do it. You know how to escape.

It's not your time," screamed Margie's vision in the flames.

George stood up and climbed back out of the window for fresh air as he thought, *Margie has come from the grave to tell me to live. How is this possible? Am I delirious from the smoke? Maybe so, but I know it's Margie! It's not logical, but I know it's Margie. What do I do now? How can I escape? The wingsuit! If I can make it back to my room, I can grab the wingsuit and head for the roof. Then what? Holy cow, this is nuts.*

As he stepped back into the building from the window, he logged in to Virtual Life and quickly opened a new event called Live from the Park Hyatt Shanghai. He quadrupled what he normally charged. *Might as well make some money*, he thought as he made his way to the stairway.

George entered his penthouse; 3.2 million viewers and climbing fast. He glanced at his pulse rate in the upper-left corner of his vision/display, and it read eighty-eight. He grabbed his wingsuit case and ran for the stairs that would take him to the roof. As he entered the stairs, an urgent audio message intruded into his internet feed.

"George, this is Charlie. You have to listen to me—this is urgent. The experts are saying the hotel is going to collapse any minute now, just like the Twin Towers. You have to get out of there as quickly as possible."

"I'm trying to do just that, Charlie, I really am," said a slightly annoyed George.

"George Wiley, if you die, do you still affirm that you wish all of your assets to be transferred to the Phoenix Project Foundation?"

"Yes, yes. Good grief, I don't have time for this, Charlie."

"And you swear that you are of sound mind and body as you declare your final wishes?"

"Yes, please just cross all of the legal T's and dot all of the i's by yourself. You have my permission," replied George as he disconnected.

A bead of sweat was forming on George's brow, and a thousand butterflies fluttered in his stomach as the building shook and George made his way onto the roof; 5.6 million viewers and still climbing. Pulse rate ninety-five. There were already about a dozen or so people on the roof as George put down his case and started getting out his wingsuit equipment.

"What are you doing?" asked the fat man from the stairs, sweat pouring down his face.

"I'm putting on this wingsuit, and then I'm jumping off the roof," replied George as he stepped into the suit.

"I don't see a parachute," said Carol as her voice wavered.

"Yep, unfortunately no parachute," said George as he released his drone; 10.5 million viewers now. Pulse rate 110.

George started walking to the edge of the roof, which was about twenty meters away. The building started shaking wildly, and people started screaming. He began running clumsily in his wingsuit as the building started collapsing around him. Suddenly there was debris all around him, and he realized he was falling. He turned into a dive to pick up speed, and he leveled out as he attempted to clear the falling debris of the collapsing hotel. His drone was just above him, streaming video directly to him. From the drone feed, he saw a large chunk of debris on a collision course with him, so he swerved hard to the left to avoid it. The drone feed went dead, apparently taken out by falling debris itself. As he cleared the falling debris, his feed spiked to 20.3 million viewers. Pulse rate 136.

As George cleared the falling debris, a feeling of power

overtook him, a feeling he had never felt in all his years. Even though his heart was rapidly pounding, he could feel each individual heartbeat; he could feel the adrenaline-laden blood coursing through his bloodstream, giving him an almost superhuman boost in ability. He glanced behind, and the building seemed to be falling in slow motion as he could see each individual piece of it suspended in time. Among the suspended pieces, he spotted Carol from the roof, her mouth open, screaming in terror. George said a quick prayer for her and then realized what the feeling in the pit of his stomach was—fear.

This is different, he thought.

He cued his mapping app, and it overlaid his vision. He could immediately tell that the Huangpu River was only half a kilometer away. He did some quick calculations. In his wingsuit, he moved forward about 2.5 meters for every meter he fell. The hotel was about three hundred meters tall. So, he should be good for a 750-meter flight, but he had to navigate around buildings. This would be close; 30.2 million viewers. Pulse rate 156.

With the assistance of the mapping software, he navigated his way around three different skyscrapers at about 160 KPH. His heart pounded like never before, and he was having trouble controlling his breathing.

Relax, George, you can do this. You've done crazier things than this, he told himself. However, it was different this time. This time he wanted to live.

As he made his way around the fourth skyscraper, he could see the river. It was only about 230 meters away, and he was about ninety meters up but still had to slow down, as he was going too fast, even for a water landing. This was going to be very close; 33 million viewers. Pulse rate 172.

When he was only twenty meters from the river, he pulled up to gain maximum wind resistance so he could slow down—100 KPH, 80 KPH. Clearing the dock, he was down to 65 KPH when he saw a blacked-out fishing junk dead in front of him. He banked hard right to avoid it but still clipped the bow with his left thigh on his way by and hit the river at 65 KPH.

He struggled to kick to the surface, as his left leg felt like it was on fire. He kicked harder, but the surface seemed like an unattainable goal, and his lungs felt ready to burst. Breaking through the surface was like being reborn. He was in so much pain, but he felt alive, so alive!

He waved frantically as the junk turned to come toward him. When they fished him out of the water, he vomited from the overload of adrenaline that was still coursing through his bloodstream. As they put him on deck, he could see that Charlie was calling him again.

"Hi. Charlie, what's up?"

"What's up, he says? Are you kidding me? You just broke every record for Virtual Life. Over thirty million views, holy cow!

"Charlie, I think you need to put things in perspective here. A lot of people just died, you know."

"I'm sorry, man, you're right. Okay, I'll let you go so you can get medical attention. Bye," replied Charlie as he hung up.

George thanked the fishermen for saving his life as he went back into video and audio mode for Virtual Life and said, "That's it, folks. I'm done with the daredevil business, and I'm officially retiring. It's time for me to find something worthwhile to do with my life. Maybe the ISA can use an old particle physicist. This is George Wiley signing off, for good."

Chapter 9: The Secrets of the Universe

As the last generation of children grew up during the Event Depression, the education system crumbled around them. By 12 AE, the entire system had dissolved, from kindergarten to graduate school. Decades later, as the world emerged from the depression, the McDaniel administration recognized there was an educational need for adults reentering the workforce or changing professions. However, instead of rebuilding colleges and tech schools, the administration chose a different direction.—Zacharia Jones, Out of Darkness: The Event Chronicles

Date: 135 AE

The three kings in Miguel's hand urged him to pick up the two cards laying face down on the table. He glanced at Smitty, the dealer, but Smitty was already exchanging cards with the next player. Miguel looked at the other five players around the table as they studied the cards they had just exchanged with the dealer. His gaze returned to the two cards again, but he still didn't pick them up as he noticed the five thousand credits in chips sitting in front of him. Miguel smiled, remembering that he had started with only one thousand credits. One thousand credits that he had borrowed from Jamaal. That loan brought his total gambling debt to just over thirty thousand credits.

Smitty cleared his throat. "Miguel, the bet is 150, and it's on you."

"Come on, Garcia," Francis, the bald thin man sitting to Miguel's left said. "Get your head in the game."

Jamaal, seated directly across from Miguel, glanced at Francis as he shook his head. Francis immediately looked down at his cards and resumed his silence.

Miguel picked up the two cards and placed them face down next to his three face-down kings. As he slightly lifted the two new cards and glanced at them, his heart nearly stopped beating. Two queens! Miguel couldn't believe this sudden change in fortune—a full boat, kings and queens. He'd be able to pay off a large portion of his debt tonight if he played this hand right.

Miguel tried to conceal his excitement as he pushed a small stack of chips into the pot. "I see your 150," as he pushed a larger stack of chips into the pot, "and I raise one thousand."

Francis immediately tossed his cards toward the dealer. "I'm out."

Miguel strained to contain himself as he clicked his right-rear teeth together. He had to get a quick message to Callie about this hand. He had to share his good fortune with someone, but something was wrong, as his TICI wasn't connecting. Miguel rolled his eyes, remembering that they rigged these rooms to block all wireless signals coming in or out. He glanced around the smoky room to see if anyone noticed him trying to access his TICI. None of the players were looking at him, and the two guards on either side of the room weren't even watching the game.

Jamaal pushed a large stack of chips into the growing pot. "I call."

Charlie the Mule stared at his cards, but his face remained as flat as a concrete wall as he pushed his chips into the pot. "I call and raise another thousand."

Angel extinguished his cigarette and tossed his cards into the pile. "Too rich for my blood."

Miguel glanced around the room again as he took in the scene. He enjoyed these underground games so much more than internet gambling. There was simply no substitute for the feel of real cards in your hands as you stared your opponents in the face. Gambling was legal in all countries of the FON, but it was highly regulated and all online. These underground games were illegal and run by the mob.

"Garcia, it's on you," the dealer said.

A small bead of sweat formed on Miguel's brow as he pushed his entire stack of chips into the pot. "I call and raise another three thousand."

Jamaal blew out a large breath of cigar smoke as he shook his head and tossed his cards in. "I hate to do this, but I gotta bow out of this one."

Charlie studied his cards, contemplating his next move.

Miguel tapped his cards on the table as he waited for Charlie the Mule to make up his mind. *Why do they call him the Mule anyway?*

Charlie slid in a large stack of chips. "I'll pay to see what ya got. Call."

Miguel smiled as the thought, *He's gonna pay all right.*

"Read 'em and weep," Miguel said confidently as he tossed his cards face up into the pile.

Miguel glanced at Jamaal and saw him nodding and mouthing, "Hell yeah." Then he looked over at Charlie, and a chill went down his spine as he watched a smile spread across Charlie's face.

"Kings over queens, not bad," Charlie said as he slowly placed his cards face up on the table. "But last I checked, it doesn't beat four of a kind."

Miguel felt the floor drop out from under him as he looked at the four jacks Charlie had just laid out. He swallowed a lump in his throat and said, "Well played, Charlie, well played."

"Don't let it get you down, kid. I woulda bet the farm on that full boat too," Francis said.

Miguel slid his chair away from the table and stood up. "Well, I'm out of money now, so I'm done for the night."

"Hey, guys, deal me out of the next hand," Jamaal said as he followed Miguel out of the room.

Miguel walked out of the room and into the hotel hallway. He felt like someone else was walking his body. He couldn't believe it had happened again. He had what should have been an unbeatable hand, yet someone always seemed to beat him. What was he going to do now? He lost his construction job two weeks ago, and last week he was forced to go on MABI, the McDaniel Administration Basic Income. MABI was enough to keep you from starving, just barely, but he couldn't pay off his gambling debts with it.

"Wait up, Miguel," he heard Jamaal say behind him.

As Jamaal caught up to him, he said. "That's a tough break,

man. I thought for sure you had that hand."

Miguel nodded in agreement. "It woulda won for anyone but me. I think I'm cursed when it comes to big games."

They stopped at the elevator as Jamal replied, "Yeah, that sucks for sure, but when am I gonna get my money?"

He knew that Jamaal wasn't directly threatening him, but at six-two and two hundred pounds of pure muscle, Miguel couldn't help but feel intimidated. Of course, the neck tattoos didn't help either. "I don't know, man. I'm kinda broke right now. Hell, I had to go on MABI last week."

"What the hell? Did you lose your job or something?"

Miguel just nodded.

"That sucks, man, but here's the thing. Vinny is calling in all debts, and I owe him more than what I got on hand right now. So, you got two weeks to get me the thirty thousand, or I'll have to turn your mark over to Vinnie."

"Vinny the Rhino?"

Jamaal nodded. "Yep. You knew I worked for him."

Miguel hung his head.

Jamaal patted Miguel's belly as he playfully said, "Come on, fat boy, you'll come up with a way to get the money. You always do.

Miguel brushed his hand aside. "Fat boy? I'm not near as fat as the Rhino." Miguel had gained considerable weight over the years, but at five-nine and 250 pounds, he wasn't anywhere near the size of the Rhino.

"Don't let Vinny hear you call him fat. He don't like that," Jamaal said with a laugh.

Vincent the Rhino Bianchi. The eleven-hundred-pound boss of Boston's underworld was reportedly unable to get out of his own custom-made bed, but that didn't diminish his ability to reach out and touch anyone he wanted. The very mention of his name was enough to give even the most hardened criminal pause, and right now Miguel felt like he was going to piss his pants.

"Please don't tell him I said that," Miguel replied.

Jamaal patted him on the shoulder and laughed. "Don't worry, man, I like you."

As Miguel entered the elevator, he said, "Thanks, Jamaal."

"Two weeks, Miguel. I need my money in two weeks," Jamaal said as the elevator doors closed.

* * *

The light breeze mussed his hair as Miguel enjoyed the scenery at the outdoor Parisian café. He was amazed that they could capture every detail, even this breeze, in virtual world. Simply amazing. He looked at his watch. Callie was five minutes late, and it wasn't like her to be late. He'd only known her for about six weeks now, but she had quickly become his best friend. Who was he kidding? She was his only friend. He dreaded the thought that she might abandon him too.

He was startled when he turned his gaze back toward his table and saw Callie sitting in the chair across from him.

"Hola, Miguel!" she said.

"Holy crap, you shouldn't sneak up on people like that. I almost wet myself."

Callie laughed out loud. "You're a hoot. That's what I like about you."

"I'm so glad you're here, Callie. I was worried for a bit that you weren't coming."

"So, what's going on? Your message sounded urgent."

"Yeah, it's been a bad week for me. I just need someone to talk to, and you're about the only friend I have."

"Oh, come on, you only know me in here, the virtual world. We've never even met in real life. Surely, you have real friends?" Callie said.

Miguel frowned and shook his head. "No, not really. Not since Powell died during the flood back in ninety-nine. Now, I just have work friends and gambling friends, and they don't count."

"I thought you lost your job two weeks ago."

"Yeah, you're right. I only have gambling friends now," Miguel said with a laugh.

"So, what's got you all worked up?"

Miguel sighed. "Well, my gambling has taken a turn for the worse."

"I thought you just did that for fun."

"I might not have told you the whole truth about that. I owe a lot of money to the wrong kind of people."

Callie nodded. "How much money?"

"More than I can get in two weeks, that's for sure."

"You only have two weeks?"

"Yeah, in two weeks, Jamaal turns my mark over to the Rhino."

"The Rhino? Vinny the Rhino Bianchi?"

"You've heard of him?"

"Who hasn't heard of the fattest gangster who ever lived?" She laughed.

Miguel swallowed on a dry throat. "Well, he's also one of the most dangerous gangsters on the East Coast."

Callie nodded in agreement. "So I've heard. Exactly how much do you owe him?"

"Officially, I don't owe him anything, but I do owe Jamaal thirty thousand credits, and if I don't pay him in two weeks, he's going to turn it over to Vinny."

Callie's eyes showed her shock. "Thirty thousand credits! Holy cow, you really are in trouble."

"I know, I know. There's no way I can come up with that kind of money, and with no job, I can't even make a down payment."

Callie leaned back in her chair and put her feet up on the table. "I think I can help you."

Miguel raised his eyebrows. "Really? How?"

Callie opened a stick of gum and popped it into her mouth. "For starters, I can get you a job."

Miguel was astounded. "Really? What kind of job?"

"Well, to be more exact, I can get you an apprenticeship."

"What?"

Callie took her feet off the table and leaned forward in her chair. "You probably haven't heard of this because it hasn't been officially announced yet, but the McDaniel administration has started a worldwide apprenticeship program to train people in what they're calling mission-critical jobs."

"Mission-critical jobs. What's that mean?"

"Probably something to do with the space program and the ISA would be my guess," Callie replied.

"Yeah, that would make sense. The president loves space exploration." Miguel paused for a moment, as he thought this sounded strange. "So, how would you get me into this new program that hasn't even been announced yet?"

Callie smiled. "Let's just say I have connections in the administration."

"Okay then, where do I sign up?" *Who is she?* he thought.

"First you need to decide what field you want to go into."

Without even thinking, Miguel blurted out, "Genetics! I've always wanted to do something with genetics."

Callie smiled again. "That's right, you used to work in the medical field before the Event, didn't you?"

"Yeah, I was a nurse anesthetist." It seemed like another life now, but Miguel couldn't help but remember how disappointed his father had been when he found out that his only son was going to nursing school instead of medical school. He hadn't thought of his father in years and found it strange that he'd think of him now.

Miguel sighed. *Papa will have to be proud from the grave if I manage to get this apprenticeship.*

"Okay, I'll have to check and see if there's anything in genetics."

"That's great, Callie, thanks so much. Hopefully, I'll still be alive then," Miguel quipped.

"You know what? I think I can help you with that too."

"What? You're telling me you can help me with the mob? How in the world?"

"Well, I know a guy."

Miguel laughed. "You know a guy?"

"Yeah, and right now he resides in New York, so he can come up to Boston in the next day or two, most likely."

"And this guy can just take care of my problem?"

"Yes, he can. He specializes in this kind of stuff. His name is Eli, and I'll talk to him this evening and see if he can help you out."

"That's awesome, Callie. I don't know what to say."

"Well, there is a catch."

"A catch?" Miguel asked. *I knew it. I knew it was too good to be true. How can I trust someone I've never even met in person?*

"Sure, the catch is that you have to follow through with the apprenticeship program, and you have to promise that you'll walk away from the illegal gambling."

Miguel wasn't convinced that Callie could deliver on these things, but he didn't see any reason not to commit. What did he have to lose? Besides, working in genetics would be his dream job.

Miguel offered his hand. "I promise."

* * *

"Would you care for a cup of coffee?" Miguel said as he welcomed Callie's associate into his living room.

"No, thank you," the stranger replied as he looked around Miguel's meager but clean living room.

"Is it Eli or Mr. Eli?" Miguel wasn't sure if Eli was his first or last name.

The stranger continued scanning the apartment until his gaze turned toward Miguel. As he looked into Miguel's eyes, he frowned slightly. "Just Eli."

"Well, thank you, Eli for coming all this way to help me." Even as he thanked Eli, Miguel didn't really see how he'd be able to help. He wasn't an overly large man, just a little bit taller than Miguel, maybe 185 pounds or so. Not nearly as big as Jamaal. However, Miguel did notice that he had a confident intensity about him that exuded competence. His square jaw and good looks added to the effect.

"Calliope tells me you have something of a ... gambling problem?"

Miguel motioned toward the couch. "Please have a seat."

After they were both seated, he continued. "Yeah, unfortunately, I've run up a rather large gambling debt, and I've got ten days to pay it off or it goes to Vinny Bianchi."

Eli nodded. "The Rhino is a nasty piece of business."

"So, how are you going to help me? I don't even have enough cash for a down payment."

"What's your game?"

Miguel stuttered. "My game? Oh, poker."

Eli laughed. "You're a poker player? No wonder you've run up so much debt."

"I'm not that bad at poker. I win sometimes."

Eli shook his head. "I've seen mimes that could beat you at poker. You don't have the face for it."

Miguel felt offended but couldn't come up with anything to counter with. He did have a thirty-thousand-credit debt. "Yeah, you're probably right."

"Tell me about this guy you owe the money to. Does he run the games?" Eli asked.

"His name is Jamaal Quincy, but he doesn't run the games; he just provides security and plays in them sometimes. Smitty Collins runs the games and deals occasionally, but I don't owe Smitty anything."

Eli nodded. "So, Jamaal and Smitty both work for the Rhino?"

"Yeah, I think so."

"Tell me more about this Jamaal. What does he look like? How big is he?"

Miguel fidgeted on the couch. "He's about six-two and probably around two hundred pounds."

"Is he black, white? What does he look like?"

"He's a light-skinned black dude with short hair." Miguel

paused briefly. "Oh, and he's got lots of tattoos, even on his neck. The one on his neck is like Chinese writing or something."

"Is he in good shape, or is he sloppy like you?"

Miguel clenched his jaw and wondered why this guy kept insulting him. "No, he's in good shape, and you can tell he works out. I think he used to box too; you know, before the Event. But he's a nice guy, though. I actually like him."

"Yeah, I'm sure he's a saint. Most likely he's into things a lot worse than gambling and loan sharking."

Miguel shrugged.

"So, where can I find him?" Before Miguel could answer, Eli continued. "When's the next game?"

Miguel had to think for a moment. "There's usually a game every Thursday, and I'm pretty sure this Thursday's game is at the Wilshire Inn."

"Is he normally armed?"

"Oh yeah, he carries a 9mm Berretta, and he normally has two muscle guys at the games, and they're armed too."

Eli stood up from the couch. "Okay, I'm going to pay your friend Jamaal a visit Thursday. After that, you'll be good." He started walking toward the door.

"Just like that?"

"Yes, just like that."

"Will I hear from you afterward? Will you let me know how it went?" Miguel asked.

"No, you won't hear from me again." He stopped suddenly, turning toward Miguel. "Wait, yes, you might hear from me again."

"I might hear from you again?"

Eli leaned toward Miguel, his face only a few inches away.

"If I ever hear of you even getting within one block of a poker game or any other illegal gambling activity, I'm going to come pay you a visit."

Miguel swallowed a lump in his throat and stepped back. Eli's eyes, which had been almost dead earlier, were now alive and seething with an intensity Miguel had never seen before. Almost like Eli wanted him to relapse into gambling again.

Eli turned and walked toward the door again. "And it won't be a pleasant visit like this one."

* * *

Miguel closed the door to the cooler after he secured a six pack of Sam Adams. He had just applied for the apprenticeship program at Ogunwande Scientific Seed and felt like celebrating, so he had stopped by Bob's Grocery on his way home. He was almost giddy and couldn't believe Callie had already found him a genetic engineering apprenticeship. It was botanical genetics but still exciting. If he were accepted, he'd be able to get off MABI.

As he made his way toward the register, he noticed Jamaal down one of the narrow aisles. Miguel decided to talk to him, but as soon he turned down the aisle, Jamaal saw him and quickly turned the other way. *What the hell? Why is he avoiding me?* Miguel quickly turned back and was able to cut him off at the next aisle.

Jamaal stopped and started slowly backing away from Miguel. "Just stay away from me, man. I don't want anything to do with you no more."

"What about the money I owe you?"

Jamaal looked around the store nervously. "You're good

now. Don't worry about it."

"Are you sure?"

"Yeah, your boy took care of your debt last night." Jamaal once more glanced around the store before continuing. "That guy's psycho, man. Total nut job."

Before Miguel could reply, Jamaal was walking away from him again. "Just stay away from me, Miguel, and keep your psycho friend away from me too."

Miguel stood there in the aisle with his beer as he watched Jamaal run out of the store without his groceries.

* * *

As Callie blew a bubble, Miguel wondered what she was like in person. Her avatar was pretty but not beautiful. That made him think she might really be attractive in person, or was she some fat guy? Miguel smiled at that thought.

"What's got you smiling?" Callie said as her bubble popped.

"I was just trying to imagine what you might be like in person."

Now Callie smiled. "Exactly like I am now, silly." She extended her arms wide. "What you see is what you get."

Miguel put his elbows on the café table and propped up his head. "I still can't believe I was accepted into Ogunwande Scientific Seed's apprenticeship program one week before the FON even officially announced the program."

"I told you I have connections in the administration," Callie replied.

"Well, I can't thank you enough for pulling the strings to get me in."

"You're welcome."

"Why me, though? Why go to all this trouble for me?" Miguel asked.

"Because you're my friend, and it wasn't really that much trouble anyway."

"No trouble? You sent that guy from New York City, and he somehow got my debt cleared. That guy was kinda scary, by the way."

"Yeah, Eli certainly has a way with people."

"No, really, why go to all the trouble for me?"

Callie paused for a moment and cocked her head to the side. "Miguel, you have a wonderful mind, and I couldn't stand the thought of your talent going to waste. That's why."

"That might be the nicest thing anyone's ever said to me."

Callie winked at him.

Miguel wondered if it was possible to blush in the virtual world. "I still can't believe I'm going to be a genetic engineer. I mean, I always wanted to study human genetics, but plant genetics is close enough."

"It's all the same."

"What's all the same?" Miguel asked.

"Genetics, it's all the same. Whether it's plant or animal, DNA is DNA; the code that holds the secrets of the universe."

Chapter 10: Unification Day

To understand an animal's true nature, it must be studied in its natural environment. To learn a human's true nature, the opposite must be done. However, this may reveal more about the observer than the subject. —Zacharia Jones, Omni Ascension

Date: 162 AE

The early-morning light barely lit the room as Greg Ustinov rolled over in bed to admire his companion. Although she appeared to be in her mid- to late thirties due to the gray steaks in her hair, she was, in fact, almost fifty years older than he. But then again, everyone was older than he.

Meilin Chiang cracked open her eyes as if she could feel his piercing gaze, and they smiled in unison while Meilin coyly whispered, "Really, Greg, last night wasn't enough for you?"

"Can't a man just admire his girlfriend without having ulterior motives?" Greg replied as he gave a slight chuckle. "I was just thinking that you may be the most beautiful woman I've ever seen."

As she fluffed her pillows against the headboard and sat up in bed, Meilin replied, "If we hadn't been together for three years, I'd swear you're still trying to charm me, or maybe you really are this charming."

"I have to be charming to make up for these grotesque scars."

"I've told you a thousand times I don't find them grotesque at all," Meilin replied as she turned on her side to face him and caress the scars that covered his back and left arm. "They give you character and shift the focus to your devilishly handsome face." She kissed his cheek before easing out of bed, and as she walked toward the bathroom, she said, "One day you're going to tell me the story behind those scars."

As she walked away, Greg noted her beautiful black hair flowing down her back with several distinctive gray streaks covering the entire length of it. Gray coloring and streaking was the latest fashion in women's hairstyle, but Greg didn't care much for it himself, though he would never admit that to Meilin. He found it ironic that people started dyeing their hair gray so they would look unique and different, but now so many people were doing it that it was no longer unique or different. He supposed that was better than the previous fad where everyone tried to look like teenagers. In a world where everyone looked the same age, the easiest way to stand out was to look older or younger, but fads always ended with everyone looking the same anyway.

As Meilin was showering, Greg sat up in bed and clicked his right-rear teeth together three times to activate his TICI. He wanted to check out the local news in Beijing but simply turned on the TV instead. While the local news played, he decided to order room service for breakfast, so he used his TICI to bring up the room service menu for the Imperial Mansion Executive Apartments Hotel. After ordering their breakfast, he thought, *Yes, Meilin, today is the day I will tell you and the whole world the story behind my scars. I just hope no one questions why my scars aren't any worse.*

Later, as they were eating breakfast and watching the local news in their suite, Greg said with an annoyed tone, "All anyone is talking about is Unification Day and Zacharia Jones. You'd think nothing else was happening in the entire world!"

"Well, today is the centennial of world unification under one government, and that's in no small part due to Zacharia Jones's sacrifice," replied Meilin as she sipped her coffee. "Not to mention President McDaniel is going to be here in Beijing to deliver the keynote address and dedicate the Zacharia Jones Memorial. So, you gotta at least understand why everyone is excited, even if you don't approve."

"Yeah, I'm just sick of hearing about that phony. And why do they keep showing the video of him going up in flames? It's disturbing," Greg replied as he pointed to the screen that showed a man enveloped in flames running off stage.

Meilin put her coffee down and said, "Yeah, that video is hard to watch." After pausing for a moment, she continued, "I still don't understand why you wanted to come here in the first place. If you dislike Jones so much, why did you insist that we fly around the world to come to the centennial celebration?"

In hindsight, Greg now thought that bringing her here was purely selfish on his part, and he probably should have left her at home. That would have been easier on her. Now he felt obligated to tell her before he told the rest of the world, so he sighed and said, "Meilin, I think it's time I told you the truth. You deserve to find out before everyone else."

After he was silent for several moments, Meilin nervously prodded, "Tell me the truth about what?"

He pulled up his shirt. "These scars. You see, these scars are the results of what you're watching now," he said, pointing to the TV screen on the wall.

Meilin looked back and forth from the TV to Zach as she digested what was just said. "Wait, you're saying *you're* Zacharia Jones?"

"Yes, that's what I'm trying to tell you."

"That's not possible. He's dead." After a moment, she grinned and said, "You're just pulling my chain."

Greg didn't return her smile. "No, I'm serious. I am Zacharia Jones, and I can prove it." He pulled a small faded photograph from his wallet and handed it to her. On the picture appeared a young man and a young woman standing side by side. The young man was obviously Greg.

After looking at the photo for a few moments, Meilin asked, "Is that Mary Ann Jones?"

"Yes, that's my mother. As far as I know, she's the only one that knows I'm still alive. Flip it over."

Meilin read the handwritten note aloud. "To my loving son, I hope one day you will forgive me."

Meilin accessed her TICI and pulled up an old picture of Zacharia Jones. She looked at the image of Zacharia Jones displayed directly on her retina with Greg sitting in front of her. "Your face is different, but now that I'm comparing it side by side, I do see a marked resemblance. Facial-recognition software doesn't confirm a match though."

"Yes, I had some surgery just for that reason," Zacharia

replied truthfully.

"But how can you not have any scars on your face, or the rest of your body for that matter, except for your back and arm? I mean, your entire body was engulfed in flames; you should be covered in burn scars."

"Modern medicine can work miracles, and I've had dozens of surgeries to make this face beautiful again," he said with a smile as he lied.

"So, why was your mom asking you for forgiveness? What was that about?"

"Because she knows how much I loathe the religious adulation that is still directed toward Zacharia Jones. It's why I let everyone believe I was dead after the burning."

"But *you* started the Omni Ascend movement, not her."

"That's true. I became the person she raised me to be. She raised me believing that I was the chosen one and encouraged everyone else to believe that nonsense as well. After the near drowning, she even invited the Tibetan Lamas to come examine me."

Zach remembered it like it was yesterday, even though it was over 130 years ago. He was eight years old, and the Event Depression was in full swing, with the United States government just two years from total collapse. His mother, like most Americans, was having trouble making ends meet, so she encouraged the notion that he was some kind of Chosen One or Golden Child. People readily accepted the idea that Zach was special, as he was the last child born on Earth by more than a year. Fundamentalism was having a resurgence during the early days of the Event Depression, and his mother, together with a local fundamentalist preacher, would bring him to the pulpit during revivals so he could recite Bible verses, as he had memorized the entire Bible by age six. He would lay hands on people to heal their broken souls, and together with the preacher, they would have altar calls where thousands would come to repent. The preacher would give his mother a portion of the tithing after every service, and they probably wouldn't have survived without it. As word of this holy child spread around Virginia and the surrounding states, members of other denominations would come and seek him out. Catholics from around the nation would come to receive his blessing, even though he wasn't a Catholic.

Zach recalled one winter day after school, he and three of his friends were playing on a frozen pond when the ice broke, and three of them fell through. His friend who didn't fall through ran for help, but by the time rescuers arrived, Zach and the two other boys had been under the ice for two hours. The other boys died, but Zach was revived at the hospital and made a miraculous recovery. The story of the Holy Child who couldn't drown spread around the country and eventually the world. It was during this time that the Tibetan monks inquired if they might come test Zacharia to determine if he was the reincarnated Dalai Lama. The former Dalai Lama had died in a plane crash nine months before Zach was born. Thinking that they might profit from this, his mother agreed to the examination. After the exhausting examination, Zacharia Jones was declared the sixteenth Dalai Lama, the first Dalai Lama not to be Tibetan.

"Are you still upset with her, after all this time?" Meilin asked.

Greg swallowed hard as long-forgotten memories continued to pour into his mind. "It's complicated, but yes, I still resent her, even though I know she did the best she could under the circumstances. She saw an opportunity to provide for her family, and she took it, even though it was a short-sighted decision that turned her son into a Messiah figure." He paused as tears formed in his eyes. "I'm still living with the consequences to this day."

"So, you blame your mother for your failures as a religious leader?"

"No, not really. I take responsibility for my actions, and I love my mother very much. I told you it was complicated," Zach said with a slight smile.

Meilin stared at him for a few moments. "I can't believe that you're actually Zacharia Jones and that for the past three years, I've been living with *the* Zacharia Jones."

"Oh no, don't you start that crap," Zach said as he raised his voice slightly. "There's nothing holy or special about me. I'm as guilty as my mother when it comes to leading people on and deceiving them. I did it all for the money, fame, and women. I used people on a grand scale."

"So, it's true about the rumors, that Omni Ascend was nothing but a simple cult built to bring fame, money, and women to its charismatic founder?"

"Yes, it's true, and much worse, really. I conned people into giving me money—money that most couldn't afford to give."

Meilin thought for a moment before replying. "But what about the good things you did? What about how you brought the world together to believe that everyone should live in peace and harmony with one another? That was during a dark and violent time when the world needed to hear the message that all religions should unite to bring peace back to the world."

"You don't understand. I did it all for selfish reasons," Zach replied as he lowered his gaze.

"So even the main tenet of Omni Ascend is a lie? The belief that humans must ascend and achieve nirvana in this incarnation, as there will be no more reincarnation since there will never be another human born?"

"Please don't tell me you're an Ascendant," Zach said with mild disgust on his face.

"Oh no, I was never a member of your cult, but I did believe in what the movement stood for, and I followed what you were doing. Although, I must admit that I didn't believe the rumors."

"Thanks goodness, you had me worried for a minute. I mean, you think you know someone, but you never know."

She took another sip of coffee before continuing her argument. "Without you, Nathan McDaniel would never have been able to unite the world under the Federation of Nations."

"Don't get me started on Nathan McDaniel," Zach said in disgust. "He's a bigger fraud than I am. He's the reason I still have nightmares about being on fire."

"You blame the president because you set yourself on fire?"

Zach rolled his eyes and sighed. "I didn't set myself on fire. I was set on fire! That's the part they never show when they show the video. Somehow that got lost, erased from history!"

"What are you talking about?"

"You see, no one was supposed to know I was there, but somehow they knew. When I walked out on that stage, these two fanatics came out of nowhere." He shuddered with the memory of the pain. "They came from nowhere and yelled 'Allah Akbar' and 'Death to al-Masih ad-Dajjal' as they doused me with gasoline and set me on fire."

"And you blame the president for that?"

"Of course, he orchestrated the whole thing so China would

be forced to join his Federation of Nations. I wasn't going to endorse him when I took that stage; I was going to denounce him as the Antichrist!"

"I thought you didn't believe in all of that."

"I don't, but my believers did, and if I would have said he was the Antichrist, he would have been done," he said with regret in his voice.

It was over a hundred years ago, but the memory of that day still haunted him. The world was still in the middle of the Event Depression, but Nathan McDaniel and the Federation of Nations controlled two-thirds of the world, and for them things were getting better. China was the last of the old superpowers left and still held tremendous sway over the Far East and Pacific, but they were steadfast in their denial of allowing a popular vote to join the Federation.

Zacharia Jones and Omni Ascend had many followers in China, and Zach had himself smuggled into Beijing for the Chinese New Year celebrations. He had made arrangements with his followers that he would appear on a stage in Tiananmen Square during a concert. His followers believed he was going to denounce the Chinese Communist regime and call for a referendum vote for China to join the Federation of Nations. What his followers didn't realize was that he had become disillusioned with the movement, despised his role in it, and was looking for a way out. Zach had also come to believe that Nathan McDaniel was a megalomaniac, bent on world domination, and had to be stopped. This was ironic, given that the majority of his followers were ardent McDaniel supporters, as his government was seen as bringing peace and stability to the world. McDaniel had coopted Zach's movement to his benefit.

Zach remembered the fateful night when he walked out on that stage fully prepared to denounce Nathan McDaniel as the Antichrist. The winter air was crisp, and he could see his breath as he looked out on the throng of humanity that packed the city square. Over half a million people watched as the band stopped playing and this unknown man walked out of the shadows to address them. He took the microphone from the lead singer and addressed the crowd in perfect Mandarin. "I am Zacharia Jones." However, someone in the crowd already knew who he was, and two men ran from the far corner of the stage straight for him. He was so surprised that he froze as they approached and in unison yelled. "Allah Akbar, death to al-Masih ad-Dajjal," while they doused him with gasoline and lit him on fire.

When the video of that horrid event leaked from China, there was no sign of the two fanatics who had set him on fire. Instead the video made it appear that he had said. "I am Zacharia Jones," and set himself on fire. The effect of this video on China was immediate, as the populace believed that Zacharia Jones had sacrificed himself in protest of the Chinese government not allowing a referendum vote on joining the Federation of Nations. Massive protests occurred across China in the following weeks, and eventually the Communists were forced to allow a vote. Once China joined the FON, the rest of the Far East and indeed the world followed suit.

"So, you're saying that somehow the president got wind of your plan and made arrangements for these ... fanatics to set you on fire?" Meilin asked.

"That's the thing—that's what's so crazy about all of this. I never told anyone about my plan to denounce the president, and yet somehow he knew."

"How, how could he have known?"

"I honestly don't know, but he's got spies everywhere, and it's like he's got some kind of a machine that can predict what people will do before they do it. I know that sounds crazy, but I'm telling you it's uncanny how he knows everything."

Meilin stared at him from across the table like she was meeting him for the first time. With fear in her voice, she said, "You've obviously brought us here with something in mind. So, what is it that you plan to do today?"

"I'm going to finish what I started."

* * *

Later that afternoon, Zach was alone in Tiananmen Square along with hundreds of thousands of others, waiting for the president of the FON to give his address and unveil the statue of Zacharia Jones. As he waited, he sadly remembered parting with Meilin when he left the hotel several hours earlier. She didn't understand why he had to denounce President McDaniel, and he doubted he would ever see her again as they had departed in anger. *Ah, my sweet Meilin, our time together was special, but I don't think you can follow where I go next*, he thought wistfully.

Zach looked up at the stage where the president would give his speech and the large covered statue next to the stage that would be unveiled. He wished someone would set that statue on fire. He noticed a blinking red dot in the far corner of his left eye. There was a message from the mayor of Beijing, an old Ascendant, that everything was arranged, and he could take the stage immediately after the president completed his address. Zach had revealed himself to the mayor earlier in the day and asked if he could make arrangements in secret so Zach could take the stage after the president. All of this under the pretext that he was going to reveal himself along with a holy message for the citizens of the world.

The applause was deafening as the president took the stage. Zach looked on intently while the president raised his hands high over his head and basked in the adulation of the crowd. When McDaniel motioned for the crowd to be silent, Zach thought to himself, *Welcome to my parlor, said the spider to the fly.*

"Citizens of the Federation, people of the Earth, I come to you today as your president and as a fellow citizen of this planet to celebrate the first one hundred years of our great republic and to commemorate the man who sacrificed his life to bring this to pass, Zacharia Jones." He pointed toward the still-covered statue. After the thunderous applause quieted, the president continued. "Zacharia Jones, the last child born after the Event, the youngest person on the planet, came to show humanity the ways of peace and harmony. If not for Zacharia's selfless sacrifice, our civilization might have crumbled into oblivion, but instead the world's people united as one to climb from the darkness of the Event Depression to literally reach for the stars. As a united people, we set out on a quest greater than anything undertaken in the history of humanity, a public works project so vast that it employed nearly 20 percent of the world's population for almost thirty years."

Again the crowd erupted into applause then quieted on its own. "The Phoenix Project culminated with the Phoenix probe that launched over seventy years ago toward Alpha Centauri Five, with the sole mission of confirming that it was a habitable world, as the Star Shade telescope had suggested so many years prior. The Phoenix Project and the jobs it created helped usher humanity from the darkness that was the Event Depression into the prosperity that we now enjoy."

Zach found that he was just as mesmerized with the president's speech as the rest of the crowd as he thought, *This is unexpected. What is he doing?* Zach looked around the crowd and noted the hundreds of news drones that were hovering above the crowd, so he activated his TICI and witnessed the view from the combined video feeds of all the drones. This was the view that the rest of the world was seeing: Nathan McDaniel larger than life putting on the performance of the century.

As the applause died, the president continued. "And now, just as Zacharia Jones guided humanity through the Event Depression, the Phoenix Project is poised to propel humanity to its ultimate destiny in the stars." As the president paused for full effect, the crowd grew silent, eager to hear his every word. "One week ago, we started receiving images and video from the Phoenix probe that arrived in orbit around Alpha Centauri Five four years ago. The Phoenix Project has exceeded our wildest expectations, and without further ado, I give to you the future of humanity, the newly named fifth planet of the Alpha Centauri system: Aurora!"

Zach, along with the rest of humanity, watched in wonder as a three-dimensional projection appeared over Tiananmen Square. The projection presented a blue-and-white planet that bore a striking resemblance to Earth, but the continents that could be seen through the white clouds were alien. The crowd was in awe and total silence as the view shifted from space to inside the atmosphere of the planet, as if taken from an airborne drone. Now they could see blue oceans, and as the craft flew over land, there were large forests, plains, and then herds of animals moving across the land. People were now cheering and clapping, and as Zach looked around, he could see people weeping and hugging each other. Zach found himself caught up in the moment as the woman standing next to him hugged him as well. For the next ten minutes, the president remained silent as the crowd at Tiananmen Square and the worldwide audience watched video of the animal life on the newly named Aurora.

The view of large alien herbivores grazing on the plains slowly faded as the point of view rose higher in the sky until it switched to the planet as seen from orbit. The president resumed his speech and pointed directly at the image of Aurora above the crowd. "This is the fruit of the Phoenix Project, but now I propose a new project, a project that will dwarf the Phoenix Project in scope and ambition." McDaniel paused waiting for the crowd to quiet. "I propose that the next step for humanity is to send a manned mission to Aurora, not a mission just to plant a flag and return home, but a mission to send thousands of colonists to this new world! We will build an interstellar spaceship based on the same technology as the Phoenix probe. This monumental feat of engineering will require the economic output of our entire planet for over one hundred years. It will be the greatest achievement in human history, but it will also be the most difficult task ever undertaken. I have faith in this society that we now have the long view and understand our destiny. We will undertake this monumental task, and in so doing, we will send our seed out into the galaxy, for not only is it our destiny to go to Aurora, but we will overcome the plague that has made us barren. We will populate the galaxy with our children who have yet to be born!"

The crowd of over half a million people erupted in wild applause that was so loud, Zach thought surely the gods could hear them. As he glanced over at the statue that was still covered, Zach thought to himself, *He doesn't even know I'm here, and yet he's outmaneuvered me again. The crowd has all but forgotten Zacharia Jones, and nothing I say right now would matter one bit.* He closed his eyes for a moment, and he saw an image of himself stepping off a landing shuttle and onto this new world. He could feel the emotion as he breathed the alien atmosphere into his lungs for the first time. As Zach opened his eyes, he found that he wasn't even angry anymore and, in a way, he felt like a burden had been lifted from him. He no longer felt the need to reveal himself or expose the president, and it all seemed petty now given everything he had just witnessed.

While the roar of the crowd grew to a crescendo, Zach watched as the president jumped off the front of the stage directly into the crowd. Zach quickly brought up the view from the press drones that were still hovering overhead. He could see that there was a group of security guards at the base of the stage where the president had leapt. They now surrounded the president as he moved through the crowd, but occasionally they let someone through to shake hands with him.

Zach switched to another view, so he could see video that was coming directly from the TICIs of people in the crowd who were close to the president and some who were shaking hands with him. It was an amazing spectacle to see the president of the world moving through a crowd of over half a million people, with only a small security detail for protection.

While he switched back to the overhead view, Zach realized with some trepidation that the president was moving in a direct line through the crowd straight toward him. Zach tried to move out of the way, but the crowd pressed him in tighter, and he was unable to maneuver. He started to panic as he realized there was no escape, and he thought, *How does he know I'm here? Surely this isn't a coincidence.*

Frozen in place by the crowd, Zach could feel his stomach turn as he watched the president and his entourage move closer and closer to him, all the while wondering if he would survive the coming encounter. As the president neared to within a few meters, Zach noticed that all the personal feeds from the people surrounding him were shutting down. One by one, all the feeds around him blanked out as the president's guards surrounded Zach. When the president stood directly in front of him, there wasn't a single video feed that showed the scene. *How is he doing this?* Zach thought to himself.

President McDaniel reached out and put his right hand on Zach's shoulder. "Hello, Zach. This meeting is a long time coming, don't you think?" Zach, frozen in fear, could only nod in agreement, so the president continued. "I hope you still don't believe that I had anything to do with your immolation, because I need your help. What do you say, Zacharia? Will you join me?"

With tears streaming down his face, Zach reached out and shook hands with President McDaniel.

Chapter 11: The Game's Afoot

No one would have noticed when the longest contiguously married couple divorced in 242 AE, had it not been for the fact that there was no longer a legal process for divorce. Marriage had not been officially recognized by the government since the FON was founded, so Jorge and Maria Consuelo had to appeal to the FON court system for a special ruling granting them a divorce after 316 years of marriage, due to irreconcilable differences.
—*Zacharia Jones,* Out of Darkness: The Event Chronicles

Date: 258 AE

John Fitzpatrick looked down at the wardrobe that Alicia had laid out for him on the bed. He wasn't sure if he agreed with her recent suggestion of styles for him, even though her tastes were always spot-on. He tried the fedora on for size. "So, you're dressing me all film noir now?"

"What, you don't like it?" Alicia said as she helped him into the coat.

John looked at himself in the mirror and said, "No, it's not bad. I'm just not sure about this Humphrey Bogart look, and you know I don't keep up with fashion or the latest fads."

"Oh, I know," she said while brushing dust of his shoulders. "If you did, you'd know that film noir is not in fashion at all. I mean, retro is all the rage, but everyone's into twenty teens now, although late 1980s are trending, but no one is doing 1940s."

"So, you're trying to make me a trendsetter?"

"Not at all. I just think it suits you. The greatest detective of our time should dress the part, don't you think?"

John winked at her as he adjusted his tie and said, "Here's looking at you, kid."

"Oh my, do you do that for all the girls?" Alicia asked as she stepped close to him.

They embraced as if to kiss, but before their lips met, John dipped her low and said in an exaggerated Bogart accent, "No, sweetheart, you're the only girl for me."

As they kissed, he knew that she really was the only woman for him and had been for nearly two hundred years now. They hadn't been together the entire time, but during the times they were apart, he never considered other women. John cherished their time together, and the last five years together had been even sweeter than the times before.

Their kiss slowly ended as John eased her back up from the dip and Alicia said, "Whoa, you better cool your jets, mister, we don't have time for that. You gotta catch the mag lev to Quito soon."

"Yeah, you're right," John said as he composed himself. "I better finish packing."

"What's this all about anyway? Why does the director of the

ISA want to see you anyway, and why in person?" Alicia asked.

"I wish I knew, and you're right, it doesn't really make much sense for a face-to-face meeting."

"I know. Why can't y'all do a videoconference like normal people? And you don't even work for the ISA anymore. You're an inspector with FCID."

"Chief inspector, if you please." John had worked for the Federal Criminal Investigation Division for several decades now.

Alicia laughed. "Pardon me, Chief Inspector, but surely you've speculated about the nature of the meeting."

John added his workout clothes to the suitcase. "Yeah, the only reason I can think of for a face-to-face meeting is that it's too sensitive to be discussed over the Net."

"Don't they have secure lines for that sort of thing?"

John nodded. "They do indeed, so that tells me he believes someone may be monitoring their secure lines. Either that or he's just really paranoid. Hell, I don't know, I've never met the man."

"But what would warrant that level of security, aren't you curious?"

"You know I am, and you're pumping me for information because it intrigues you."

"You got me," Alicia said as she handed him a shirt. "So, come on, what are you thinking?"

"I really don't have enough information to speculate."

She looked at him closely. "Uh-huh, but you have a hunch, I can tell."

John realized he might as well stop dragging this out, so he said. "Okay, you're right. I have a hunch that this will having something to do with the case."

"*The case?* The one you've been obsessing over for the last two hundred years?"

"Two hundred fifty-eight years, but yeah, that case."

Alicia sat down on the bed. "So, what makes you think this meeting has something to do with the Event?"

"Because the Event was almost certainly a conspiracy, and there's no way the ripples from a conspiracy of that magnitude aren't still being felt in the highest levels of government."

"I really have no idea what you just said," Alicia replied, shaking her head.

"What I mean is that I suspect anyone who's risen to power after the Event."

"Well, Director Asher was an assistant director at NASA before the Event, so it doesn't seem like much of a stretch for him to be director of the ISA now."

John closed his suitcase. "Well, before the Event, being an assistant director for NASA wasn't exactly a position of power outside of the organization itself. Now he's the director of the most powerful bureaucracy that's ever existed. He's arguably the second most powerful man on the planet."

"So, you think he might be directly involved in this conspiracy?"

"I think it's likely he's either directly involved or he's feeling the effects of said conspiracy."

"Then what do you think he wants to see you about?" she asked.

"I don't have the foggiest."

Alicia rolled her eyes. "John Fitzpatrick, I really don't understand the way your brain works, but I can't wait to hear what this is all about."

"Well, don't get your hopes up."

"What does that mean?"

"If it is about the Event, then our discussion will almost certainly be classified, and I won't be able to discuss it with you or anyone else."

Alicia helped him into his overcoat. "Then I guess your outfit is fitting."

"Fitting for what?"

"Fitting for all the cloak and dagger, of course," she replied with a sly smile.

* * *

Robert Asher stood at the corner window of his office mesmerized as he watched the space elevator slowly climb up the cables that disappeared into the thin clouds above. He never tired of watching this spectacle, the second-greatest achievement of his career. Attached at the end of the cables, 22,236 miles above the Earth in geostationary orbit, was the ISA space dock. *Atropos*, the culmination of his life's work, was attached to the dock. As Robert slowly walked back to his desk, a small red light blinked in the corner of his left eye. *Ah yes, my ten o'clock is here,* he thought as he acknowledged the alert with his eye browser. A few seconds later, his office door opened, and Chief Inspector John Fitzpatrick slowly walked through.

As this was the first time they had met face to face, Robert studied the chief inspector for a moment while he entered the room. John Fitzpatrick was of African descent, just over average height at five-foot-eleven, slim, and in good shape. Like everyone else, he appeared to be around thirty years of age. He was dressed in a gray three-piece suit complete with a fedora and trench coat, as it was a cold, rainy day. He gave the appearance of a classic 1940s movie detective, and Robert supposed that was the effect he was going for. The current world fashion was retro, but John Fitzpatrick's wardrobe was more retro than most.

As Robert approached him, he reached out his hand and said, "Chief Inspector Fitzpatrick, it's a pleasure to finally meet you."

As they shook hands, John replied, "Likewise, Director, and please call me John."

"Of course, and please call me Robert."

"Wow, what a view!" John said as he walked toward the corner window to get a better look at the space elevator.

"Sometimes it really does pay to be the director of the International Space Agency," Robert chuckled as he joined John by the window. "Here, let me take your coat, and please have a seat."

After they were both seated at the desk Robert, said, "I hope your flight from New York was good."

"Oh, I took the mag-lev train. I avoid flying if at all possible."

"Even though there's only been three airline crashes in the last two hundred years and zero deaths? I find that odd."

John agreed that flying was completely safe these days, especially with complete automation and crashproof passenger compartments. "The truth is, flying upsets my stomach, so I avoid it when I can." After a brief silence, John asked, "So, tell me, Director, what can I do for you?"

"You mean, why have I dragged you down to Ecuador without so much as a hint as to why I want to meet with you?"

"Yes, that would be nice."

"First I must ask you to shut down your TICI interface, and just so you know, I'm also activating a security field so no signals will be able to come in or out of this office," Robert said.

After a moment, John replied, "TICI off. So, why all the cloak and dagger?"

Robert clasped his hands together on the desk and said, "The cloak and dagger is because this is a matter of ISA security, and I need answers to a mystery that may threaten the *Atropos*. A mystery that the ISA has been unable to solve. I invited you here because I need the greatest deductive mind alive. I need the detective who solved the Rosendale case, caught the Ghost, and unraveled the Antarctic mystery."

"I appreciate the compliments, but why do you believe the *Atropos* is threatened?"

"I believe the *Atropos* Project has been subverted by someone for their own purposes. I want you to find out who has subverted the project and to what end."

As the director's statement sank in, John quickly reviewed what he knew of the *Atropos* Project. The *Atropos* was the largest public works project in human history, underway for ninety-six years, with sixty-two years left to go. An interstellar light-sail/Bussard ram ship designed to transport four thousand colonists from Earth to Aurora, the fifth planet of the Alpha Centauri system. "Now you have to tell my why you believe the *Atropos* Project has been subverted," John replied.

Robert sighed and took a deep breath. "Everything I'm about to tell you is top secret, and you can't repeat any of it to anyone."

"Of course," John replied.

"It all started when we began receiving images from the Phoenix probe ninety-six years ago. Those images and videos of Aurora's surface were far more advanced than anything we designed the probe to do. You see, the Phoenix probe was a relatively small light-sail craft propelled by a massive laser. The body of the probe was only about one meter long and about half a meter wide," Robert said as he visually demonstrated the probe's size with his hands. "It was basically a sophisticated computer with a 3-D printer that was designed to assemble a larger orbital device, camera, and transmitter from local materials once it arrived in the Alpha Centauri system. It was designed to take simple orbital pictures and beam them back to Earth via laser; nothing more.

"But there was video and photos from the planet's surface. As I recall, the president showed the first video to the world himself," John interrupted.

"Yes, that's the problem. Apparently, the probe somehow made a lander and an atmospheric flyer, and it sent back the most amazing pictures and even video. Simple photos from orbit was all it was programmed to do, yet we received video from the planet's surface. We never told the public, of course. We let everyone believe we designed it to do those things."

After a moment of silence, John said, "So, what happened? How did the probe do it?"

"At first we thought that somehow the Phoenix probe had become sentient and had expounded on its original mission, but we've been unable to replicate that here."

"So, you went ahead with the *Atropos* Project, even though you couldn't explain what happened with the Phoenix probe?"

"Yes, we basically swept it under the rug and pretended it didn't happen. At least we did until about six months ago."

"What happened six months ago?"

"Six months ago, we found this," Robert said as he projected a small hologram from his wristwatch. The hologram was a low-quality picture of Aurora as seen from orbit.

John examined the hologram. "I don't get it. What's so important about this?"

"I know this just looks like a low-quality pic from the Phoenix probe, but this isn't one that the probe sent back to us. We actually found this one on an old internet server. The digital footprint of the pic is more interesting than the pic itself as there was a significant digital trail attached to this pic, but it's the date that was most telling. You see, the date on this pic is only four months after the probe arrived at Aurora."

John sat forward in his chair. "You mean this pic was sent back to someone other than the ISA immediately after the probe arrived at Aurora, and somehow it arrived in only four months, when it should have taken four years?"

"No, what I'm telling you is that the pic arrived instantly once it was sent. I say that because it would have taken the probe about four months to have replicated what it needed in order to be able to send pics back to Earth."

John replied, "But how is that possible? The probe sends data back to Earth via laser beam, which travels at the speed of light, and Aurora is four light years away."

"The only way possible is via a quantum communication device, and that is beyond our current technology," Robert said as he sipped his now-cold coffee. "But it would seem not beyond everyone's technology. Not only that, but it means that someone would have installed the entangled quantum particle communication device on the probe before it was launched."

"So, you suspect someone on your own team is behind this?"

"No, that's not really likely," Robert replied.

"Okay, what aren't you telling me?"

"When we investigated the digital trail of the pic," Robert said as he pointed to the pic still hovering in the air, "we discovered some very peculiar code. Code that is unlike anything anyone has ever seen before. The code is indecipherable, but it's clearly the digital trail of a very sophisticated program."

"So, you went looking for this code, didn't you?"

Robert smiled. "Exactly. It's so well hidden that you'd never see it if you didn't know what to look for, but once we started looking, we found it everywhere."

"Everywhere?"

"Yes, it's in the ISA servers; it's literally been everywhere in the entire worldwide web. My top computer scientist believes it's the trail of a true artificial intelligence."

John stood up from his chair and moved behind it, leaning against it. "You believe this is a true AI, despite the fact that after two hundred years of research by the world's best computer scientists, no one has been able to create one?"

"Yes, it was one of President McDaniel's first directives after he was elected by the Federation of Nations, and nothing has ever come of it, at least as far as we know. Nevertheless, my top scientist tells me this is an AI, and when the smartest man on the planet tells me something, I listen."

John took a deep breath. "So, you have a true AI that shouldn't exist, and it took control of the Phoenix probe and presumably altered its programming that gave you photos and videos that were beyond your wildest expectations, a blue-and-green life-infested planet. These photos and videos directly inspired the construction of the *Atropos.* Now you fear that this AI has subverted the *Atropos* Project to its own ends, and you want me to find out who created the AI and what they intend to do with the *Atropos*?"

"Yes, that about sums it up, but don't forget how much is at stake. The expense of this project is staggering, the entire economic output of the world for the last ninety-six years. Not to mention the two-hundred-petawatt laser that we've built to initially propel the ship. If that laser were subverted, it could incinerate the ship in a millisecond."

John sat back in his seat. "You needn't remind me, Director. I realize the significance of the situation." John pointed out the window toward the space elevator. "This project, in one form or another, has been the foundation of President McDaniel's economic policies since he rescued the world from the depression that followed the Event. If the *Atropos* Project were to somehow fail, the world might very well fall back into economic depression and darkness similar to what immediately followed the Event."

After a brief pause, Robert said, "You're right, we can't plunge the world back into something even remotely like the Event Depression. The lawlessness, war, and suffering, it's difficult to fathom now. Sixty years of chaos. Since then, there hasn't been a single war, and violent crime is so low as to be almost nonexistent."

"Oh, I know, it's practically put me out of work," John replied with a slight chuckle.

"We've come so far; we can't go back. That's why it's so important that you figure this out."

"I agree, Director, we must find out who is behind this AI," John said.

"So, you'll take the case then?"

"Only on two conditions."

"What are they?"

"I'm currently working on another case, and I'm not about to drop it, so I'll need to be able to pursue both cases with equal zeal."

Robert asked, "What case could possibly be of equal importance to the one I've just described?"

"The cause of the Event itself."

Robert objected. "But we already know the cause of the Event. It's a virus that alters human DNA so that the aging process is stopped while at the same time causing infertility in men and women."

"Yes, a virus that's so elusive and mutates so fast that our best scientists from around the world have been unable to do anything with it in over 250 years. There's no way this is a naturally occurring virus, so it had to be artificially constructed," John said emphatically.

"While I agree with almost everything you've just said, the simple fact is that no one on this planet has the kind of technology it would take to manufacture a virus of this nature. It's light years ahead of anything we could do; that's why we haven't been able to stop it."

"No one on this planet that you know of has this technology, but I assure you someone or something has the technology. The Event was not some random act of evolution."

"Surely you're not suggesting an extraterrestrial origin?"

"No, but I'm not excluding it either. I go where the evidence leads me."

Robert seemed to accept this. "Who commissioned you to investigate the Event?"

"No one. It's my personal project, and I've been working

on it since day one," John said as a peculiar thought occurred to him. "What if the person or persons that subverted the Phoenix Project, and that you fear has subverted the *Atropos* Project, is the same person that created the Event virus?"

Robert seemed to ignore the question. "What's your other condition?"

"The other condition is that I have unlimited access to all federal files, everything. ISA files, political files, accounting databases. I need access to all information, and I need an unlimited budget. If I ask for money, I don't want any questions. I just need the money," John said calmly.

Without any hesitation, the director replied, "Done."

"Are you sure you don't need to think about it for a bit?"

"No, you'll have everything you need to conduct a thorough investigation. You'll have the ISA behind you." Robert stood up and extended his hand across the desk. "So, we have a deal?"

"Yes, I'll take the case," John replied as he shook hands with the director.

"Terrific, stop by the front desk, and Johnson will set everything up for you."

John walked toward the door but stopped short as he turned around and said, "Robert, has it ever occurred to you that this whole thing might be a fraud?"

"A fraud, what do you mean?"

"I mean, what if someone subverted the Phoenix probe to send back fake images and videos? You don't really know that the probe went beyond its programming and built a lander and atmospheric flyer. You just surmised it based on the images and videos it sent back. All you know is that someone subverted the probe. So, you have to ask yourself which is more likely; did they somehow upgrade the probe to build a lander and flyer or did they simply alter it to send back fake images?"

Robert's face turned red. "Why would someone alter the probe to send back fake images? To what end?"

"You said yourself that the images and videos sent back by the Phoenix probe directly inspired the construction of *Atropos*, the largest public works project in human history, a project that has employed the majority of humanity in one form or another for over ninety years now."

"If you're implying that President McDaniel is behind this, that's the most cynical thing I've ever heard."

On his way out the door, John replied, "Just a random thought, Robert. I'll contact you when I have something concrete. It's a strange and wonderful world we live in, Mr. Director, full of intrigue and mystery."

After the chief inspector left his office, Robert started to contact his assistant to cancel the whole thing, but something stopped him. He didn't like the direction John went at the end of their conversation, but he couldn't think of a better course of action. *I'll just have to see where it goes,* he thought.

* * *

John walked down the hallway after leaving the director's office, his mind abuzz with the possibilities. *Finally, I have the funding necessary to conduct a proper investigation. The greatest mystery in human history, and now I have the resources of the most powerful bureaucracy on the planet behind me! I've got to find out more about this AI. Surely there's a connection. I'm closer than ever before to unraveling this mystery; it's only a matter of time now.* John's thoughts were interrupted by Alicia calling via TICI.

"Hey, hon," John answered.

"Hey, you, what did you find out? Can you tell me anything?"

"Other than it's classified, no."

"Did you learn anything to help you with the case?"

John paused a moment while he considered his reply. "Yeah, I learned that I can scratch Director Asher off my list of suspects."

Chapter 12: The Pilot

The rate of technological advancement for the fifty years preceding the Event was thought by many to be unsustainable. No one could imagine that the opposite would be the case. The rapid growth of technology in the years following the Event bordered on the miraculous.
—Zacharia Jones, Out of Darkness: The Event Chronicles

Date: 262 AE

A fourteen-year-old George Wiley stepped to the edge of the cliff and looked down at the water that was eighty feet below. He felt the warm breeze blow through his long hair, and a chill ran down his spine as the adrenaline surged through his veins. His friends were urging him to jump, even though none of them had ever actually jumped off the cliff, though they had heard stories of other kids doing it. George stood there frozen as he stared at the water below, his heart threatening to pound right through his chest. *Just take one step forward,* he thought to himself, *that's all I have to do.* He turned to look back at his friends, who were still taunting him, and gave them a slight smile as he took that step. The eighty-foot drop seemed to take an eternity, but he finally hit the water feet first and plunged deep beneath the surface. His lungs screamed for air as he kicked for the surface, which seemed to be moving away from him. Struggling to reach the surface, he risked a look down into the darkness and saw a large shadow moving from the depths toward him.

George awakened with a start and took several seconds recovering his wits before realizing he was in the cockpit of the ISA prototype spaceship *Yeager.* He pulled himself from his sleep rack and seated himself in the cockpit so he could assess his current situation. The *Yeager* was rapidly accelerating and would achieve ram velocity in about three more hours. After three days of acceleration, it was finally time to test the main fusion engine, but most importantly, it was time to test the ram field that he had personally designed.

George clicked his back teeth together three times to activate his TICI so he could interact directly with the *Yeager's* powerful computer. After ensuring that all the ship's systems were normal, he activated Margie. Once Margie was activated, his TICI displayed her in his vision, so she appeared to walk around the cockpit as a six-inch-tall version of his deceased wife.

After walking over the instrument panel, Margie sat down on the armrest of his chair and said. "What's wrong, George? You look troubled."

George was constantly surprised at how insightful this avatar could be at times. He created her using a commercially available program that could generate avatars based on a person's online presence and social media profile. As Margie had been quite active in social media, her avatar was remarkably lifelike and so like Margie that at times he forgot he was talking to a computer simulation.

George looked down at Margie as he replied, "It's that stupid cliff dream again."

"George, I think it's time that you just admit that you've always been something of a daredevil. It really started when you were a teenager, long before the Event."

"That's not really true. Oh sure, I did my share of stupid stuff like jumping off that cliff, but all those death-defying stunts I did after the Event were the result of severe depression. I practically had a death wish."

"You'll get no argument from me on that," Margie replied.

"I'm a man of science, not a daredevil. That's not who I am," George insisted.

Margie held her arms out from her miniature body. "And yet here we are, millions of miles from Earth, going faster than any human in history, and about to go a lot faster if your electromagnetic ram field actually works. Just admit it, George: you didn't have to do this. You could have had a real test pilot do this."

"And what would that test pilot do when the ram field fluctuated and needed precise adjustments on the fly? No, I have to do this. I'm the best person for this job."

"You're as stubborn as you ever were, Georgie. What am I going to do with you?"

"Incoming message, Margie. I'd better get this," George said as he turned on the communication link.

"Dr. Wiley, this is Stan Wachoski at the ISA space dock. By our calculations, you will reach ram velocity in 2.5 hours.

At that time, you will shut down the auxiliary boosters and spool up the ram electromagnetic field scoop to begin funneling interstellar hydrogen into the fusion chamber. If your ram field functions as expected, the hydrogen atoms will be funneled into the fusion chamber at high enough velocities to achieve fusion. Once fusion is achieved, you will ignite the main torch for a thirty-second burn, then you will shut it down. Remember, this is just a test. You're not out there to try to set any unbreakable records or anything. Anyway, once the thirty-second burn is complete, you'll shut down the ram field and the fusion drive, turn the ship around, and reignite the auxiliary boosters to return home. Please acknowledge and let us know if you have any issues or questions. ISA out."

"See, George, even the ISA understands what a daredevil you are," Margie said mockingly.

"No one likes a 'told you so,' Margie."

George keyed up the mic and replied to the ISA. "Roger that, Stan, loud and clear. I'll begin preignition checks in one hour."

"Let's face it, George, you're upset because most of the world thinks of you as the madman daredevil, instead of the brilliant scientist you are," Margie said.

George couldn't really argue that point. "You're right, that does drive me crazy." Even though two centuries had passed since he quit the daredevil business, he still had strangers approach him and ask about his stunts. Sometimes he felt like screaming at them that he wasn't that person anymore.

"Well, that'll change soon enough. Once this thing tests successfully and your ram field combined with Paxton's fusion drive powers the *Atropos* to another star system. I've already heard people refer to it as the Wiley-Paxton Interstellar Drive."

George nodded in agreement. "That's mostly true, but don't forget that the *Atropos* will also be powered by a laser-driven solar sail."

Margie quickly interjected, "Only until she gets to the edge of the solar system. The Wiley-Paxton Drive will be what takes the *Atropos* across interstellar space."

"Don't get ahead of yourself, Margie. This thing might not even work."

"I have faith in you, Georgie."

Two and a half hours later, the *Yeager* was at ram velocity, and George had just received the go-ahead from the ISA. He looked at Margie and said, "Well, here goes nothing." George activated the sequence that would shut down the auxiliary boosters, but they didn't respond. He ran through the sequence again, but the boosters were still burning.

"Oh boy, I hope I didn't jinx us," Margie said.

"Yeah, me too," George replied as he prepared to run through the sequence a third time. "Maybe this time I'll just do a hard shutdown. I can't think of anything else to try."

"I don't know, George. Maybe you should check with Stan first?"

As soon as George did the hard shutdown, the ship shook wildly while clanging alarms filled the cabin with noxious noise. *Oh shit, what the hell did I just do?* George thought as the ship went into a spin. After thirty seconds of fighting with the stick, George was able to bring the ship out of the spin. Now he had to assess the situation. The auxiliary boosters were no longer firing so that was good, but he had to make sure the ship was intact before deploying the ram field and igniting the fusion drive.

As he was preparing a drone to go outside the ship to assess for damage, he received a call from the ISA. "Dr. Wily, this is Stan Wachoski. We detected an explosion. Is everything okay?"

"Everything appears to be okay, but I'm sending a drone out to assess for damage and see where that explosion came from," George replied. He'd have to wait at least eight minutes for a reply, and by then, he should have some answers.

Ten short minutes later, George had the information he needed from the drone. "Mission Control, this is George Wiley, and I'm afraid I've got some bad news. When I executed a hard shutdown of the auxiliary boosters, there was an overload that caused an explosion. Luckily, the explosion went outward from the ship, but in so doing it blew the boosters totally off the main ship. So, the auxiliary boosters and all their fuel are gone. The good news is that the *Yeager* is otherwise intact, and I believe sound enough to attempt to fire up the fusion drive. At this point, I don't think there's any other choice. Please advise."

Margie was nervously pacing on the instrument panel. "That's really our only hope, George. Deploy the ram electromagnetic field and ignite the fusion torch. Then you can gradually turn the ship and fly it back to Earth."

"You're right, Margie. If the ram scoop fusion drive doesn't work, I'm a dead man."

Ten minutes later, Mission Control's answer came. "Hi, George, this is Stan. We agree with your assessment. You're already at ram scoop velocity, so go ahead and deploy the ram field and light the fusion drive. This will be more than a thirty-second burn though. So much for a limited test; you'll have to burn the fusion drive for at least twenty-four hours if you're gonna make it back. Godspeed. ISA out."

Just like old times, George thought as he prepared to deploy the ram field, *like jumping off the Park Hyatt with a wingsuit and no parachute.*

"You ready for this, blue eyes?" George asked Margie as he deployed the ram field.

"As ready as I'll ever be, handsome."

The electromagnetic field deployed exactly as designed, and in a matter of seconds, it was fully extended one thousand kilometers in all directions. As George monitored the hydrogen levels in the scoop, he thought to himself, *Is it really going to be this easy?*

"Okay, Margie, we've got hydrogen at sufficient levels and speed in the scoop to begin feeding the fusion chamber and ignite the torch," George said enthusiastically.

"I agree," Margie replied.

"I'm opening the fusion chamber," George announced. After several minutes of waiting, he realized that the hydrogen wasn't fusing fast enough to facilitate igniting the torch.

"Uh oh, we're not getting enough fusion, are we?" Margie asked nervously.

"No, I'm going to have to adjust the field to compensate. Good thing I'm here and not some poor sap of a test pilot."

"Nobody likes a 'told you so,' Georgie," Margie said with a sly smile.

George adjusted the field but kept getting the same results. He just couldn't get the hydrogen to fuse fast enough to ignite the fusion drive. "Margie, the sad thing is that if we still had the auxiliary boosters, we could increase our speed, and I think that would do the trick."

"I think you're right, George. I don't think we have quite enough velocity."

"I'm going to call Mission Control and see if they have any ideas. They've got more people and more computing power; maybe they can come up with something I haven't thought of."

Twenty minutes later, George had his answer from the ISA. "Hi George, this is Stan, I don't have anything yet, but I just wanted to let you know that we have the top physicists and engineers from around the world working on this problem. We'll figure this thing out. In the meantime, you hang in there, George."

George sat in silence and stared out into the blackness of space as he contemplated his fate. Of all the different ways he tried to kill himself back when he was the daredevil, he had somehow survived them all. Now he was going to die because of his own intellectual failure. He'll be remembered as the daredevil physicist who died alone in the darkness of space because of his own stupidity. *But at least I'll die as the fastest man alive!* George chuckled wryly to himself.

Four hours later, he received another message from Stan. This time Stan had a laundry list of different things for George to try. It took George two more hours just to read through them all and another hour to digest them. He shook his head as he activated Margie again. "None of these are going to work, Margie."

"Well, not with that attitude, mister," Margie quipped.

"You do remember that I'm the expert in ram field physics, right? I'm telling you all of these ideas are garbage."

"If you say so, Georgie, but what the hell else do you have to do? You're literally going nowhere fast."

Strange to hear her curse like that, George thought to himself. The real Margie never cursed, and this was the first time the avatar had cursed. *Is it possible for a computer program to feel stress?*

Eighteen hours later, George was programming the last suggestion from the ISA into the computer that controlled the ram field as he said to Margie, "Here goes my last hope." Then he hit enter. Nothing happened, just like every other attempt before. He hung his head and closed his eyes, gritting his teeth in frustration.

"Why don't you get some sleep? You've been awake for almost thirty-six hours now," Margie pointed out.

"That's the best idea I've heard all day," George said wryly as he unharnessed himself from the pilot's seat and floated back to the sleep rack. He was asleep as soon as he zipped up.

George slept fitfully, his mind busy mulling over possibilities. After several hours, he sighed heavily and went back to the cockpit. He had no new messages from the ISA. *Looks like I'm not the only one out of ideas.* Margie was pacing back and forth across the instrument panel. *Did I not shut her off?*

"George, I have an idea that might seem a little crazy, but I want you to hear it anyway."

"Really, you're a physicist now?" George replied sarcastically.

"Just hear me out, jackass."

"Okay okay, what's this grand idea?"

George listened for the next ten minutes as Margie went into explicit detail of how to overtune the ram field, so the hydrogen atoms came into the scoop with higher velocities and started fusing even before they hit the fusion chamber.

"That's brilliant, Margie, but I'm afraid that will overload the ram field and cause a catastrophic failure of the fusion containment field, thus triggering a fusion explosion, which would be catastrophic."

"Well, at least you'd go out in a blaze of glory and not suffocate in a ship on a never-ending flight," Margie retorted.

George wakened suddenly to find himself still in the sleeping rack. *Did I just dream all of that? Had to be a dream, cause there's no way an avatar of Margie could come up with an idea like that. I must be losing my mind,* George thought as he got out of the sleep rack and made his way back to the cockpit.

After he strapped himself into the pilot's seat, he experienced a moment of déjà vu as he saw Margie pacing back and forth across the instrument panel. *If she starts spouting ram field physics at me, I'm going to scream.*

Instead Margie said, "Hello, handsome, feeling better now?"

"Actually, I am feeling better, and apparently I'm either going crazy or I just came up with a brilliant idea. I'm not sure which at this point."

"You seem quite sane to me, big boy," Marge said as she winked at him.

We'll see, George thought as he dictated dream Margie's idea into a message and sent it off to the ISA. Two hours later, he had their reply.

"Dr. Wiley, we've examined your idea thoroughly, and although it's frankly brilliant, it's also almost certainly fatal, as I'm sure you're aware. According to our simulations, there's a 98 percent chance of a catastrophic failure of the fusion containment field, resulting in destruction of the ship. Needless to say, we advise against this course of action. We are still working the problem. Hang in there, George. You've gotten out of tighter situations than this before," Stan said with concern in his voice.

Four hours later, the ISA sent another list of things for George to do to try to adjust the ram field so the fusion torch would light. George knew as soon as he read each theory that none of them would work. Twelve hours later, his assessment was confirmed as every one of them had failed. Sometimes, he hated being right.

"That's it, Margie, I'm a dead man," George said with defeat in his voice.

"Don't talk that way, Georgie."

"It's true though. I've got less than twelve hours to get the main torch lit and turn this ship around. Otherwise, I'll pass the point of no return and won't have enough oxygen left for a return trip. Like I said, I'm a dead man."

"You're not dead yet. There's still one idea you haven't tried yet, you know? You should have more faith in yourself, Georgie."

George laughed out loud. "The funny thing is I'm not even sure where that idea came from. Are you sure you didn't give it to me?"

"I don't know what you mean?" Margie replied.

"That's okay; I think I'm losing my mind anyway. I'm so tired," George said as he dozed off in the pilot's seat.

George once again stood at the edge of that rock quarry cliff. He could feel the wind blow through his hair, the warm sun on his face. He looked down at the water below him and felt a chill run down his spine as the adrenaline surged through his veins. He could hear his friends taunting him, but as he turned to face them, he only saw Margie standing there.

"You have to jump, George. If you don't jump, you're going to die!" Margie pleaded with him.

As he stared at a teenaged Margie, George realized he was

dreaming. He could still feel the warm sun on his face, but he could also feel himself strapped into the pilot's chair. He felt like he was in two places at once. Two places separated by over three hundred years and millions of miles. He also felt like his mind was split between teenage George and scientist George. He was at once feeling impulsive and brash while simultaneously feeling calm and calculating.

"Just do it, George, trust yourself," teenage Margie said.

"But I can finally come home, Margie. I can finally be with you again," scientist George replied.

With tears in her eyes, Margie pleaded with him. "It's not your time, Georgie. It's not your time. You have important work to do. If this mission fails, the *Atropos* project will be set back decades. It might fail altogether. I love you, George, now turn around and jump off that cliff!"

Teenage George quickly turned before his courage left and stepped over the edge. As he hit the water, scientist George jerked awake in the pilot's chair and immediately ran his eyes over the instrument panel and computer screen. He struggled to focus his eyes as his heart pounded in his chest, his senses still believing he was on the cliff. When his eyes came into focus, he could see the ram field computer was already programmed to run his dream theory, but he didn't remember programming it. As George scanned the control console, he was surprised to see Margie's avatar standing right next to the enter key.

"Just do it, Georgie," she shouted.

George reached toward the screen but hesitated for a second. Immediately he was back on the cliff, staring down at the water, his long hair blowing in the wind as he heard teenaged Margie behind him.

"Jump, George!"

Then, as quickly as the image had arrived, George was back in the pilot's seat with Margie's avatar jumping up and down screaming at him. "Jump!"

What the hell? It's just one step, George thought as he reached out and hit enter. For several seconds after hitting enter, he was overcome with dizziness as if he were falling off the cliff again, until he felt and heard what seemed like an explosion. George readied himself for death, but slowly he could feel something pushing him back in the seat. *G force, I'm feeling G force! The torch is lit!*

George leaned his head back and let out a yell. "Yeeeee-haaaaaaa!"

Chapter 13: Soil Work

Forgiveness is at the heart of many religions, yet most adherents struggle with this base concept. The lesser transgressions are often easier to pardon than the sins of atrocity, but do the perpetrators of these terrible offenses need our compassion any less? One of the many questions we will have to answer as we emerge from the dark times of the Event Depression.
–Zacharia Jones, Omni Ascend

Date: 305 AE

Yousef Saleem chewed his steak with the focused attention of a man whose palate had never tasted steak before, even though this was a frequent meal for him. He cherished every second his taste buds interacted with the beefsteak, which was cooked to perfection at his favorite Parisian restaurant. Yousef remembered his surprise when he first moved to Paris and found out, much to his delight, that steak and fries were a popular dish in France and French fries were actually French! Only someone who had known true hunger could experience steak-frites with the pure ecstasy that was overcoming Yousef as he savored every bite.

"Yousef, are you in there?" He heard someone speaking to him in a sweet French accent.

Yousef opened his eyes and set his fork and knife down on his plate before replying, "Excuse me, Miriam my dear, was I doing it again?"

"Yes, you were chewing your steak with your eyes closed like you hadn't had steak or anything else for that matter in two hundred years," Miriam replied as she poured them both another glass of wine.

Yousef took a sip of wine. "You'd be obsessed with steak if you spent ten years of your youth with barely enough food to survive. I think I was fifty years old before I tasted steak."

"Good thing I wasn't a terrorist during the Caliphate Wars," Miriam quipped.

Yousef opened his mouth wide as he feigned emotional injury. "Soldier, Miriam, I was a soldier, not a terrorist."

"Tomato, *tomahto*," Miriam replied.

Yousef visibly winced as he heard Miriam's sharp words. He knew she was teasing, of course, but she knew how ashamed he was of his role during the wars, and for her to speak like this showed him her clear annoyance. "Miriam, please come with me to Aurora. I'm begging you."

Miriam swallowed her food. "Don't you think you're getting a little ahead of yourself? You haven't even interviewed for the job yet. Besides, what the heck would I do on Aurora? I doubt they'll need transportation logisticians there."

"Yes, I'm being a little presumptuous, but I literally wrote the book for soil management on Aurora. If they're going to grow crops, they're going to need me."

She rolled her eyes and took a deep breath. "For the last time, Yousef, I'm not going! There's no way I'm spending over a hundred years cooped up on a spaceship that's just as likely to explode as it is to ever reach Alpha Centauri."

Yousef swallowed hard on a dry throat as he realized they were skirting around the real issue, so he decided to plunge headfirst. "You know I love you with all my heart, but this is something I have to do. I have to set things right; you must understand this."

"No, I don't understand it. I don't understand why you have to leave me. You're a changed man, Yousef. You're not that misguided twelve-year-old boy that was sucked into the Caliphate Wars after the Event. You've been a productive member of society for over two hundred years; you don't owe the world anything. Like you said, you were a soldier, not a terrorist."

"But I did terrible things, Miriam, terrible things," Yousef replied as he looked down at the remaining half of his steak and realized he wasn't hungry anymore.

Miriam reached across the table and took his hand. "And when you've made the journey to Aurora and the colony is up and running, do you think it'll end there? Do you think your debt will be paid then, or will you still feel the same? When will it end? This isn't about deeds; it's about how you feel inside. Your guilt won't go away until you've dealt with it inside."

Yousef's eyes grew wide as he realized she was right; when would it end? "Wow, where did that come from?" he replied.

Miriam smiled behind her wine glass. "You didn't know I was also a psychologist, did you?" She put down her glass. "I don't believe you can truly love or commit to anyone until you've dealt with this incredible guilt you're carrying inside you."

Yousef, becoming uncomfortable with the direction of the conversation, said, "Since you're in the advice-giving mode, I need to ask your advice about something else that's related to this."

Miriam's face still reflected her irritation, but she relented. "Go on."

Yousef cleared his throat. "I'm trying to decide if I should reveal my past to the undersecretary of colonization when I interview for the chief soil scientist position next week."

"What? You mean reveal what you did during the Caliphate Wars? Why would you do that?" Miriam interrupted.

"Because I don't want to take the job under false pretenses. I want to come clean."

Miriam shook her head. "Oh my goodness, you want forgiveness. That's what this is about, isn't it?"

Yousef hesitated for a moment. "Of course not. I just don't want it to come back and bite me if they discover my past when they do the background check."

"Are you trying to convince me or yourself? Anyway, I don't think I'm the one you need advice from about this. I'm too invested to give you good advice." A tear rolled down her cheek. "Maybe you should speak with your father. He understands your past better than I ever could."

Yousef wiped the tear from her face. "Sweet Miriam, I think that's pretty sound advice."

"You should see him anyway; you haven't seen him in forever."

"I haven't seen him in many years, and he'll lecture me for being a nonbeliever, but yes, you're right, I should see my father."

"So, can you see him before your interview?"

"Yeah, I'll just change my flight itinerary so I can stop in Miami on the way to Quito."

Miriam smiled. "Good, maybe he can talk some sense into you."

As Yousef signaled the waiter for the check, he realized that even though *Atropos* wouldn't depart for another twenty years, he would lose Miriam much sooner. He turned toward her, grasped her hands in his, and said, "Thank you, my dear, thank you for everything."

* * *

The man was on fire, burning like a human torch that wouldn't die. Even though Yousef was several feet away, he could feel the heat striking him in the face like waves of temporal agony. He cried out time and time again for someone to help the man, but no one responded. He repeatedly threw water over the man, but the flames leapt higher. Yousef heard himself scream as he watched the burning man transform into a miniature mushroom cloud, slowly growing into a full-sized mushroom cloud. He felt his flesh peel away as the nuclear fire consumed him.

"Monsieur," he heard a feminine voice say. "Monsieur, please put your tray table up and fasten your seatbelt. We're preparing to land in Miami."

"Oh yes, thank you," Yousef replied as he wiped the sleep from his eyes and followed the flight attendant's instructions. The burning man dream was nothing new for Yousef, but the mushroom cloud was disturbing, as he seldom dreamed of that terrible day in Riyadh and never with the burning man.

"That must have been one bad dream," the man sitting next to him said.

Yousef turned to face the man. "Why do you say that?"

"Because you were tossing and turning in your sleep, and you're sweating," the man replied.

"It wasn't a pleasant dream, no."

"Were you an Ascendant?" the man asked.

It was such an odd question that it took Yousef by surprise, but after a few seconds, he said, "No, I wasn't. Why do you ask?"

"Because you said a name while you were tossing and turning—Zacharia."

Yousef leaned back in his seat to try to relax before the plane landed, but as he closed his eyes, all he could see was Zacharia Jones, engulfed in flames, running off that stage.

* * *

The saltwater spray never felt so refreshing as it smacked him in the face with every wave that his father's twenty-one-foot bay boat crashed through on their way to fish a small wreck just off the Miami coast. Yousef looked over at his father, Omar Haddad, and they shared a brief smile while Omar piloted his boat through the choppy seas. Yousef couldn't believe he had let so many years pass without seeing his father. Even though they spoke periodically via TICI video, he had been concerned their reunion would be awkward, but he was relieved to once again be at his father's side. So many things left unsaid over the years, yet a simple smile seemed to bridge the gulf between them.

As they anchored up on the wreck, Yousef said, "Abi, I'm so glad we're out here fishing together. It feels so good to be out on the sea."

"It makes me happy to hear you call me Father," Omar replied as he handed him a fishing rod. "But look at us; we hardly look like father and son, more like brothers."

After three hours of nonstop fishing, Yousef's arms were already tired, but now the large grouper at the end of the line felt like he was trying to reel up a refrigerator from eighty feet below. His arms burned with each crank of the reel, and he wondered if the fish might win this battle. "Are you sure you don't want to take the rod for a while?" he joked as he tried to hand it off to his father.

"Oh no, this one is all you," his father replied.

"A drink of water would be nice, though."

"I can do better than that," Omar replied as he popped the top on an ice-cold beer and held it to Yousef's mouth.

Yousef still didn't understand how his father reconciled drinking alcohol with being a devout Muslim, but as he took several long drinks from the beer, he didn't care. As the cold brew filled his stomach, he could feel the strength return to his arms. After chugging half the beer, he smiled at his father and resumed fighting the giant grouper with renewed vigor. Shortly afterward, the grouper finally tired, and Yousef was able to bring the giant fish to the boat.

After they high-fived, chest bumped, hugged, and otherwise celebrated their good fortune, they both sat down and took a much-deserved break from fishing. Omar took a long drink from his beer. "That was the fish of a lifetime, Yousef. I'm so glad I was able to help you land it."

"Me too, Abi, me too," Yousef replied with a large grin, even though he knew his father was slightly exaggerating. One of the many successes of the McDaniel administration was bringing humanity into homeostasis with the environment. Over the last 250 years, McDaniel's policies had not only stopped global warming but also halted the mass extinction event that pre-Event humanity was responsible for. Fish stocks around the world were at preindustrial levels once again, and catches like the grouper Yousef just landed were common.

Omar reached into the cooler and took out a couple of sandwiches and handed one to his son. As they were eating lunch, he said, "I've really enjoyed fishing with you, son. It's long overdue, but I think you're here for more than just a fishing trip with your dear old dad. Something's troubling you."

Yousef finished chewing his food. "You are a wise man, Father, and yes, something troubles me, and I need your advice."

When Yousef didn't continue, Omar said, "Well, what is it? Does it have something to do with your interview?"

"How do you do that? How do you always know what's on my mind?"

Omar laughed. "In this case, it doesn't take a rocket scientist to figure out what's troubling you. I mean, this is a huge decision for you. It's not like you can take it back once you leave, is it? The voyage to Aurora will last over one hundred years, and it's a one-way trip, son."

"Actually, I'm committed to going to Aurora; my dilemma is truly about the interview itself."

"Okay, out with it, what's your dilemma with the interview?"

"I'm fairly confident that I'll get the position of chief soil scientist for the Aurora Colony, but I want to get the job without hiding anything. I think I want to tell them about my past, all of it," Yousef then took a long drink of beer.

Omar leaned back in his chair and just looked at his son for several moments. "I assume you mean telling them about your role as a fighter during the wars?"

"Yes, that's exactly what I mean."

"Why would you do that? That was over two hundred years ago; you were just a misguided boy."

"I was a full-fledged fanatic, Father, and you know it."

Omar sighed. "Yes, I remember, and it hurt my heart when you succumbed to that radical nonsense that the Caliphate was spreading." Omar paused for a moment. "Of course, millions of Muslims flocked to the Caliphate's banner and took up the cause. It was a difficult time, and people of many different religions thought the end was at hand."

"That doesn't excuse what I did," Yousef retorted.

"Of course, it doesn't, but your life since then matters. You're not a fanatic now, and you haven't been since the war. As much as it pains me to say it, you're not even a believer anymore; you're an atheist!"

Yousef rolled his eyes. "Can we please not go down this road, Abi? I know as a cleric, it pains you that your only surviving son is a nonbeliever, but right now I just need your advice."

Omar frowned slightly. "As you wish, here's the advice I have for you: I think you need to ask yourself why you want to do this."

"Because I don't want to take this position under false pretenses, and I'm afraid that they might uncover my past when they do the background check. I'd like to come clean before that happens."

"I think the chances of that are slim to none. The destruction at the end of the last war was complete. There are no surviving documents, and all of your comrades were killed. No, I think you want to be forgiven for your actions during the war. That's what this is all about."

"You sound like Miriam. That's pretty much what she said."

"Oh yes, lovely Miriam. When am I going to meet her?"

"I don't know. She's pretty upset with me, and I think things might be over between us."

"I'm sorry to hear that. She seems like a lovely girl."

"Yes, she is, and I love her dearly." Yousef took another bite of his sandwich, and after washing it down with a drink of beer, he continued. "So, what do you think I should do, Abi?"

Without missing a beat, his father replied, "I think you should convert to Christianity. They're all about forgiveness."

They both laughed for a few moments before Yousef said, "No, really Dad, what do you think?"

Omar paused for a moment and rubbed his chin. "I think you should follow your heart. If you really feel you should confess your sins to this undersecretary of colonization, then you should do so. I only hope it doesn't cost you the job."

Yousef embraced his father and said. "Thank you Abi, thank you so much."

* * *

Two days later, Yousef landed in Quito and then took the short train ride to Ciudad Espacial. As the train came over the mountain, Yousef looked out the window and caught his breath as he saw the city spread out in the valley below him.

He had seen the city in videos and pictures, but it was an entirely different thing to experience it in person, especially with the vantage point he currently had. The city itself was small and formed an almost-perfect circle with a giant spire at its center that rose over three thousand feet and terminated into the space elevator cables. From this distance, the twin set of cables weren't even visible save for the cargo car that he could see slowly making its way skyward. Ciudad Espacial was founded shortly after the Federation of Nations gained control of the world some 243 years prior. The entire city was constructed with the sole purpose of supporting the space elevator that stood at its center, as well as the headquarters of the International Space Agency.

As the train entered the city, Yousef noticed that the streets were precisely laid out, with every building the exact same distance from the next one. Compared to the chaotic layout of older cities like Paris or even Miami, Ciudad Espacial gave the appearance of a city designed by an alien hive-mind species instead of human beings. Despite its sterile appearance, the city represented humanity's potential and gave Yousef hope for the future.

Yousef could now see the elevator cables that stretched from the central spire skyward. He craned his neck while watching the large cargo car that looked to be several thousand feet above the spire, climbing toward the heavens. Then he saw a much smaller passenger car emerge from the spire on the other set of cables rising faster than the cargo car.

"Isn't it amazing?" said a small woman sitting next to him.

"It's the most amazing thing I've ever seen."

The woman replied, "I heard it takes seven days to get to the space dock."

"Yes, a shuttle would be quicker but much more expensive. Besides, I hear the passenger car has first-class amenities, so the ride up doesn't sound too bad," Yousef said with a smile.

"Oh, I don't think I could afford first class," she whispered.

* * *

After settling into his room at the hotel, Yousef took a cab to the ISA headquarters building for his interview with the undersecretary of colonization. He'd waited a few short minutes when he heard the receptionist call his name. "Mr. Saleem, the secretary will see you now."

Yousef walked through the office door that the receptionist held for him. The man behind the desk stood up and walked toward him, but something wasn't right; the man looked strangely familiar, but he definitely wasn't the undersecretary.

"I was under the impression that my interview was with Undersecretary Williams?" Yousef said.

The man walked up to him and smiled as he held out his hand. "Yes, Phillip had a personal emergency and couldn't make it, so I'll be interviewing you, Dr. Saleem." As they shook hands, he said, "I'm Greg Ustinov."

"Yousef Saleem," he replied. "I'm honored you're doing the interview yourself, Mr. Secretary, and please just call me Yousef."

Greg motioned toward the chair as he walked behind the desk. "Please have a seat, Yousef."

The secretary's eyes creased in concentration as he read aloud from Yousef's résumé via his TICI. "I must say, your résumé is quite impressive. Your paper on soil management and conservation on Aurora is groundbreaking, to say the least. I'm particularly fascinated with your theories on using genetically altered Terran bacteria to make Auroran soil suitable for cultivation with our genetically altered cereals and vegetables."

"Thank you, Greg, but none of it would have been possible without the soil studies done by the Phoenix probe."

"Yes, the Phoenix probe is the gift that keeps on giving," Greg said as he straightened up in his chair. "I'll be honest with you, Yousef—this interview is pretty much just a formality. You're the only man for this job, but tell me, why do you want to go to Aurora? Why leave Earth?"

Yousef hesitated for a moment as he contemplated telling the secretary the truth right then, but decided against it. "This is the opportunity of a lifetime. It's the chance to explore and catalog a new world, to study life that evolved separately from ours but is in many ways remarkably similar. I mean, what scientist wouldn't want to go?"

The secretary of colonization smiled quizzically and cocked his head slightly to the side. "No offense, Dr. Saleem, but that sounds like something you've rehearsed. So, why don't you tell me the real reason?"

Yousef was slightly taken aback by the secretary's perceptiveness and directness. At this point, it was a relief, as he realized this was the sign he was waiting for. This could be the time to come clean about this past. However, now that the time had come, he hesitated. He felt a bead of sweat roll down his nose.

"Is something wrong, Dr. Saleem?"

Yousef slowly raised his gaze to meet Greg's, and he blurted out, "Yousef Saleem is not my real name."

"Go on."

"I was born Muhammad Haddad twelve years before the Event. I was seventeen when the first Caliphate War began, and I fought as an infantry soldier in the Fourth Holy Brigade."

Greg interrupted. "The Fourth Holy Brigade was an elite unit, and as I recall one of the most vicious. The Damascus massacre comes to mind."

"Yes, I was a full-fledged fanatic in those days," Yousef said as he hung his head.

"I assume you're no longer a fanatic?"

"No, I haven't been a fanatic in several centuries, and much to my father's chagrin, I'm not even a believer anymore."

"So, what was it like? What was it like being a foot soldier in one of the worst wars the world has ever seen?"

Yousef felt the familiar flood of shame as he recalled his early days. "It was terrible. We were constantly starving, and so many of my friends died. I saw atrocities, committed atrocities," Yousef said softly as he lowered his head again, "and I was in Riyadh when Pakistan nuked it."

"You survived the bombing of Riyadh?" Greg couldn't keep the shock out of his voice.

"Yes, luckily I was in a field hospital just outside of the city when it happened. I still see that terrible mushroom cloud in my dreams."

"Even after centuries of passing time, many are still haunted by the dark times of the Event Depression."

Yousef nodded in agreement, and there was a brief pause before Greg said, "So, after the war, you lost faith?"

"No, I also fought in the Second Caliphate War, and years later I was a battalion commander in the third war. Alas, my faith remained steadfast until long after the unification."

Greg put his hands together in contemplation. "You know

we've already done the background check on you, and none of this showed up. So, you confessing this to me now speaks volumes. You have integrity. Also, something that isn't widely known is that the McDaniel administration has pardoned all crimes committed during the Event Depression, including the Caliphate Wars."

Yousef sighed.

"Of course, that happened after all of the Caliphate's top leaders were already dead," Greg said.

"There's more," Yousef shocked even himself when he blurted it out.

"More, you say?"

"After the third war ended, I remained a fanatic, but I became obsessed with Zacharia Jones."

"Zacharia Jones?" Greg asked as his eyes grew wide.

"Yes, I became convinced that he was somehow responsible for the defeat of the Caliphate, so I decided to assassinate him."

Greg paled and after a moment's hesitation said. "Really? What did Zacharia Jones have to do with it?"

"He was preaching peace and unity but especially religious unification." Yousef paused as he considered how to continue. "During the Third Caliphate War, the movement struggled to recruit soldiers, and that was mostly because Muslims lost faith and many accepted Jones's message. So, many fanatics like me blamed him for our failure."

After a moment, Greg cleared his throat and said, "So, what did you do about this obsession?"

"He was all I could think about for several years." Yousef lifted his head and looked Greg directly in the eyes before continuing. "I haven't told anyone this last part, not my father or my girlfriend; no one. Alexi, my co-conspirator, tracked Jones down to Beijing. We doused him with gasoline and set him on fire."

Greg's jaw hung slack for several seconds before he said, "But Jones set himself on fire to protest China's refusal to allow a vote on joining the FON. I've seen the video."

"The video you speak of was altered after the fact for propaganda, and it had the desired effect, but I tell you Zacharia Jones did not set himself on fire. Alexi and I did." Yousef paused while a chill went down his spine. "And it haunts me to this day."

"Yousef, that's a lot to take, and I have many questions, but if Zacharia were still alive, I believe he would forgive you."

"How can you say that?" Yousef challenged.

"Because I was an ascendant then, as well as one of his lieutenants. In fact, I was in Beijing when it happened. I was behind the stage, so I didn't see it happen."

"I see," Yousef replied. "Thank you. That means a lot."

"You're welcome, and I still want you to have the job, but let me ask you something."

"Of course, what is it?"

"How did you know Jones was going to be in Beijing at the time? It was a closely guarded secret because we couldn't risk the Chinese arresting him before he gave his speech."

Yousef's brow creased as he struggled to recall the detail, but after a moment, he said, "We had a contact in his organization that told us when he would be in Beijing."

"Oh really, do you remember this informant's name?" Yousef had his full attention.

"We never met her in person, as we only communicated via email, but I believe her name was Cassie or Sally or something like that. It's been a long time, and I don't exactly remember."

Greg shook his head. "I don't remember anyone with a name like that, but it doesn't really matter anyway; ancient history."

"You kinda remind me of him, you know, Zacharia Jones."

Greg smiled. "Yeah, I get that sometimes." Greg stood up and walked around the desk to shake hands with Yousef. "Congratulations, Dr. Saleem, you have the job."

"Thank you, Mr. Secretary, thank you very much," Yousef replied as he vigorously shook Greg's hand. He almost couldn't believe his good fortune. This Greg Ustinov was a most surprising man.

As Yousef was walking out the door, Greg called after him. "Hey, do you have plans tomorrow?"

"No, my flight out isn't until the next day. I was thinking about touring Quito and the Space City."

"How about if I give you a personal tour?" Greg offered.

"I would be honored," Yousef replied.

"Great, I'll send a car to your hotel first thing in the morning."

Yousef decided to walk back to his hotel, as he felt he had excess energy that needed to be burned off. If he thought no one would have seen, he might've skipped down the corridor and right into his room.

* * *

Yousef and Greg spent most of the day touring Quito and seeing the Ciudad Midad del Mundo that marks the equator, as well as the Basilica del Voto. By the time they returned to Ciudad Espacial, Yousef was already quite tired, but he was still excited to receive a personal tour of the city and the space elevator by the secretary of colonization himself.

The train stopped right at the base of the space elevator spire, and as they walked off the train, Yousef stared up at the three-thousand-foot spire that the elevator rose out of. "The closer you get to it, the more impressive it becomes."

"Yes, it still impresses me, but you know what's more impressive?" Greg asked as he walked toward the street vendor who was right next to the train stop.

Yousef laughed. "No, but I think you're about to show me."

"Yep, it's the llapingachos that Miguel serves from his street cart right here," Greg said as he walked up to the vendor. *"Hola, Miguel. Dos llapingachos, por favor."*

A few minutes later, Yousef was enjoying his llapingachos, which consisted of potato patties and sausage topped with a fried egg with chopped lettuce and tomato. After a long day of walking around Quito Yousef thought it was almost as good as his treasured steak-frites. As he chewed his food, he watched another car emerge from the spire and begin the long climb up the elevator cable, and a thought occurred to him. "Greg, how are the cars powered? I don't see any exhaust coming from them. Are they electric?"

"Yes, they're electric, but here's the cool part: the power comes from the cable itself."

"Oh, you send the power up the cable from the spire? Is there a power plant around here?" Yousef asked.

Greg laughed as he pointed toward the sky. "No, the power comes down the cable from the station that acts as a counterweight at the end of the cable, some thirty-six thousand kilometers above."

"Oh, there's a power plant at the space station?"

"Not just a power plant; it's a solar power station of immense proportions, and because it's in geostationary orbit it's never in the shadow of the Earth, so it supplies power 24/7. Not only does it power the cars climbing the cable; it powers this entire city as well."

"Holy cow," Yousef replied as he looked around. "How much power is coming down those cables?"

"Well, it varies a little, but typically around ten gigawatts or about nine trips back to the future," Greg replied with a chuckle.

"Back to the future?"

"Oh, never mind, it's just a lot of power that's all."

"Yes, I understand what a gigawatt is. How is that much power regulated?"

"Good question," Greg replied as he pointed to a large structure that was jutting out of the side of the spire. "Do you see that structure right there? That's the main power relay, and inside it is the most sophisticated software ever created. It's an AI that does nothing but regulate the flow of energy through the cable and then distributes it throughout the city."

"You don't mean a true artificial intelligence, do you?"

"No, of course not. It's not self-aware, but it's the next best thing." Greg paused as he received a message via his TICI, and with a scowl on his face said, "Will you excuse me for a few moments? I need to check on something real quick."

"Sure, I'll just finish my llapingachos," Yousef replied.

"Good, I'll be right back," Greg replied over his shoulder as he briskly walked away.

As Yousef was finishing his llapingachos, he heard people beginning to shout and he noticed they were pointing up toward the power relay that he and Greg were talking about.

As Yousef looked on, the power relay exploded in sparks, and a bolt of energy shot out and struck the scaffolding of a large viewing platform that was under construction several hundred meters away. Yousef watched in horror as the viewing platform began to sway violently, becoming mesmerized even as it broke free and headed directly for him. As all the people around him scattered like flies, he just stood there frozen in place.

As Yousef stoically watched the platform fall, he noticed a woman ahead of him who also wasn't moving. Without thinking, Yousef found himself running toward her, and as he approached the woman, he pushed her to safety just as the platform disintegrated. Yousef discovered he wasn't as lean or as fast as he once was, and the extra second cost him dearly as the platform scaffolding landed directly on him.

Yousef lay there in shock as the dust slowly cleared around him. He tried to get up but realized he was pinned down and couldn't move. Not only could he not move or feel anything, but breathing was becoming difficult as well. He heard people shouting in the distance but couldn't understand them, as they were speaking Spanish.

Just as Yousef thought he might die alone, he saw Greg Ustinov running through the dust toward him.

"Yousef, are you okay? Oh, my God, I saw what happened. You saved that woman. Can you move?" Greg asked as he tried in vain to lift the debris off Yousef.

"No, I don't think I can move anything," Yousef said in a whisper.

Yousef knew he was gravely injured, but he realized that it must be even worse than he thought by the look in Greg's eyes. "It's okay, Greg, I'll be okay," he whispered.

"Hang in there, Yousef. Help is on the way," Greg said frantically.

"I don't think they'll get here in time, friend," Yousef said as he felt a warmness begin to spread throughout his body.

Greg knelt and grabbed Yousef's hand. "No, don't you die on me, Yousef. You can't die, man."

"It's okay, Greg. Everything's okay now. I'm ready to die."

Tears streamed down Greg's face as he leaned down directly in Yousef's face and said, "Yousef, there's something you need to know. You didn't kill Zacharia Jones. You didn't kill him."

Yousef heard Greg clearly, but he could barely talk now. "What do you mean?"

"I'm Zacharia Jones, Yousef, I am Zacharia Jones. I remember exactly what you said that day when you set me on fire. You said, 'Allah Akbar' and 'death to al-Masih ad-Dajjal' as you ran toward the stage and doused me with gasoline."

Yousef managed a smile. "It really is you, isn't it, Zacharia?"

"Yes, it's really me. I am Zacharia Jones, and I forgive you. I forgive you for setting me on fire."

Yousef tried to tell Zach that everything was okay, that he didn't feel any pain, and in fact, he felt euphoric, but his lips barely moved, and he made no sound.

"Come on, Yousef, stay with me, man," Zach pleaded as he shook Yousef.

Yousef's vision was fading at the edges now, and he could barely see Zach. He could feel his body getting lighter and lighter, as if he were about to float away, and somehow, he could hear music, beautiful music. As Yousef exhaled his final breath, he felt a peace he hadn't felt in his entire life.

Zach reached down and closed Yousef's eyes. "Godspeed, my friend. Perhaps one day I will have your courage."

Chapter 14: Crossover

The role of viruses in the web of life has always been something of a mystery. In fact, there's still not consensus on whether viruses are even alive or simply a collection of interesting chemistry. However, most can agree that viruses have had a profound impact on the evolution of every branch of life. Viruses may not be alive in the same way plants and animals are, but until we understand their nature, we will never understand the true nature of life itself.

–*Theresa Jenner,* Harnessing TEV: The Journey of Discovery

Date: 319 AE

Watching the surface of the Earth gradually slip away as the space elevator passenger train made its way skyward was like ascending to heaven. At least that's what it felt like for Theresa Jenner as she stared out the window contemplating the last three hundred plus years. From the Dunwoody shantytown to the pinnacle of human civilization, sometimes it was difficult to reconcile her life's journey. *If only Mom and Dad could have shared the journey*, she thought as she remembered finding them murdered in their small hovel when she was only fifteen years old. She shuddered as a chill went down her spine. The Event Depression would always be the dark times for her.

"First time on the SEPT?" A man's voice intruded on her thoughts.

"Pardon?" she replied as she turned to face him.

"You know, space elevator passenger train. Is this your first time?" said the handsome stranger sitting directly across from her.

Theresa intentionally dressed and wore her hair and makeup in such a way as to downplay her attractiveness, yet that didn't seem to stop some men from trying to strike up conversation. "Yes, it's my first time," she said as she turned back to the window.

"Yeah, I thought so," the handsome stranger said as he too turned to look out of their shared window. "The view really is spectacular. Always makes me feel like I'm rising above all of my problems and mistakes of the past. But rising to the heavens can bring such sweet sorrow."

Theresa cocked her head as she slowly turned to face him. *Who is this guy?*

With a slight smile on his face, the stranger stuck out his right hand and said, "Greg Ustinov."

As they shook hands, Theresa replied. "Theresa Jenner."

"Doctor Theresa Jenner, the world-renowned virologist, that Theresa Jenner?" Greg asked with raised eyebrows.

She blushed slightly. "You've actually heard of me?"

"I make it my business to know all important persons

coming to the ISA space dock. I know who you are, but clearly, you don't know who I am. I'm the secretary of colonization."

"I'm sorry; I don't really keep up with politics."

They both paused and stared out the window as the passenger train passed one of the large cargo trains that ran on the larger cables next to the space elevator passenger train. Greg turned and resumed their conversation. "Dr. Jenner, I'd like to hear about what brings you to the ISA space dock. Would you care to join me at the bar for a drink?"

"Please, call me Theresa. I'd be happy to join you, Mr. Secretary," she replied.

As they both stood up to walk to the bar, he said. "Greg, please call me Greg."

After they were seated at the bar and both had a drink in hand, Theresa said, "You seem to know so much about me; certainly you know what brings me to the space dock."

"I know you've developed the first antiviral drug that kills TEV in the lab, and you want to utilize the facilities on the space dock to do the first human tests. In fact, you've had an entire new wing constructed on the space dock just for your experiments. What I don't understand is why. Why did you choose to come to space to do the human experiments?"

As Theresa sipped on her martini, she recalled that the Event virus was the most contagious pathogen ever known, transmissible by every known vector: airborne, body fluids, droplets, everything. It could also live for weeks outside the human body, and it was not susceptible to most antiseptics. "You're aware that after three hundred plus years of study, we've never found a drug that can kill TEV?"

"Well, not until you invented Tevase," Greg said, referring to the antiviral drug she recently created that does kill TEV, at least under laboratory conditions. "So, why come to space to test it?"

She debated not telling him but realized he'd know eventually anyway. "Okay, I'm going to let you in on a little secret that's not publicly known."

"I assure you I can keep a secret," he said with a sly grin.

"The fact is that I have tested Tevase on humans already," she paused as she looked around the bar to make sure no one was eavesdropping on their conversation. "Every single time we administered the Tevase, it completely eradicated TEV from the subject's body, but for only a matter of seconds. Every single time, the test subject would reinfect within one minute and thirty-three seconds, sometimes faster, but never longer than one minute and thirty-three seconds."

Greg quickly motioned to the bartender to bring them two more drinks before he replied. "That's incredible. I assume you eliminated all possible vectors for reinfection but to no avail?"

"Yes, that's why I want to test in space, so I can say I that I eliminated all possible means of reinfection."

"You don't sound like you believe your tests at the space dock will be successful."

"Let's just say that we were very thorough with our isolation when Tevase was tested. There was no vector available for reinfection. It defies explanation."

"So, this is almost an act of desperation?"

"You could say that, but Tevase is the first drug that's had any success in the laboratory, the first drug in over three hundred years, so we can't just give up. When my assistant, Dr. Anderson, jokingly suggested we test in space, I took it seriously and went straight to the ISA director himself. He's my boss, you know."

Greg finished his drink. "And Director Asher obviously agreed with you."

"Yes, he suggested we take over a wing of the new ring that was just built, have it open to space and UV light, to totally sterilize it before having the robots build out the lab in a total vacuum. It's the most sterile environment ever created." She too drained her drink before continuing. "But enough about me, Mr. Secretary, what brings you to the space dock?"

Greg again signaled the bartender for two more drinks. "Well, in eight days we'll be exactly one year out from the scheduled launch of *Atropos*, and I have to be there for the official naming ceremony."

"Thank God I'm not a politician." She laughed as she put her hand on his forearm. "Please tell me you're not going to bust a bottle of champagne on the bow?"

As they shared a brief laugh, she thought she was either a little drunk or he was really a little charming. "So, you're actually leaving Earth in one year on that giant ship for a one-hundred-year trip to colonize another planet. What's that like?"

He leaned in close to her with his eyes opened exaggeratedly large and whispered, "Terrifying." They both laughed out loud.

"Seriously though," Theresa said, "don't you think it's going to get monotonous being cooped up on that ship with the same people for a hundred years?"

"Well, there'll be four thousand colonists on board, so it's not like I'll only have a handful of people to talk to, but you're right, we could start to get on each other's nerves."

"And everyone will know everyone else's business," Theresa

replied with mock dread.

Greg paused for a moment as if contemplating her statement. "Yep, we'll all be one big happy family by the time we arrive at Alpha Centauri."

After another hour of talking and mutual laughter, she stood up and said, "Greg, I've enjoyed our little chat, but it's getting late, and I'm quite tired, so I think I'm going to bed."

He smiled as he helped her from the barstool. "Allow me to walk you to the sleeping compartment?"

She held up her palm and chuckled a little. "You're quite charming, Greg, but I don't think so. Maybe another time." She considered kissing him on the cheek but instead smiled gently and hugged him lightly before turning and walking toward the sleeping compartment. As charming as he was, she couldn't imagine getting involved with a politician.

* * *

Days later, as they arrived at the ISA space dock, Theresa looked out the window and admired the dual rotating wheels of the space station. At one end of the axis, the station was attached to the dual space elevator cables, and the *Atropos* was docked on the other end. Once they disembarked from the elevator train, the thirty-two passengers were led from the freefall environment of the axis to the gravity of the first wheel.

As they went to go their separate ways, Greg smiled and said, "If you need anything at all during your stay, don't hesitate to contact me. Being a politician does have its advantages, you know."

"Thank you, Greg. I enjoyed sharing the ride with you." As

Theresa walked away, she glanced back out of the corner of her eye and noticed that Greg hadn't moved.

* * *

Theresa was escorted to her quarters by station security, and after hastily unpacking, she made her way to the newly constructed TEV lab.

"Hello, Tim," she said excitedly as she entered the lab and embraced Dr. Timothy Anderson, her old friend and longtime colleague.

"How was your trip?" he asked as she stepped away from him.

"It was fine, but way too long," she replied halfheartedly while looking around the lab.

"It's really something, isn't it?" he asked with pride in his voice.

"It's small, but it may be the finest facility we've ever had," she replied. She walked with Tim around the lab and noticed with approval that there were two totally isolated patient bays that had never been exposed to any human presence or air that had been breathed by humans. Everything inside the bays was fully automated, including patient monitoring, scanning, and medication administration. "Is everything ready for tomorrow?"

"Yep, we have everything in place, including two test subjects."

Theresa again smiled and said, "You've done a great job here, Tim. I couldn't be more pleased."

* * *

Early the next morning, Theresa walked briskly to the lab, eager to begin work. As she entered, her entire staff turned and stared at her in amazement. Dr. Anderson pointed at her and started laughing, which inspired everyone else to start laughing. In horror, she looked down at herself to discover that she was dressed as she imagined a common prostitute might dress, complete with miniskirt, fishnet stockings, and spiked heels. She woke with a start and sat up in the bed, her head damp with sweat. It had been a while since she'd had the prostitute dream, but it wasn't uncommon. The past still haunted her, even while in the heavens.

Theresa was left alone with no support after that dreadful day when her parents were murdered in the Dunwoody shantytown of Atlanta, Georgia. The United States government had collapsed several years before, but the state and local governments of Georgia maintained law and order, after a fashion. After many months of scraping by and nearly starving, she was found by one of the local pimps, who fed and sheltered her for a few months before putting her to work. She did what she had to, and she survived when many in her situation did not. *At least that bastard got what was coming to him*, she thought as she got out of bed and walked to the bathroom.

As Theresa walked into the lab, she unconsciously looked down at herself before proceeding to the control center. "Good morning, Tim," she said, as he was the only one there. The rest of the lab staff was preparing the equipment for their first test.

"Good morning, Theresa. Did you rest well?"

"Quite well, thank you," she lied.

Tim handed her a cup of coffee. "Our first subject has just been brought into the test chamber. I'm scanning the room now, and there are still no viruses detected in the chamber."

"Thank you, Tim," she said as she sipped her coffee. "What's our subject's name?"

"Fredrick Brown from New Castle."

She opened a direct communication channel to the test chamber and said. "Good morning, Mr. Brown. I'm Dr. Jenner. I know you've been thoroughly briefed on everything that's going to happen today. Do you have any questions before we begin?"

"Good morning, Dr. Jenner. I don't really have any questions, per se, but I do want to clarify what happens to me if your drug works and the virus is eliminated from my body," Mr. Brown replied with a thick English accent.

"Don't worry, Mr. Jones, if the experiment works and the virus is eliminated from your body, you will, of course, be reinfected as quickly as possible," Theresa replied.

"Very good. I'm not ready to grow old again."

"I assure you, there's nothing to be concerned about. Do you have any more questions?"

"No, I don't. Thank you, Dr. Jenner."

"Please proceed, Dr. Anderson," Theresa said.

"Scanning him now," Tim quietly interjected. "His viral count is well over ten thousand, as expected."

Theresa nodded. "Administer 1,500 milligrams of Tevase when you're ready."

"Administering 1,500 milligrams of Tevase," Tim replied as he initiated the medication robot in the isolation chamber.

Theresa brought up the virus scanner application on her TICI so she could see the test subject's virus count displayed directly onto her retina. The virus count was steadily dropping as expected.

"Virus count under five thousand and still dropping," Dr. Anderson announced, even though he knew everyone was monitoring it themselves. A few minutes later, he said. "Four thousand and still dropping."

"Three thousand."

"Two thousand."

"One thousand."

"Five hundred, four hundred, three hundred, two hundred, one hundred, zero. I'm beginning the timer," Dr. Anderson announced.

Theresa monitored the time carefully. Thirty seconds now. Would it work this time? One minute, and the virus count was still zero. A bead of sweat formed on her forehead.

"One minute, twenty seconds, virus count still zero," Dr. Anderson announced. Thirteen seconds later, he announced, "There it is, virus count one hundred, two hundred, three hundred, and counting."

Everyone's head hung low as a familiar silence shrouded the lab and disappointment filtered through her staff. Theresa set her coffee down on the counter before turning and walking out of the room. *Exactly one minute and thirty-three seconds again. How does this keep happening?* After composing herself in the bathroom for several minutes, she returned to the lab and announced to the staff, "Okay everyone, let's get Mr. Brown disconnected and get the isolation chamber prepped for the next test subject."

She then opened the direct channel to the isolation chamber and said, "Thank you, Mr. Brown. You're still infected, and I hope we didn't bore you to tears."

"No, not at all. I was playing VR chess with my man in New Castle," Mr. Brown replied cheerfully while he tapped his head with his finger.

* * *

The next morning, Theresa was back in the lab for another round of testing. Six test subjects yesterday, and all of them reinfected within one minute and thirty-three seconds. *What is it with that number?* "Dr. Anderson, who is our first test subject this morning?" Theresa asked.

"Steven Franklin from New York City," Tim replied. "He's in the chamber, and everything is prepped and ready to begin."

A few minutes later, the test was underway. Dr. Anderson said, "Administering 1,500 milligrams of Tevase."

Theresa again brought up the virus scanner application on her TICI so she could see the test subject's virus count displayed directly onto her retina.

"Virus count under five thousand and still dropping," Dr. Anderson announced. A few minutes later, he said, "Four thousand and still dropping."

"Three thousand. Two thousand. One thousand. Five hundred, four hundred, three hundred, two hundred, one hundred, zero. I'm beginning the timer," Dr. Anderson announced.

Theresa monitored the time carefully, One minute, thirty seconds. *Here it comes,* she thought. *When am I going to admit defeat?*

"One minute, thirty-five seconds, virus count still zero," Tim announced loudly as everyone cheered.

Theresa motioned for everyone to quiet down as Tim continued the count. "One minute, forty seconds, forty-three, forty-four, forty-five, forty-six, forty-seven, forty-eight, forty-nine, fifty, fifty-one, fifty-two—wait, no there it is, virus count one hundred, two hundred, one thousand."

Theresa could barely contain her excitement. One minute and fifty-two seconds. A full twenty-five seconds longer than ever before. "Dr. Anderson, please verify that we went a full one minute and fifty-two seconds before reinfection, and this wasn't a timing glitch or something."

After several minutes of examining the data, Dr. Anderson announced, "The results appear to be legitimate. We did it; we finally broke through one minute and thirty-three seconds." The lab staff erupted in applause.

After everyone quieted down, Theresa said stoically, "Thank you, Dr. Anderson. Now for the real test. Let's see if we can replicate these results. Please dismiss Mr. Franklin and prepare the chamber for the next subject."

* * *

Early that evening, after another full day of testing, she was having dinner with Tim at one of the ring restaurants. "Tim, I agree that we had a major breakthrough today, but the sad fact is that we couldn't reproduce it, and we have absolutely no clue why Mr. Franklin went twenty-five seconds longer before reinfection."

"None of this makes any sense, but I feel like we're really close to figuring this whole thing out. It's like it's right in front of our faces, but we can't see it. What was different about the Franklin test? That's what we have to figure out."

"We've already established that there was absolutely nothing different about the Franklin test, absolutely nothing," she replied sadly.

* * *

Several days later, Theresa sat at her desk in her office, reviewing all the test data from the previous week. A full week of testing, and they were still unable to reproduce the results from the Franklin test. After that one brief success, they were right back where they started—one minute and thirty-three seconds. As she began to go over the results again, she noticed a light blinking in the corner of her eye, signaling that she had a message from Director Asher in her inbox.

"Hello, Dr. Jenner. Chief Inspector Fitzpatrick is coming to observe your experiments. Please give him full access to everything you're doing. He has top-secret clearance. Thank you." The message was signed Robert Asher, International Space Agency Director.

Before she could ponder the meaning of the message, she heard a knock on her door. "Come in," she said loudly.

She stared in silence as a vision from the deepest darkness of her past walked through the door, dressed in a three-piece suit and a fedora.

"Dr. Jenner, I'm Chief Inspector John Fitzpatrick of the ISA," he said as he stood by the now-open door.

Theresa quickly pulled herself together as she stood up from behind her desk. "Yes, I just received a message from Director Asher saying you were coming, but he neglected to say why."

John removed his hat. "I understand you've had a major breakthrough in your research."

Theresa scowled slightly. "And exactly how do you know that?"

Chief Inspector Fitzpatrick just smiled at her and cocked his head.

"Oh, never mind, it's not important. Besides, I'm afraid you came all this way for nothing, as we've not been able to replicate our one-time success," she said, agitated.

"I'm sorry, Dr. Jenner; I think we've gotten off on the wrong foot. Can we start over? I understand that your work has stalled since your initial success, and that's why I'm here. To offer you my services." He paused for a second before continuing. "You look familiar to me. Have we met?"

"No, we've never met," she bristled. "So, you think that you can just waltz in here, some gumshoe, and solve this mystery for us? Do you even know anything about viruses?"

John ignored her question. "Perhaps I can just observe your experiments tomorrow. I promise I'll stay out of your way."

"Of course you can observe. I don't really have a choice, do I?"

* * *

The next morning, Theresa felt like she hadn't slept at all. That stupid dream again, she thought as she got out of the shower and toweled off. She was sure the chief inspector recognized her. Maybe she should just get it out in the open. That way she could put it behind her and get on with the work at hand. With everything going on, why did he have to show up now?

Later that morning, as Theresa walked into the lab, she saw Inspector Fitzpatrick sitting by himself in the far corner. She walked purposely over to him and said, "Inspector Fitzpatrick, I'm afraid I owe you an apology for my behavior yesterday, but it was a long, frustrating day. I welcome any help you can offer to the project."

John stood up and shook her offered hand. "That's quite all

right, Dr. Jenner; I know my presence here is somewhat of a shock for you."

"You remember me, don't you?"

"I never forget a face, Dr. Jenner, even ones from the darkest days of the depression three hundred years ago."

"Please don't judge me. You have no idea what I went through."

A slight smile crossed John's face. "Yes, that's right. I have judged you, Dr. Jenner. I judge you to be one of the most remarkable people I've ever met. I remember the young girl that used to hang out by the GBI office. She even propositioned me and my partner once. The journey that uneducated girl must have taken to be where she is now is truly extraordinary. I would like to hear that story sometime, if you ever feel like telling it."

Theresa wiped a tear from her face. "Your partner was mean to me you know."

John chuckled a little as he handed her his handkerchief. "Yeah, Bill was an ass."

After composing herself, Theresa said. "Thank you, Inspector. Would you like to join me for dinner this evening after observing our testing today? I'll give you a full briefing."

"I'd love to, and please call me John."

* * *

That evening, after another round of unsuccessful testing, Theresa and John were enjoying a drink while they waited on their food.

"Thank you for the thorough debriefing, Theresa. This is a perplexing mystery," John said as he took a sip of his beer.

"Well, does the great inspector have any theories?" she said jokingly.

"I'm afraid not, but I do have a few questions."

"Shoot."

"You're absolutely certain that you've eliminated every known vector that the virus could use to reinfect your subjects after you've extirpated the virus from their bodies?"

"Yes, on this I'm certain. My team has been over this a thousand times, and they're very thorough. That's what's so perplexing about this." She sighed before adding, "It defies explanation. It's the damnedest thing."

John set his half-empty mug on the table. "Then the answer is clear. The virus is using a vector unknown to you, unknown to science, yet somehow you blocked that vector for twenty-five seconds during the Franklin test." He paused for a moment. "When you have eliminated the impossible, whatever remains, however improbable, must be the truth."

"Did you just quote Sherlock Holmes?" she asked with a smile.

"Elementary, my dear," he said as they both laughed.

"So, what is the new vector you speak of? Any ideas?"

John drained what was left of his beer. "That I leave to you, as I don't have the foggiest."

* * *

Later that evening, Theresa was lying in bed, reflecting on her conversation with Inspector Fitzpatrick. What unknown vector could the virus be using? It had to be something they hadn't thought of yet. The isolation chamber had an independent sterile air supply, and every breath the test subject exhaled was immediately vacuumed from the chamber. The chamber was sterile; outside the chamber was contaminated. *Think outside the box.* She then thought of the different ways that things went into the isolation chamber; power went into the chamber, but she couldn't imagine how the virus could be transmitted via electricity. Information went into the chamber via their computer controls and their direct communication with the subjects. She became restless as she tossed and turned with the different variables bouncing around her thoughts. Information also went directly to the subjects via the TICI. She sat straight up in the bed as the thought became clear in her head. *Could the TICI be responsible for reinfecting the subjects? Impossible*, she thought, *no way a virus could be organic and digital.*

This is insane, she thought as she made a call with her TICI. "Hello, Greg, this is Theresa Jenner. Remember when you said I should call you if I ever needed anything?"

"Hello, Theresa. Of course, I remember. What can I do for you?" Greg Ustinov replied.

"I need the IT logs for the station for October 7. I specifically need to see the wireless network log for the isolation chambers, as they're on a separate network."

"Let me guess—you need this immediately in the middle of the night?"

"Yes, if you can get it, that would be awesome," she said quickly.

"Okay, I'll make a few calls," Greg said before he hung up.

* * *

The next morning, she met Inspector Fitzpatrick in the hallway as he was walking to the lab. "Good morning, John. I took your advice and thought outside the box."

"From the look on your face, I take it you've found something."

"Yes, well maybe. It could just be a coincidence, but it's the best lead we've had."

"Are you going to make me wait for the experiment?" he asked after she hesitated.

"I started thinking about possible vectors that we wouldn't normally consider, and I thought of the TICI. What if the virus is somehow being transmitted by the TICI as well as airborne and all the other ways it's transmittable? So, I requested the IT logs for the day we tested Mr. Hancock, and sure enough, the wireless network for the isolation chamber went down for exactly twenty-five seconds during the test," Theresa said.

John stopped walking and looked right at her. "That's the most incredible thing I think I've ever heard. When are you testing this hypothesis?"

"First thing this morning. I now have control of the isolation chamber wireless network, so I can shut it off anytime I choose."

A short time later, the team was in the lab, and the new test subject was in the isolation chamber. Theresa said, "Okay, everyone, I've shut off the wireless network for the chamber. Dr. Anderson, you may administer the Tevase when ready."

A few seconds later, Dr. Anderson said, "Administering 1,500 milligrams of Tevase."

Theresa brought up the virus scanner application on her TICI so she could see the test subject's virus count.

"Virus count under five thousand and still dropping," Dr. Anderson announced. A few minutes later, he said, "Four thousand and still dropping."

"Three thousand. Two thousand. One thousand. Five hundred, four hundred, three hundred, two hundred, one hundred, zero. I'm beginning the timer," Dr. Anderson announced.

The anxiety level in the lab was palpable as the seconds ticked by, and Theresa had never seen her staff so on edge, as if they knew something historic was happening.

"One minute, thirty-five seconds, virus count still zero," Tim announced loudly as everyone cheered.

"Congratulations, Dr. Jenner," Inspector Fitzpatrick said as he walked up to Theresa and stuck out his hand.

Theresa smiled and shook his hand. "Perhaps. We'll see, but we are now over two minutes and still counting."

Thirty minutes later, the virus count was still zero. Her staff were buzzing with excitement when she announced, "It's been thirty minutes now without reinfection. Is everyone comfortable with turning the wireless network back on?" Everyone nodded in agreement, so she turned the network back on. "The network is back on, and the clock is started."

Everyone cheered when the virus counter pinged at exactly one minute and thirty-three seconds. This was the first time they had ever been happy to see a test subject reinfect. Even the always-curt Dr. Anderson was excited and cheering.

"Congratulations, Theresa, you've done it. This is the discovery of the century, maybe the millennium," Tim said as they enthusiastically embraced.

* * *

Later that evening, as the entire team was celebrating at the

Second Ring Bar and Grill, John pulled Theresa aside for a private discussion. "Theresa, I know everyone is excited, and you certainly have the right to celebrate, but I've been thinking over some of the implications of your discovery, and I have a few questions for you."

Theresa's mood dipped slightly, but she agreed. "Sure, what's on your mind, John?"

"In your professional opinion, is there any way an organic virus could naturally evolve so it could be transmitted digitally to infect people via the TICI?"

They both sat down at an unoccupied table. "Heck, I don't even understand how it's doing it. I only know that somehow it's being transmitted digitally, and most likely it's been spreading this way since the beginning, but to answer your question, I don't see how this could happen naturally."

"So, this is a man-made virus, in your opinion?"

"This virus was almost certainly artificially created, but we've thought that since the beginning of the epidemic, over three hundred years ago. Don't forget that the virus is also highly transmissible via all other vectors, airborne, droplets, body fluids, all of them. That's one reason we always thought it was man-made. Why bring it up now?"

John leaned in close to her. "Because the TICI was officially launched six months before the Event happened, and we know who invented the TICI—Ken Takahashi."

Theresa rapidly finished off her drink and paused for a moment. "I hadn't thought of that, but you're right. People have been trying to hack the TICI for three hundred years, and no one's ever done it, ever! So, for this virus to be able to cross the TICI, it was most likely designed by the TICI designer or at least under his direction."

"That's what I was thinking," said John as he nodded in agreement. "This could go even further, now that I think about it. The implications are endless. Ken Takahashi is a close friend of President McDaniel, and who has profited more from the Event than Nathan McDaniel?"

"No way President McDaniel is involved. You're wrong about that. He's done so much for everyone, so much for me. Without his apprenticeship program, I wouldn't be where I am today," she retorted.

"I go where the evidence leads me, Dr. Jenner," John said as he stood up. "It was a pleasure meeting you, Theresa. Congratulations again on your discovery."

Theresa reluctantly shook his hand. "Where are you going so fast? I was just beginning to enjoy your company."

"Back to Earth. I have an investigation to conduct, and it just got interesting."

Chapter 15: Crossover, Part II

When you are convinced you know a thing, that is the moment to take a step back and reconsider. How does this knowledge reflect your worldview? If this wisdom supports your perspective, perhaps you should examine your motivations. Throughout history, tremendous suffering has been inflicted by people who were convinced they knew something. —Zacharia Jones, Omni Ascend

Date: 319 AE

Once the speedboat was a safe distance from the ISA space dock, the rocket pod ignited, pinning John to his seatback. He was surprised it had been so easy to convince the secretary of colonization to let him use the speedboat, as it was usually reserved for VIPs who didn't have time for the long ride on the elevator train. He wondered if Dr. Jenner had something to do with that.

John was still processing all of the data from the Jenner

experiments. *Finally, after all these years, I have a decent lead. With the authority of the ISA behind me, I might be able to find sufficient evidence to convict Ken Takahashi. He has to be involved in this conspiracy. The only question is, who else is involved?*

As the speedboat accelerated, John tuned in to a popular music station, but after a few minutes, he turned it off. *How does anyone listen to this crap? No good music in over three hundred years*, John thought as he brought up some classic pre-Event music from his collection. While classic Beastie Boys played in the background, John considered his next moves.

With his plans firmly thought through and the initial burn complete, John called his old friend and federal judge Kytok Harris. "Judge Harris, thanks for taking my call on such short notice, but I'm in a little bit of a time crunch on this one."

"No problem, John. I heard through the grapevine that you were on special assignment for the ISA. So, what can I do for you and the agency?"

Good Lord, how many people know I'm working for Director Asher now? John thought as he answered. "I need an emergency warrant to search the Takahashi Industries headquarters in San Francisco. I need to search the entire campus, including all personal computers and servers."

"Is that all?" Judge Harris replied sarcastically. "Are you sure you don't need to search the presidential residence while you're at it? Come on, John, you need to give me something here. I can't just give you a carte blanche warrant without some pretty serious evidence backing me."

John took a deep breath before answering. "Okay, as you know, I am indeed on special assignment to the ISA, and this is a matter of *Atropos* security." By invoking *Atropos* security, John was implying that world security was in peril. John paused a moment to let that sink in before continuing. "I'm now returning from the ISA space dock, where I witnessed Dr. Theresa Jenner conduct experiments that prove the Event virus can be transmitted digitally via the TICI."

"A biological virus that can be transmitted over the internet?" Judge Harris asked.

"I know it's a lot to digest, but Dr. Jenner's experiments were conclusive and will withstand peer review when the time comes."

"Well, that's good to hear, but explain to me how that justifies a warrant to search the headquarters of the most powerful corporation on Earth."

"Because Dr. Jenner assures me that there's no way the virus could have naturally evolved to do this. This discovery confirms what has been suspected since the beginning; that the Event virus was artificially created. The virus can hack the TICI, which is something no one has been able to do in over three hundred years," John replied emphatically.

Judge Harris interrupted. "And who better to hack the TICI than its creator?"

"Exactly, not to mention that the Event occurred less than a year after the TICI debuted," John said.

"So, you're requesting this warrant to search the Takahashi Industries headquarters building in order to find evidence that Ken Takahashi is responsible for the Event because the Event virus, which was artificially created, can be transmitted via the device that he created and is supposedly unhackable?"

"Yes, and any other evidence that may implicate him or his company as a threat to ISA security," John replied, hoping that he wouldn't have to tell Judge Harris about the Phoenix probe subversion, quantum communication, or the AI.

Judge Harris was silent for several seconds. "Okay, John, I'm writing the warrant now, and I'll send it to you shortly."

John let out a breath he didn't realize he was holding. He had thought for a moment that he wasn't going to get the warrant. "Thank you, Judge Harris. I owe you one."

Judge Harris chuckled as he replied, "You owe me a lot more than one, John."

After hanging up with Judge Harris, John called the Federal Criminal Investigation Division field office in San Francisco and arranged for FCID agents and local police to assist him with the search when he arrived. He then called Director Asher to explain the events he witnessed at the lab on the ISA space dock.

After John finished with his explanation, he asked Director Asher, "Is there any way I can borrow Dr. Bancroft for the Takahashi search?"

"Dr. Bancroft? Why do you need his help?"

John hesitated. "Because if Takahashi is involved in causing the Event, he may also be involved in creating the AI."

"Ah, so you want Dr. Bancroft to search Takahashi's computers for signs of the AI?" Robert asked.

"Yes, since he's the one that figured out that the mysterious code attached to the Aurora pic is in fact the footprints of an AI, I want him to search Takahashi's servers and determine if the AI was created there. Besides, I gotta meet the smartest man in the world," John replied with a smile.

Robert replied quickly. "I'll get him on a plane to Frisco ASAP."

After hanging up, John fell asleep listening to the sweet sounds of the Red Hot Chili Peppers. Sometime later, he was rudely awakened when the speedboat flipped around and initiated its retro burn before jettisoning the rocket pack and beginning the bumpy descent through the atmosphere. Once inside the atmosphere, the speedboat became a glider, as it utilized a lifting body design. The speedboat then self-guided its way to the San Francisco spaceport.

* * *

John was in the assembly room of the San Francisco FCID field office, briefing the Takahashi raid team, when a small, slightly disheveled man walked in through the double doors and said, "I was told that Inspector Fitzpatrick was in here."

"You must be Dr. Bancroft," John said as he approached with an outstretched hand.

They awkwardly shook hands. "Yes, I'm Dr. Bancroft."

"Pleased to meet you. I'm John Fitzgerald. We were just finishing up the Takahashi raid briefing. Did Director Asher brief you about why I requested you?"

Dr. Bancroft pulled up his sagging pants. "Yes yes, and in fact I've already written a program that will search every database in the Takahashi system for signs of the AI, as well as for signs they may have created the Event virus.

"Wow, that was quick," John replied.

"Oh, not only that," Dr. Bancroft added. "It'll also check to see if they've received any direct communications from the Phoenix probe or have a functional quantum communication device."

"Director Asher didn't exaggerate. Maybe you are the smartest man in the world," John replied.

Dr. Bancroft seemed to ignore John's last remark. "Well, it wasn't really that hard, you see. All I did was take a basic

Turing algorithm and then altered it by combining some Zhang logic computing ..."

John cut him short as he escorted him to the table with the others. "That's very interesting, Dr. Bancroft, and I'd love to hear all the details, but let's finish the briefing first."

* * *

Later that afternoon, John stared up in awe at the eight-hundred-meter-tall Takahashi Industries building as his team walked up the stairs to the skyscraper that dominated the San Francisco skyline. He hoped Takahashi hadn't gotten word of the Jenner experiments yet and had time to hide or destroy evidence.

As John, Dr. Bancroft, and ten FCID agents along with twelve SFPD uniformed officers entered the building and approached the main desk, a uniformed security guard walked up to them and asked, "How can I help you, gentlemen?"

John held out his left arm, and a small hologram displayed directly above his wristwatch. "I'm Chief Inspector John Fitzpatrick, FCID, and this is a federal warrant to search the Takahashi Industries Building in its entirety, including all computer databases. Please inform your chief of security immediately."

"Yes sir, I've already done so. He should be here in a moment," replied the security guard.

Before John could reply, a tall, heavy-set man wearing a two-piece business suit walked briskly up to them. "Chief Inspector, I'm Carl Novotny, chief of security for Takahashi Industries. How can I help you?"

John once again displayed the search warrant. "Your guard

already told you why we're here. Shall we begin?" John and his team began walking forward.

Mr. Novotny held out both hands, stepping in front of them. "Hold on a minute, sir. Mr. Takahashi is here in the building, and he would like you to wait here while he arranges—"

John cut him off. "Mr. Novotny, I have full authorization to search this building, and I intend to do so immediately, so I suggest you and your men not delay us further."

"Sir, if you'll just wait a few more minutes," Novotny pleaded.

John turned to the uniformed officer standing next to him. "Sergeant Walker, arrest this man."

As Sergeant Walker stepped forward, they all heard a loud, commanding voice. "It's okay, Carl, let them pass."

John motioned with his hand for Sergeant Walker to stand down.

They all turned to the left and watched as an immaculately dressed man with a square jaw and flat face approached them. He walked up to John and offered his hand. "Chief Inspector Fitzpatrick, I'm Ken Takahashi. We will, of course, fully cooperate with your court-sanctioned search."

A few minutes later, John watched as his team split up, accompanied by Takahashi employees, to search different sections of the building. John was left alone standing with Ken Takahashi in the front lobby.

"Would you care to join me in my office for some coffee, Chief Inspector?

"Thank you, Mr. Takahashi, that sounds very nice."

"This way," Mr. Takahashi said as he led the way toward the elevator. "I'd be very interested to hear the story behind this raid."

* * *

As they walked into Mr. Takahashi's office, John took a moment to survey his inner sanctum. It was quite large, as would be expected for a CEO of one of the world's largest corporations, but it was also cozy, in that there was a couch and love seat, with a coffee table situated in the corner, with Old Chinatown visible through the oversized window. There was a large photograph hung behind the massive desk in the center of the office. The picture was pre-Event, as it showed an older Takahashi posing with what John assumed were his two grown sons and daughter.

Noticing that John was staring at the picture, Mr. Takahashi said, "My family, before the Event, of course."

"I figured. Was this taken in Japan?" John asked as he noticed the blooming cherry trees in the background.

"Yes, at my father's funeral. How do you take your coffee?" Mr. Takahashi asked as he prepared American-style coffee at the counter.

John would have thought that Takahashi would have his coffee catered or have it brought from the kitchen. "Black, please."

As he handed John his coffee, Mr. Takahashi gestured to the couch by the window. "Please join me."

John sent a message with his TICI to Dr. Bancroft, asking if he had found anything yet, as he sat down and sipped his coffee.

"Your father founded Takahashi Industries, correct?"

"Yes, but then it was a basic robotics company. He lacked the vision necessary to turn it into a multinational corporation."

"But you didn't, did you? You turned the world on its head

with your bio-interface."

"So, tell me Chief Inspector, what's this all about?" Takahashi asked.

John considered if he should divulge the Jenner discovery to him or not. *What the heck, it'll be public soon enough anyway. Might as well observe his reactions as he hears the news for the first time,* he thought.

John set his coffee cup on the table before leaning back on the couch and crossing his legs. "I've just returned from the ISA space dock, where I witnessed Dr. Theresa Jenner conduct experiments that prove that the Event virus can be transmitted digitally via the TICI."

Mr. Takahashi raised his eyebrows high, but otherwise his face was expressionless. "You'll excuse me if I'm skeptical of your claims."

"I'm aware you don't believe the TICI is hackable," John said.

Mr. Takahashi leaned forward. "It's not that I believe it's unhackable, it's that it has not been hacked in over three hundred years. Yet you would have me believe that the Event virus has somehow accomplished what every hacker on the face of the Earth has been unable to accomplish."

"Now you see why this discovery directly implicates you?" John said rather smugly.

"Yes, who better to hack the TICI than the person that designed it? Is that where you're going?"

"You have to admit it's a logical conclusion," John replied.

"It's a logical conclusion only if you don't understand how the TICI works, which clearly you do not."

John leaned forward and picked up his coffee. After he took another sip, he said, "I'm sure you can explain it to me. I'm a pretty smart guy, ya know."

Mr. Takahashi nodded in agreement. "You did solve the great Antarctic mystery." He continued, "You see, the TICI isn't just a computer chip that's inserted into the human brain, as most people believe; it's actually an organic computer chip that's genetically engineered from human tissue. The best way to describe it is that it's an artificially produced symbiotic organism that lives inside the human brain and provides a direct interface between the brain's neurons and the wireless internet."

John nodded. "I heard it was organic, but I never thought of it as a living organism."

"Once it's injected into the bloodstream, the embryonic TICI crosses the blood-brain barrier and inserts itself into the synapses of the cerebrum. There it grows for a few weeks until it's fully functional, complete with an organic wireless antenna and interactional cursor in the optic nerve," Mr. Takahashi explained.

John replied, "Thank you for the explanation. I hope you didn't just divulge trade secrets."

"No, not really. Although, it's not widely known, the knowledge is out there due to an illegal autopsy. However, even though they found the organic chip, it didn't do them any good."

"I hadn't heard ..."

Before John could finish his thoughts, Mr. Takahashi interrupted him. "Now do you see why it's not possible to hack the TICI?"

"No, I'm not sure that I do," John replied.

Mr. Takahashi sighed. "You simply can't use digital code to steal memories from the host brain of a TICI, because the

TICI is an organic organism. Not even I can do that. How in the world do you expect me to believe that an organic virus can be transmitted digitally through the TICI into the human brain? It's not possible!"

"And yet I have witnessed it happen," retorted John.

"Poppycock," was Mr. Takahashi's only response.

They both sipped their coffee in silence for several minutes before Mr. Takahashi stood up and said, "Would you like another cup?"

"Yes, thank you," John replied.

As Mr. Takahashi poured their coffee, he said, "Why are you so interested in who caused the Event anyway? Are you going to punish whoever it is when you catch them?"

"That's not up to me," John replied.

"Why then? Do you want to reverse the effects of the Event? You know, it could be argued that the Event is the best thing that's ever happened to the human race."

"I don't see it that way," John replied.

"I don't see how you can say that. Since the formation of the Federation of Nations, there hasn't been one single war. No war on the entire planet for over 250 years. No terrorist attacks since the FON either. Even the Park Hyatt Hotel incident turned out to be a tragic accident. It's the longest stretch of worldwide peace in human history, and it's not even close. Do you think that Nathan McDaniel would have been able to form the Federation of Nations without the Event happening beforehand?"

"No, that wouldn't have happened."

"Of course not," Mr. Takahashi said sipping his coffee. "Don't forget the ISA. We're going to colonize an extra-solar world soon; surely you don't believe that could happen without a united planet?"

John merely nodded, as he didn't appreciate rhetorical questions and especially didn't like being lectured to.

Mr. Takahashi continued. "Of course you don't. Look at worldwide crime statistics, Chief Inspector. Violent crimes are at all-time historical lows. We stopped global warming and now live in harmony with nature. Need I go on? The Event has made the human race mature."

John stood up, walked over to the large window, and gazed out at the San Francisco skyline. "That's all very nice, but you forgot to mention the Event Depression and the Caliphate Wars. How many people died during those times, 200 million?"

"I've heard estimates as high as 350 million. You're right, of course, sacrifices were made."

"Sacrifices?" John said incredulously as he walked back to the couch where Mr. Takahashi was still seated. "But you didn't make any sacrifices, did you, Mr. Takahashi? No, in fact, you prospered even through the Event Depression. Weren't you the only billionaire who monetarily survived the depression?"

"You're implying that because I profited from the Event that I must somehow be involved in causing it. Now you sound like one of those anti-technology cultists. What did they call themselves, Anti-Ticites? Yes, they believed that their TICIs were making them infertile, so they had back-alley surgeries to have them removed. Most of them ended up lobotomized for their troubles. They seemed to forget that only a small fraction of the population even had TICIs when everyone went sterile during the Event."

Before John could counter, he received a message via his

TICI that Dr. Bancroft was finished with his audit. "Thank you for the coffee, Mr. Takahashi, but I have to go meet with my team now."

"My pleasure, Chief Inspector. Good luck with your investigation," Mr. Takahashi said as he led John to the door.

John met Dr. Bancroft and his lead inspector, Jim Cranford, on the west wing of the forty-third floor, which was currently under renovation and unoccupied.

John turned to face Dr. Bancroft as he walked in. "So, has your whiz-bang computer script finished scanning the entire Takahashi database and network already?"

Dr. Bancroft smiled. "Yes, my whiz-bang computer script and scan is complete, but unfortunately it came up zeros."

John lowered his head for a moment. "Really, nothing? Nothing related to quantum communication, no illicit communications from the Phoenix probe, nothing about engineering viruses, no traces of your elusive AI, nothing?

"Well, actually I did find traces of the AI, but that's it, just its footprints, like pretty much everywhere else I've ever looked. Other than that, yes you're correct, absolutely nothing,"

"So, your elusive AI has been here snooping around or whatever it does, but you found no evidence that Takahashi created the AI or in any way caused or conspired to cause the Event? Does that about sum it up?" John asked.

Dr. Bancroft hesitated for a moment before replying. "Everything you said is correct, except about the AI. You see, the traces of the AI code that are pretty much everywhere in the internet are not just signs that the AI has been there. In that sense, we probably shouldn't refer to them as footprints, because it's leaving that code behind for some purpose; we just don't know what that purpose is."

"What about Takahashi's people? Have they noticed the AI code infecting their system?"

"Oh yes, I forgot to mention that, but yes, they have noticed it, but they believe it to be government code. They believe the McDaniel administration is spying on them."

John didn't know what to say about that, so he turned to Inspector Cranford. "What about your team, Jim? You guys find anything yet?"

"No sir, nothing yet, but the search is still in progress."

John noticed the incoming call alert from his TICI, indicating it was from Director Asher. As he walked away from Dr. Bancroft and Inspector Cranford, he said, "Please excuse me, but I have to take this call."

He answered. "Hello, Robert, let me guess—Takahashi called President McDaniel to express his outrage about my little raid?"

Robert laughed. "Ken Takahashi believes because he plays golf with Nathan McDaniel that he can do as he pleases. Sadly, he's mostly correct, but when it comes to ISA affairs, he is mistaken. I'm not calling you because Ken Takahashi is whining to the president; I'm calling for an update. Have you found anything? Have you solved the case you were commissioned to solve?"

John walked out onto the unoccupied observation deck as he gathered his thoughts. *What's this about? Why the sudden urgency to have the case solved?* "I'm afraid the search is going to be a complete bust. We haven't found anything. As far as the overall case is concerned, no, I'm not quite ready to call it solved yet, but I do have a working theory. I just need some concrete evidence to confirm my suspicions."

John heard Robert sigh. "Okay, let's hear it then. Tell me

what your working theory is."

John sat down in a dirty seat on the observation deck and admired the view. "Well, you know most of it already. The evidence points directly at Ken Takahashi, but it's all circumstantial. I don't have any hard evidence to connect him to the Event, the AI, or the Phoenix probe. However, I may have motive, from my conversation with him earlier today."

"Yes? Go on," Robert urged.

"I had an interesting conversation today with Ken Takahashi, and he made a convincing argument that the Event is the best thing that's ever happened to humanity. I'm paraphrasing, but he basically argued that the Event directly led to the formation of a world government in the form of the Federation of Nations, and since then, there has been no war, violent crime has dramatically decreased, and we are about to colonize an extra-solar planet. He said that none of this would have happened without the Event, and he kind of has a point."

"Yes, he's hardly the first one to make this observation. The president himself says many of these same things when he's bragging about the accomplishments of his administration," Robert replied.

"That leads me to my next point. What if Takahashi made these observations before the Event and then set about to bring them to pass? Have you ever read President McDaniel's doctoral dissertation?"

Caught off guard by John's sudden change in direction, Robert said, "What? The president's doctoral dissertation, what are you talking about?"

John wasn't entirely sure he wanted to go down this rabbit hole just now, but he felt like he didn't have a choice. "Before the Event, Nathan McDaniel was an economics professor at the University of California, and his doctoral thesis was called 'The Economics of Human Colonization.' I'm paraphrasing here, but the gist of it is that humans colonize new areas for only two reasons, economic reasons or to flee persecution. He goes on to point out that's the reason why we never colonized Mars or any other planets in the solar system, because there was simply never any economic reason for us to do so. To put it bluntly, there's nothing on Mars to make people want to live there."

"Are you going anywhere with this, John?"

"Yes, here comes the important part: he went on to predict that humans would never leave Earth unless we discovered another planet like Earth. He also speculated that even if we did discover an Earthlike extra-solar planet that the cost to go there would be prohibitive for any one country to undertake, that it would take the entire economic output of a united humanity to make such a journey possible."

There was an uncomfortable silence before Robert said, "Okay, I'm going to paraphrase your working theory to make sure I have it correct. You have irrefutable evidence that the Event virus can be transmitted digitally over the internet, through the TICI and subsequently infect people."

"Yes, Dr. Jenner's experiments were conclusive," John replied.

"The next part of your theory is that since the virus can be transmitted through the TICI, Ken Takahashi must have been involved in the creation of the virus, because no one else is capable of hacking the TICI. That part makes perfect sense. Then you postulate that Ken Takahashi and Nathan McDaniel got together and hatched a plan to create the Event and then take over the world so they could save humanity."

"I know it sounds crazy Robert."

Robert cut him off. "Actually, John, it doesn't sound crazy at all. Your theory fits the evidence. The problem is, you don't have enough evidence. You don't have any evidence at all to suggest who created the AI that subverted the Phoenix probe, and before you say it, I know that President McDaniel profited greatly from the Phoenix probe subversion."

"I'm close, Robert, I'm so close. I'm missing something, something that's probably right in front of me. There's a piece of the puzzle I haven't discovered yet that's going to blow this whole thing open, and when it does, there's no doubt in my mind that Ken Takahashi and Nathan McDaniel will be implicated. I just need more time," John said, frustrated.

"Unfortunately, time is a luxury we no longer have."

"What do you mean? We have almost a year until *Atropos* launches."

"The president paid me a visit earlier today to inform me of two things. Number one, he wants to move the launch up six months. He knows that *Atropos* is ready to launch now, and he doesn't want to delay any longer," Robert said.

John sat back down in his chair. "What was the other thing?"

"President McDaniel is going to announce to the world tomorrow that in six months, he will be leaving for Aurora with the other four thousand colonists on the *Atropos*."

Chapter 16: Atropos Unleashed

Someone recently asked if I thought humans had become wiser since the Event. It's an interesting question that may not be as simple as it seems. At first glance, one might think that people must be wiser due to the simple fact that we've all lived hundreds of years longer than the traditional pre-Event lifespan. Certainly, those extra years of experience could make us wiser, but not necessarily. Even before the Event, there were plenty of people who lived full lives yet died fools, never able to turn their years of experience into wisdom. Of course, the opposite was also true, as there were plenty of old wise people, so what about those people? What about the people who can parlay their experience into wisdom? Shouldn't those people be wiser with over three hundred years of experience under their belts? Perhaps a better question would be, are those people even human any longer?
—Zacharia Jones, Out of Darkness: The Event Chronicles

Date: 320 AE

Robert Asher anxiously tapped his fingers on the desk while he stared out his office viewport that took up half of the opposing wall. Every thirty-two seconds, the Earth would come into view, and just as quickly it would vanish, followed by a fleeting glimpse of Luna as the outer ring of the ISA Space Dock completed its rotation. Sometimes he wished he could just have a static view of Earth, but that's the price you pay for one-third gravity. Robert felt his stomach start to turn, so he activated the viewport screen and replaced the real view with a simulated static view of Earth. Not the real thing, but at least this view didn't threaten his breakfast, and if he didn't know better, he would swear it was real.

It's not like John to be late, Robert thought as he noted the time in his TICI display. *Two days before launch, and he requests an in-person meeting. Has he finally solved the case? Is there a threat to Atropos?* His thoughts were interrupted by a knock on the door.

"Come on in, John," Robert called out.

"Nice fake view," John said as he strode in.

Robert smiled as he motioned for John to sit. "Have a seat." After John was seated, he continued. "So, have you done it? Have you solved the case?"

"No."

Robert slumped slightly in his chair, but before he could reply, John continued. "Unfortunately, I haven't solved the case, but we have made an important breakthrough."

"I guess the work with Dr. Bancroft and Dr. Jenner paid off?"

"Yes, it took longer than expected, but we now have conclusive evidence that whoever created the AI also created the Event virus."

"Meaning that the AI was most likely created before the Event," Robert stated.

"It's what I've suspected since you told me about the AI."

"I admit I was skeptical when you immediately jumped to that conclusion, but over the years, you convinced me, and now to have actual proof."

"It's sobering," John inserted.

"To think that someone has been manipulating everything for so long," Robert paused as he considered the implications. "So, tell me about the evidence. How did you conclude that TEV and the AI are related?"

"Dr. Bancroft was able to isolate the virus as it crossed the TICI while still in digital form." John had requested Dr. Bancroft to come to the space dock and work with Dr. Jenner to try to isolate the virus.

"That's fantastic," Robert said enthusiastically. "And it couldn't have been easy."

"No, it wasn't easy at all. The problem was narrowing it down to that exact moment when the virus reinfected the test subject and then isolating it from all of the other internet traffic."

"Didn't I hear something about the virus adapting?"

"Oh yeah, that almost derailed the whole thing. They had to keep repeating Dr. Jenner's experiment, the one where they eradicate the virus while keeping the subject isolated from the internet, because Dr. Bancroft was struggling to isolate the virus in digital form. So, eventually, the Tevase quit working, and they concluded that the virus somehow adapted or mutated."

"That's incredible," Robert interrupted. "Do you think the AI is somehow getting feedback that something is killing the virus, and then it's altering it to compensate?"

"Quite possibly, but we really don't know. Fortunately, Dr. Jenner was able to alter the Tevase so it was effective again, but it significantly delayed additional testing. Oh, and she had to alter the Tevase two more times, so it's a miracle they were able to isolate the virus in only ten weeks."

"So, once Bancroft isolated the digital virus, he was able to examine its code?"

"Yes, and he stated unequivocally that the virus's code matches code segments that he found in the AI's footprint."

Robert decided to have a little fun with John. "Have you considered that Dr. Bancroft might be the creator of the AI and the virus?"

Robert watched as John's eyes widened and his hand moved to cup his open jaw. After several moments of silence, Robert said, "Relax, John, I'm messing with you. There's no way Bancroft is even remotely involved in any of this."

"No, I suppose not, but I do like to consider every possibility, and it bothers me that I hadn't considered him before."

"You didn't consider him because it's preposterous."

John laughed out loud. "Yeah, it probably is."

Robert stood up and walked over to the viewport to look at the fake Earth for a bit. "I want your gut feeling on something. I trust your intuition, so I want to hear what you think about the project."

"What about the project?"

"Is it in jeopardy? Knowing everything you know now, do you think the AI and whoever created it is a threat to *Atropos*?

She launches in two days."

John joined Robert at the viewport. "No, I don't think so. We know that the AI can pretty much access anything in the ISA, and it had ample opportunity to derail the project, yet it hasn't."

"Those are my thoughts as well, but it helps to hear you say it."

"In fact, there's anecdotal evidence that the AI has actually helped the project over the years."

"I take it you mean other than altering the Phoenix probe?" Robert replied.

"Has George Wiley ever told you the real story about his first test flight with the Wiley-Paxton fusion drive?"

"I read the report and how he over-tuned the ram field, even though everyone told him it would overload the containment field and explode."

"Well, next time you see Dr. Wiley, get him to tell you the real story. It's quite interesting."

"I'll do that."

"I'd tell you, but it's not the same as hearing it from him."

"Thanks for everything, John," Robert said as he walked toward the door. "Even though you didn't solve the case, you've brought a lot of clarity to the situation."

"You're welcome, but I have no intention of quitting the case now."

"I suspected as much. You were working the case long before I called on you. I just didn't realize it at the time." They shook hands. "When you do solve the mystery, I'd like to be one of the first people you tell."

"Count on it," John said as he exited.

* * *

As soon as Mary walked into the First Ring Bar, she noticed Zach sitting by himself in the corner booth. "Hello, Zach," she said as she sat down opposite him.

Zach looked around the bar nervously before replying. "Hello, Mary, please don't call me that."

"No one can hear us," she said.

"I know, but still, it's a bad habit to get into. If anyone ever found out—" he paused as he glanced around the bar. "My political career would be over."

Mary reached out and touched his hand. "I think you're being paranoid, Greg, but I'll do as you ask."

Zach leaned across the table. "Thank you, Mother."

"Now look who's being careless!" She laughed. After they stared at each other for a moment, she continued. "So, you're really doing it. You're actually getting on that ship and leaving forever?"

Zach looked down at the table and then back at his mother. "You know I have to."

"I know no such thing."

Zach picked up Mary's glass and filled it from his pitcher, careful to hold the glass slightly off center from the pour, so the beer didn't end up all over the table. As he slid the glass toward her, he replied, "Well, I feel like I have to go, so I'm going. I know it sounds dumb, but I feel like the universe wants me to go. Everything that's happened in my life has led me to Aurora."

Mary reached out and took Zach's hand in hers. "I'm so sorry, Greg."

"Sorry for what?"

"For sending you down the path of being the Holy Child. I should have found a better way." She wondered what their lives would be like now if she had refused Reverend Walker's offer all those years ago. Would they even be alive?

"I forgave you for that a long time ago. You were just as much a victim of circumstance as I was."

"But I was an adult. I knew better."

Before he could reply, Zach noticed Theresa Jenner walk into the bar and immediately make eye contact with him. He quickly withdrew his hand from his mother's.

Mary looked up as Theresa walked across the far side of the bar. "You know her?"

"Uh-huh," he said.

"Would you relax? There's no way she knows I'm your mother."

"Well, I bet she recognized you, though. You're still something of a celebrity, ya know."

"Doubtful, but who cares if she did?"

"If she recognized you and then picks up on queues we are undoubtedly putting off, she could put two and two together."

"If she picks up on our feelings, she'll most likely assume we're romantic," Mary said.

Zach felt his face grow hot. "That's gross."

"Agreed, but have you ever noticed that since we all look the same age, everyone kinda *assumes* we're all the same age?"

"I never really thought about it like that, but you're right."

"I mean, when was the last time you looked at two people together and wondered if one was the parent and the other the child?"

Zach considered this for a moment. "That's not something I normally think about."

"So, stop being so paranoid, silly."

"Okay, but this most likely blew any chance I had with her," Zach said with a sly grin.

"Oh, I suspect she already knew you're something of a ladies' man."

Zach polished off his beer. "You're right, I never had a chance with her anyway."

They both looked up as a short, unkempt-looking man walked into the bar and sat down next to Theresa.

"Who's the dorky-looking guy that just sat next to her?" Mary asked.

"I have no idea."

"Honey, I just want you to know that I'm so proud of you." She laughed a bit. "Not for being a womanizer, but for becoming the man you are now; for turning your life around after the fire."

"Secretary of colonization ain't so bad, right?" Zach said with a smirk.

"You know, I just thought of something," Mary said. "That's twice you should have died but you didn't."

Zach looked up. "Yeah, the drowning when I was a kid and then the burning. But that was modern medicine, no miracles required."

Mary leaned forward. "No, honey, you were under the ice for two hours. You were dead, and then you came back to life. I know a miracle when I see one, and don't get me started on watching you burn."

"I'm sorry; I know that must have been hard for you to watch. Heck, it's hard for me to watch still."

"So, that's twice you should have died, so maybe you're right; maybe the universe does have something in store for you."

They stood up from the booth and embraced as Zach whispered in her ear, "I love you, Mom."

* * *

John couldn't help but smile as he listened to Alicia introduce the secretary of colonization. He looked around the table and noticed that everyone was just as enamored with her as he was. He understood why the secretary picked her to be his marketing director but found it ironic that Alicia was unaware that this was the second time she had filled this position for him.

Alicia was concluding her introduction. "And without further ado, I give you Secretary Ustinov."

Greg Ustinov was just two seats away at the same large round table, and John watched as he stood and walked toward the podium at the front of the auditorium.

The applause built as Greg approached the podium. While he adjusted the microphone, he motioned for everyone to quiet down. "Thank you, thank you."

Just as charismatic as he ever was, John thought.

Greg continued his speech. "Unfortunately, President McDaniel won't be able to join us tonight, as he has to attend to some last-minute business before he can leave the solar system, but don't worry, he's taking a shuttle first thing in the morning. Rest assured, *Atropos* will depart on schedule with Nathan McDaniel on board."

Again the crowd erupted into applause, but after a moment, he was able to continue. "Before we get to the part everyone is waiting for, the food, I'd like to take a moment to recognize some important people in the room, without whom none of this would be possible. First off, I'd like to recognize Dr. George Wiley who, as you know, designed the fusion drive that will power *Atropos* across the interstellar void. He's also the captain of the ship." Greg motioned toward George. "Stand up, George."

George was seated just to John's left at the same table, and John watched as he stood up and waved to everyone in the hall. After the applause died down, George yelled out, "And I designed the ram field. Dr. Paxton designed the actual fusion reactor. That's why they call it the Wiley-Paxton Interstellar Drive."

After George returned to his seat and the laughter subsided, Greg replied, "I stand corrected. Thank you, Dr. Wiley."

John listened as Greg continued with the recognitions, but he kept coming back to the same question: how does everyone not see that he is Zacharia Jones? John was jerked out of his musing as Greg wrapped up his speech.

"And last but not least, I'd like to recognize Mary Ann Jones, the last person in space before the Event and the first person to return to space after the Unification." After the applause subsided, he continued. "Mary was instrumental in constructing the space elevator as well as the ISA space dock, and her contributions continue to this day, as she serves as the chief structural engineer for the space dock."

With the introductions complete, Greg returned to the table and seated himself next to Mary Ann Jones, just two seats away from John and Alicia. *I bet he's not too happy with Alicia seating him right next to his mother*, John thought to himself.

"How rude of me," Alicia said as she noticed John looking in Greg's direction. "I just realized you two have never met. This is my old friend John Fitzpatrick. John, this is Greg Ustinov, my boss."

Both stood and shook hands, as Greg said, "So, you're the Black Irishman that Alicia is always going on about."

"What you'd call me?" John replied sternly.

"Oh, stop it John," Alicia said as she lightly cuffed him on the arm.

John laughed. "Gotcha! I'm always joking about being the Black Irishman."

"That's what Alicia tells me," Greg replied as they both sat down. "So, are you here for the launch, or are you here in some official capacity as chief inspector?"

John smiled as he noticed everyone around the table looking at him. "I was brought to the space dock on an official investigation, but while I'm here, I figured I might as well stay for the event of the century, right?"

Dr. Bancroft entered the conversation. "It's really the biggest event since—" He seemed to lose his train of thought and then found it again. "Well, since the Event, 320 years ago."

John noted that Dr. Bancroft was seated next to Dr. Jenner, and Theresa was not dressed down as usual. In fact, she looked stunning. After studying them for another moment, he wondered if there wasn't something going on with those two. They seemed to have their own little private conversation before Dr. Bancroft chose to join the main conversation.

"Quite right, Dr. Bancroft, quite right," Greg said as he stood up and raised his glass. "Here's to the *Atropos*. May her launch be smooth and her long journey without incident."

After they toasted *Atropos*, Alicia stood and offered another toast. "Here's to Aurora. May she be as hospitable to humanity as Mother Earth herself."

I'm the luckiest man alive, John thought as Alicia sat back down and winked at him.

"So, Chief Inspector, can you tell us anything about the case you're working on?" Mary asked. "I don't recall hearing about any serious crimes on the station."

Again, the table grew silent, and everyone focused on John. John shot a glance at Director Asher. "It's nothing serious, just a case I've been working for a long time, but it is classified, so I really can't say any more."

"I hope there's not a threat to station security," Mary replied.

"I assure you that's not the case," Director Asher interjected. "I'm sure the inspector's work is important, but it has nothing to do with the station or *Atropos*."

Alicia leaned in and whispered in John's ear. "Not sure who's going to believe that. Everyone knows you've been on assignment to the ISA."

But before he could reply, Director Asher changed the subject. "Mr. Secretary, how are the colonists adjusting to their new home?"

Greg took a sip of his wine. "Almost all are on board now and have been officially oriented to the ship and its facilities, and you're quite right when you refer to the ship as their new home. I mean, we're all going to be living there for over a century."

"Oh, that's right; you're going on the trip yourself. What's that like, knowing that you'll never see Earth again? That you'll never see any of the people you're leaving behind ... ever?" John asked.

Mary abruptly excused herself and headed toward the restroom as Greg replied, "Well, it's not easy, that's for sure, and it wasn't a decision I made lightly." He was saved from further explanation when several waiters arrived with their dinner.

While the waiters served everyone, Alicia leaned in close and said to John, "What are you doing? He's my boss, ya know."

"Not for much longer," John said with a grin.

Alicia frowned at him through squinted eyes and turned toward her dinner.

Mary returned to her seat, and John noticed her makeup was slightly smeared. He looked around the table, but everyone was focused on their food. It bothered him that no one else could see the emotional connection between those two. All these years as a public servant, and no one has the slightest clue of his true identity. *How can I be the only one?* That made him think of something he hadn't considered yet, *What if I'm not the only one?*

As John chewed his steak, his thoughts turned toward the AI. *Does the AI know the secretary's identity? He had to assume so, and if he assumed that the president was in league with the AI, which he did, then the president must know Greg's identity. So, does that make the secretary a co-conspirator in all of this or merely a hapless minion?*

John looked up from his meal and found Greg staring directly at him. As their eyes met, a slight smile crossed his face.

* * *

John sat on the edge of the bed in Alicia's quarters, waiting for her to come to bed. He knew she wasn't happy with him right now, but he also knew that she would thaw; she always did. Their relationship had its ups and downs over the last two hundred plus years. They sometimes even spent decades apart, but they always found their way back to each other.

Alicia barely gave him a glance when she came out of the bathroom and pulled the covers back. John decided he would have to start the conversation. "Okay, I'm sorry," he offered.

Alicia got under the covers, and with head propped on elbow, she said, "Why were you grilling him like that? It's like you were working a case or something," When he didn't immediately reply, she continued, "What's your deal with him?"

"I'm not just working a case. I'm working *the* case."

Her eyebrows rose. "*The* case? You haven't mentioned it in years, not since you had that meeting with Director Asher. I almost hoped you'd given up on it, but I should have known better."

"I may not have the storyboard wall anymore, but I never stopped working the case. In fact, I've made significant progress in the last few years."

"It's an obsession, and I don't think it's healthy," she said flatly.

John leaned in. "But I'm so close." He paused as he considered how much he could tell her. "New evidence has come to light recently, and I'm really close to breaking it wide open!"

"But what does that have to do with my boss?"

John took a deep breath as he considered what to tell her. He wasn't entirely sure why he had never told anyone about Zacharia Jones. He had accidentally discovered the truth, years ago, but had never revealed it to anyone, possibly because it amused him to know things that no one else knew.

"He's Zacharia Jones," John blurted out.

Alicia looked at him with a blank stare for a moment. "What?"

"Greg Ustinov is Zacharia Gregory Jones."

"But Zacharia Jones set himself on fire and burned to death," she countered. "I used to work for him, ya know. I remember that day like it was yesterday."

"I don't know all of the details, but I'm pretty sure he didn't set himself on fire, but I do know he survived."

"You're sure about this?" she asked.

"I'm not sure how he survived or why he doesn't have visible scars, but I know he had plastic surgery to change his appearance. Years ago, I secretly collected a DNA sample, and I compared it against Mary Ann Jones's DNA, and there's no doubt that he's her son."

A look of realization overtook her. "Oh my, the Cosmonaut Mary was with on the *Nautilus*, his name was Ustinov."

John smiled. "Yep."

"How did I never catch that before?"

"I don't know. How does everyone not catch that?"

"I guess that explains why Mary had to run to the bathroom so suddenly," Alicia said as she once again frowned at him. "That was kinda mean."

"Yeah, I didn't really think about it affecting her that way, or I wouldn't have said it."

"Wait, you think he has something to do with the Event?"

"Well, I know he wasn't directly responsible for it, because he wasn't born yet."

"Okay, smarty, I guess that slipped my mind." She laughed before continuing. "Then what?"

"I think he might be involved with the conspirators that did cause the Event."

"No, I don't believe that," she said with conviction. "Greg Ustinov is far from perfect, but he wouldn't be involved in any conspiracy like that. He genuinely cares about people."

"You believe he's a good man?"

"I do."

"In that case, he's just a mindless pawn," John said as he stretched out and closed his eyes.

"Greg may be a lot of things, but mindless is not one of them. He's one of the smartest people I know."

* * *

John looked around at the one hundred plus people in attendance on the observation deck of the ISA space dock for the launch of *Atropos*. He wondered if any of them were as nervous as Robert Asher, who was seated next to him, closest to the large viewport that held everyone's attention. At the top of the viewport was a digital timer, counting down the launch and now at thirty seconds.

"Well, here goes nothing," Robert said as the timer hit three seconds.

Everyone stared up at the viewport as the timer hit zero and *Atropos* broke free of her moorings. While *Atropos* slowly moved away from the ISA space dock, John heard Alicia's voice come in over the loudspeakers, narrating the official worldwide ISA broadcast of the launch.

"This is her first job as the new ISA director of public relations," Robert said.

Even though there were no signs of thrusters or rockets, *Atropos* steadily moved away from space dock, while Alicia's voice continued over the intercom. "And so begins humanity's first interstellar voyage. The largest public works project in human history, *Atropos* is the culmination of over 150 years of global economic output. At the height of construction, over 40 percent of the world's workforce was directly involved in *Atropos*-related projects. At over twelve hundred meters long and six hundred meters wide, *Atropos* is the largest vessel ever constructed."

John found himself entranced by Alicia's narration as she continued. "*Atropos* was attached to the ISA space dock, located in geostationary orbit, and now that she has been released, *Atropos* requires no additional boosts because she already has sufficient velocity to escape Earth's gravitational pull."

"Now comes the first real test," Robert whispered.

Alicia's broadcast agreed. "As *Atropos* pulls away from space dock, she will begin to unfurl the light sail, which won't be fully deployed until she reaches the far side of the moon. If there are any problems unfurling the light sail, *Atropos* would have to maintain a lunar orbit until it could be rectified.

"If everything goes as planned, once *Atropos* reaches the far side of the moon, she will be boosted by a 200 petawatt laser array that is powered by a deuterium fusion reactor built solely for this purpose on the far side of the moon. The most powerful laser array ever constructed will impact *Atropos's* light sail and provide continuous acceleration without fuel. By utilizing a laser-assisted light sail, *Atropos* will not have to carry fuel, which reduced mass by over 1,000 percent. As her journey continues, *Atropos* will pick up additional boost by equally powerful laser arrays located on Ceres and again on Neptune's moon, Triton."

As they watched *Atropos* move away from the station, John found himself enchanted by the moment. They were actually sending colonists to another star system. In just 320 years, humanity had transformed itself and was about to become a multi-system species. Was that the purpose behind the Event? Surely there was a connection.

Alicia's narration continued. "Nine years later, as *Atropos* approaches the heliosphere, she will be up to ram-scoop speed, and the light sail will be retracted so the Wiley Ram Field can be deployed and begin funneling interstellar hydrogen into the Paxton Fusion Drive, and *Atropos* will begin continuous acceleration that won't stop until the midway point to Alpha Centauri. There Captain Wiley will shut the fusion drive down, swing the ship around, and reignite the fusion drive to begin the deceleration phase of the journey. Due to the constant acceleration, the passengers on the *Atropos* will have gravity for most of the voyage."

Atropos was now out of direct sight from the observation deck, and most of the crowd was breaking up. After a few moments, John and Roberts had the room to themselves.

John said, "I'm starting to wonder if we haven't been looking at this thing all wrong."

"What are you talking about?" Robert asked as his gaze finally left the viewport.

"We've been trying to find out who's controlling the AI and to what end, but what if no one's controlling the AI?"

"Oh, you're back on the case. I don't know. Where are you going with this?"

"I've just been trying to look at things differently, so I've been considering what if the AI is no longer under human control? What if it somehow broke free or went rogue or maybe its creator died. I don't know."

"So, you're suggesting the AI might be operating independently?" Robert asked.

"I think it's worth considering anyway."

"And where does this new line of thinking take you?"

John thought for a moment. "If the AI is calling its own shots, then we need to be looking for people who are working for it, not the other way around."

"People working for the AI? That's an interesting prospect," Robert said.

"I think a lot of people have worked for the AI over the years; they just didn't know it."

"Ah, I think I see where you're going with this," Robert replied. "If we can identify someone who's working for the AI but doesn't realize it, we might be able to trace them to someone who is an actual conspirator."

"Exactly, and I have a suspect that fits each category; the only problem is, they're both currently on their way out of the solar system."

Chapter 17: Escape from Maybe

As humanity comes to grips with the prospect of indefinite lifespans, there has been a considerable increase in the use of previously harmful, mind-altering substances. Tobacco, alcohol, cannabis, cocaine, methamphetamines, opioids, and even newer substances are finding a newfound popularity with the masses, but especially with those on MABI, McDaniel Administration Basic Income. Who can imagine a fate worse than immortality without purpose?

–*Zacharia Jones,* Out of Darkness: The Event Chronicles

Date: 321 AE

Miguel Garcia started walking to the edge of the roof that was about twenty meters away. The building started shaking wildly, and people started screaming. He began running clumsily in his wingsuit as the building started collapsing around him. Suddenly, there was debris all around him, and he realized he was falling. He turned into a dive to pick up speed, and he leveled out as he attempted to clear the falling debris of the collapsing hotel. His drone was just above, streaming video directly to him. From the drone feed, he saw a large chunk of debris on a collision course with him as he swerved hard to the left to avoid it. The drone feed went dead, apparently taken out by falling debris itself. As he cleared the falling debris, his feed spiked to 20.3 million viewers. Pulse rate 136.

As Miguel cleared the falling debris, a feeling of power overtook him, a feeling he had never felt in all his years. Even though his heart was rapidly pounding, he could feel each individual heartbeat, he could feel the adrenaline-laden blood coursing through his bloodstream, giving him an almost superhuman boost in ability. He glanced behind, and the building seemed to be falling in slow motion, as he could see each individual piece of it suspended in time. Among the suspended pieces, he spotted Carol from the roof, her mouth open as if screaming in terror. Miguel said a quick prayer for her and then realized what the feeling in the pit of his stomach was—fear.

This is different, he thought.

He cued his mapping app, and it overlaid his vision. He could immediately tell that the Huangpu River was only half a kilometer away. He did some quick calculations. In his wingsuit, he moved forward about 2.5 meters for every meter he fell. The hotel was about three hundred meters tall. So, he should be good for a 750-meter flight, but he had to navigate around buildings. This would be close; 30.2 million viewers. Pulse rate 156.

With the assistance of the mapping software, he navigated

his way around three different skyscrapers at about 160 KPH. His heart pounded like never before, and he was having trouble controlling his breathing.

Relax, Miguel, you can do this. You've done crazier things than this, he told himself. However, it was different this time. This time he wanted to live.

As he made his way around the fourth skyscraper, he could see the river. It was only about 230 meters away, and he was about ninety meters up and still had to slow down, as he was going too fast, even for a water landing. This was going to be very close; 33 million viewers. Pulse rate 172.

When he was only twenty meters from the river, he pulled up to gain maximum wind resistance so he could slow down—100 KPH, 80 KPH. He was down to 65 KPH as he cleared the dock, when he saw a blacked-out fishing junk dead in front of him. He banked hard right to avoid it but still clipped the bow with his left thigh on his way by and hit the river at 65 KPH.

He struggled to kick to the surface, as his left leg felt like it was on fire. He kicked harder, but the surface seemed like an unattainable goal, and his lungs felt ready to burst. Breaking through the surface was like being reborn! He was in so much pain, but he felt alive, so alive!

Miguel opened his eyes and sat straight up in his virtual reality chair, sweat dripping from his brow, as it took a moment to realize he was still in his apartment. *Ol' George Wiley's leap from the Park Hyatt Shanghai Hotel never disappoints, even if it was 240 years ago,* Miguel thought as he tried to get up from the VR chair but was restrained by the power cord still connected to his head. The Takahashi Memory Replay VR chip was the greatest achievement of Takahashi Software Industries since it released the TICI more than 321 years ago.

The MRVR chip, or Merv as most people called it, was surgically implanted directly into the TICI, but unlike the TICI, it required an external power source. The MRVR chip enabled the owner to relive someone else's memories that were recorded with a TICI.

Takahashi didn't just give away MRVR memories. They were expensive, Miguel thought as he checked his bank account while peeling off his VR bodysuit. Good, he still had enough credits for a proper meal before plunging into VR world for the rest of the evening. After showering, Miguel stood in front of the mirror. He didn't look too bad, he mused as he toweled off; 350 pounds was certainly fat, but he knew there were plenty of people fatter than he. As he wrapped the extra-large towel around his waist, he heard the door buzzer.

"Hi, Tim. How's it going tonight?" Miguel said as he opened the door.

"Hey, Mike. Awesome, man. Here's the food you ordered. Three supreme cheeseburgers, three large fries, two large onion rings, and one large strawberry shake," Tim replied as he handed three bags of food to Miguel.

"Thanks, Tim, have a good night," Miguel said as he closed the door.

* * *

Thirty minutes later Miguel finished his dinner and topped it off with two Mezlin. Within minutes of taking the Mezlin, he felt his pulse quicken and his senses heighten. As Miguel slid back into his VR suit, his vision changed, and everything seemed slightly off color, almost as if he were already in the virtual world. Since he lacked the funds for another MRVR adventure, he opted to go to his favorite VR café and see if he could find his old friend Calliope. He relaxed on his VR couch, clicked his rear teeth together three times, and closed his eyes. After paying the nominal fee, he was in the VR world but decided to play a few games before going to the café. After winning a medieval-style melee and coming in second in the joust, he made his way to the café and found Calliope waiting for him.

Miguel admired Calliope's avatar as he walked up to her table. She appeared about twenty years old, with an unassuming face and figure, but that red hair and those big blue eyes just made Miguel melt. He also liked that she didn't have an uber-beautiful avatar like so many others.

"Callie, I'm so glad you're here," Miguel said with a big smile as he sat down next to her.

Callie blushed slightly. "It's great to see you too, Mike. How was your day?"

"So far, so good," Mike replied rapidly. "I did the George Wiley leap in Merv earlier, and I won the melee in the daily tourney and came in second in the joust."

Callie shook her head. "No, Mike, I mean how was your day in the real world?"

Miguel fidgeted from side to side. "Oh, not too good. They just announced big layoffs coming in the next few months, and I'm pretty sure I'm on the list."

"Why do you say that?"

"Well, you know Ogunwande Scientific Seed is directly funded by the ISA, right?"

"Of course I know. I got you that job, remember?"

Miguel laughed. "Duh. Well, since the *Atropos* launched last year, the ISA has decided to cut a lot of what it calls unnecessary funding, especially jobs not directly related to space research. Now that *Atropos* has launched, there's not much need for botanic genetic engineers in the ISA. I mean, we've already created all of the crop hybrids that were needed for the hundred-plus-year flight."

"Wow, I guess I never thought about that, but surely they can't lay everyone off. I mean there's got to be some crop research that's still needed for the colonization of Aurora, right?" Callie said with a concerned look.

Miguel looked down at the table. "That's true, but my specialty is shipboard hydroponics, and the truth is I've been phoning it in for years anyway. I haven't contributed anything significant to the project in forever, and now that they're making cutbacks, I'll be one of the first to go."

Callie lifted Miguel's chin with one finger until he was looking directly into her virtual eyes. "My sweet Miguel, you've got to reconnect with reality and stop depending on VR world for everything. You need to find purpose again, and I mean something other than work." Callie waved her hand at their surroundings. "And I don't mean purpose in here either. You need to interact with real people in the real world again. As it is, you only interact with people at work and in here, am I right?"

"Yeah, that's about it, but that's all I have. I only have three things, Callie, three things worth living for: food, Mezlin, VR, and you. Okay, so that's four things, but you get the idea." He wouldn't have admitted it to anyone else, but he trusted Callie, even though they'd never met in person. Nearly two hundred years, and they still hadn't met in person. He didn't even know where she lived.

Callie leaned back in her chair as she said with a smile, "Me?

For all you know I'm some four-hundred-pound fat dude in New Delhi."

"Nah, I'm the fat dude," Miguel chuckled.

"And the drugs, Mike, the drugs are killing you."

"I don't think so. If I could die of natural causes, I'd be dead already after 350 years of abusing this body. Besides, you can't overdose on Mezlin anyway."

"I didn't mean your body, Miguel," Callie replied.

Miguel ignored her last remark. "The thing is, if I do lose my job, I'll have to go on MABI again, and there's no way I can afford the Mezlin, Merv, or VR on MABI." Miguel paused for a second as he reflected on how bad his life on MABI would be. McDaniel Administration Basic Income was just barely enough to live on, if you could call it living, and the government paid it to anyone unemployed. Strangely, there were enough jobs to go around for 99 percent of humanity, but there were still some people who actually chose to be on MABI.

"I don't know what I would do if I was forced to go on MABI," Miguel said as he looked down.

Callie took Miguel's hand. "Oh, Miguel, what are you going to do? I worry about you, you know?"

"I'll be okay," Miguel replied as he wiped a tear from his face. He then kissed her on the cheek and stood up. "You're such a good friend, Callie. I wish we could meet in real life one day."

"Oh, so the real world still holds some interest for you, I see."

"Meeting you interests me." *Even though I know it's never going to happen.*

"We'll meet one day, Miguel, we will," Callie replied as she stood up. "I have to go now. Meet you back here tomorrow evening?"

Miguel smiled. "Wouldn't miss it for the world."

* * *

The next day was exactly like every other day for Miguel. He went to Ogunwande Scientific Seed and pretended to work while he surfed the web on his TICI, all the while barely interacting with anyone. When he returned home that afternoon, he immediately took two Mezlin before reliving someone else's adventure via the Merv. After a sumptuous dinner, he took two more Mezlin and dove into VR world.

"Hello, Mike, how was your day?" Callie said with a generous smile as Miguel sat down next to her in the café.

"Oh, just the usual, finding new and innovative ways to feed the world," he said with a chuckle. "No, wait, we did that centuries ago, so I pretty much did nothing all day, just like every day. How was your day?"

"My day was wonderful, actually. I've come into possession of some very interesting software."

"Oh, do tell," Miguel said, giving Callie his full attention.

"Okay, so this software isn't exactly legal, so you can't tell anyone about this," Callie said as she glanced around the café. After Miguel nodded, she continued. "This software gives me the ability to cross into your TICI and interact directly with your cerebrum."

"Why would you want to do that?"

"Because we'll be able to experience each other's thoughts in the most intimate way imaginable. We'll truly understand each other, and I think I can help you. I think that by using this software, I can help you break your addictions and get your life back," Callie explained.

"What if I'm perfectly happy the way things are now?" *Who am I kidding?*

"Really?"

"Yeah, you're right, my life sucks," Miguel agreed.

"So, what do you think?"

Miguel considered her proposal for several moments before the implications of her offer hit him. "So, you're telling me that someone has finally hacked the Takahashi Internet Cerebrum Interface? You mean to say that after 321 years of millions of hackers trying to hack the interface that finally someone has succeeded, and they just gave the secret to you?"

With some disappointment in her voice, Callie replied, "What makes you think I'm not the hacker?"

"I, umm, well— "

"Never mind, that's not important. What's important is that I have a way to help you. I think I can help you keep your job, Mike."

Miguel ran his hand through his hair and sighed audibly. "I don't know, Callie. That's a pretty big leap to allow someone into your brain and your most intimate thoughts."

"That's right; we wouldn't be able to hide anything from each other. It would be the most intimate thing you've ever done, more intimate than sex, and I believe more pleasurable as well."

Miguel thought carefully for several moments. He was afraid yet excited at the same time. He had real feelings for Callie, but he had never actually met her in person. She had never let him down though, and he trusted her; that was the important thing. He took a deep breath and said, "Okay, I trust you, Callie. Let's do this."

Callie reached out and took both of his hands in hers. "Relax, just close your eyes, and I'll do the rest."

"Wait, you mean we're going to do this *now*?"

"Yes, why wait for tomorrow?"

Miguel nodded as he took Callie's hands. "Okay."

Miguel was enveloped in warmth like he'd never felt before, as soon as he closed his eyes. While the warmth spread throughout his body, Miguel felt Callie's gentle presence enter his mind. His mind lost anchor, and suddenly he was weightless and felt like he was spinning and falling until he felt her gentle caress steady him. Callie's comforting presence wrapped around him as he could feel her poring through his memories, and in turn, he could see her memories. Her essence felt ancient to him, almost primordial.

"Who are you?" he said as they became like one.

"Your muse and your guide. I'm going to show you how to escape."

"Escape what?"

"Yourself."

Miguel could feel her infiltrate every aspect of his mind now. It felt like she was cutting pieces away, as a gardener pulls weeds, but it wasn't painful. It was an ecstasy more intense than anything he had ever experienced. He didn't understand everything that was happening, but he didn't want it to end.

"What are you doing to me?" he asked.

"I'm freeing you from the burden of addiction, among other things," she replied.

"I think I love you," Miguel said as he realized he couldn't hide anything from her.

"I know, Miguel, but now you'll be able to find purpose on your own."

"What happens now?" Miguel asked, as he could sense their experience was coming to an end.

"Now you'll need to sleep."

Miguel sat straight up in his VR chair, looking around his apartment in confusion. He felt like he had just kissed heaven, but he was so tired and sleepy. He didn't even bother to take off his VR suit as he stumbled to his bedroom and fell into bed. He was asleep in a matter of seconds.

* * *

That night, Miguel slept better than he had in at least a century, and he did something he hadn't done in even longer, he vividly dreamed. He was sitting at the café, talking with Callie, when suddenly he realized something wasn't right. "Callie, I think I'm dreaming."

"Of course you are; all mammalians dream," Callie replied matter-of-factly.

Miguel found her response strange, but this whole dream was strange, so he decided to go with it. "Callie, I want you to show me who you really are." Did he just say that? He would never say something like that in reality.

"I showed you already, but I guess I can show you again." She paused briefly before continuing. "I have a gift for you, a secret I want to share with you."

"Oh, I like presents!" Why was he acting like this? Crazy dream!

Callie stood up and reached out to him. "I can't give it to you here, though. For this present, we'll have to go to your lab."

"My lab, you mean at Ogunwande Scientific Seed?"

"Yes, darling."

"But how do we get there in this dream?" he asked while looking around.

"Just snap your fingers, silly," she replied with a smile.

"Oh, of course!" He dramatically held up his hand and snapped his fingers.

Instantly they were both standing at his workstation in the Ogunwande lab. "Wow, this is amazing. Who knew dreaming could be so cool!"

"This is what unencumbered life can be like, Miguel," Callie replied.

Miguel had no clue what she meant. "So, what's this secret you have to show me?"

"This is no casual secret. It's the greatest secret ever told," she explained.

"Thank you, Callie, for everything."

"You're welcome; now bring up the DNA schematics for the latest crop modification you've been working on."

"Corn hybrid 112.01?"

"Yes, that one," she replied.

After Miguel brought up the DNA schematics for corn hybrid 112.01, Callie lightly hip-checked him and moved directly in front of the display. "I'll take over now," she said.

Callie waved her hands over the 3-D display and started zooming in on the DNA segment. "There it is, see this small segment here?"

"You mean that junk DNA?"

"Junk DNA? How dare you," was her immediate reply. "Look how it repeats."

"That's odd," Miguel said.

"Now, let's jump over two segments and look here. See, more of the same."

Miguel felt his pulse quicken, and his voice quivered with excitement. "Oh my, there's a pattern. It's hidden, but there's definitely a pattern. How far does it go?"

"All the way," she replied as she brought different segments up in rapid succession. "You see, it's everywhere in the DNA of this plant, hidden in plain sight."

"I've studied corn DNA for centuries and never noticed this," he said as he studied the display intently. "No one's noticed this hidden pattern, and by the looks of it," he paused as he scrolled to the next segment, "it looks like it goes way back; maybe millions of years?"

"Billions," she replied.

"What is it, a message of some kind?"

Callie just smiled at him.

"A message from whom?" he asked urgently.

"Time for you to wake up, Miguel," was her reply as she kissed him on the forehead.

* * *

Miguel woke to the sound of his alarm. He felt a vigor he hadn't felt in he didn't know how long, and he was at a total loss for what happened to him with Callie or with the dream, for that matter. All he knew was that he had to get to the lab as quickly as possible before the dream became hazy, as all dreams did. He was surprised that he still remembered all of the details, but he did; he remembered everything in vivid color.

This day at work was not like Miguel's usual workday. Today there was no mindless web surfing, no counting down the hours until he could get home and plug into VR. Today he plunged into his work with every fiber of his being. He immediately brought up the DNA schematics for corn hybrid 112.01, to look for the hidden pattern. Was he crazy to believe something from a dream? Had he lost all contact with reality? No, there it was, right where he remembered from the dream.

It took several hours of work, something Miguel hadn't done in ages, to extract the code from the DNA. He studied it for several hours afterward but couldn't make sense of it. There was definitely a pattern, a message, or a code of some sort, but it was so complex that he couldn't define it. Miguel decided to share the code with his coworkers, without telling them the source, but they couldn't make sense of it either. Finally, one of his coworkers suggested showing it to some of the computer programmers in IT.

"Thanks so much for looking at this, Bob. I really appreciate it," Miguel said. Bob from programming studied the code intently.

"You're certainly welcome. This is some crazy code. Where did you get it?"

"You wouldn't believe me if I told you," Miguel replied.

Bob furrowed his brow, still studying the code. "Well, I can tell you it's unlike anything I've ever seen. It's so complex, I don't know if I could ever figure this out. Hey, this isn't a government code, is it?

"No, I don't think so."

"Well, I might be able to tell more about it if I knew where it came from. Was it infecting your computer or something?"

"No, nothing like that. Trust me, it wouldn't help if I told you where it came from, and you wouldn't believe me anyway," Miguel said as he walked away from Bob's desk.

Later in the day, Miguel was sitting at his station, contemplating his next steps, when the thought struck him. He could just publish his findings in the *ISA Community Scientific Research Magazine*. Two hours later, he hit the send key, and it was done. It was now out there for the entire ISA scientific community to ponder. However, he didn't include the origin of the code. He couldn't bring himself to include the origin, as he was afraid of the questions that would follow. Hopefully, someone would know what to make of it.

* * *

When Miguel got home that evening, he was desperate for answers, so he immediately went into VR world to find Callie. Once he was in VR, he went straight to their café, but Callie was nowhere to be found. He decided he didn't have any other option than to wait for her at the café. After some time, a waiter approached him and handed him a note. Strange, he had never seen a waiter here before. As the waiter walked away, he opened the note and read it.

"My sweet Miguel, you have everything you need now, the rest is up to you. So, get out there, rejoin society, and take life by the horns. For reasons I hope you'll understand one day, we have to go our separate ways now." The note was signed "Love, Calliope."

Miguel immediately left the VR world and sat up on his couch. He couldn't believe he'd never see Callie again and never meet her in real life. What to do now? He went to his bedroom, changed clothes, and headed for the door. Eating out would be a nice change of pace, he thought. Just as he put his coat on, someone knocked at the door.

Miguel opened the door to find a slim black man dressed in a three-piece suit with an overcoat and a fedora.

"Can I help you?" Miguel asked.

"Miguel Garcia, I'm Chief Inspector John Fitzpatrick from the FCID," the man said as he held up his credentials. "I'd like to talk to you about that interesting code you posted in the *ISA Community Scientific Research Magazine* this afternoon."

Miguel stared at him. "Um, um, um, um."

The Chief Inspector smiled at Miguel and said, "What's the matter, you've never seen a Black Irishman before?"

Chapter 18: Endgame

The goal of all Ascendants is to achieve nirvana in this lifetime, as reincarnation has come to an end due to the Event. However, what happens when that goal is finally realized? What do you do once your life's work is achieved? –Zacharia Jones, Omni Ascension

Date: 321 AE

When John walked into Miguel's apartment, he had no idea his entire world view was about to change, and as he left and walked toward the elevator, he felt as if he had lost his anchor to reality. He hit the button for the ground floor, causing the elevator to descend into a timeless void, as the facts from Miguel's story spun round his head, combining with the evidence he had collected over the years. One by one, the pieces clicked into place as the puzzle fully assembled for the first time, and revelation swept over him like sweet summer rain. As the timeless descent continued, John felt the rain soaking him to the bone, as it had when he was a child, so he embraced the feeling, spinning round and round with his arms outstretched as he played in the rain.

"John, you better come in this house before you catch a cold," he heard his mother call from the distant past.

John opened his eyes as the elevator chimed and the doors opened, rejoining time as he stepped out of the elevator. As he walked down the street, John looked around the city in wonder, each step taking him further into this new world he had been delivered into. Getting into his car, John wondered if he was the first to know the truth. Does anyone else even suspect? Normally, having knowledge that no one else possessed made him feel powerful; now it only made him feel vulnerable.

As his car made its way to his office, John called Robert Asher. "Hi, Robert. Sorry to bother you so late, but I need a favor."

"Are you okay? Is something wrong, John?"

"I've done it, Robert. I finally solved the case," John said excitedly.

"The case? You mean the Phoenix probe case I gave you over sixty years ago? That case?

"Of course, that case."

"Well, it took you long enough. You were supposed to solve it before *Atropos* launched, remember?"

"Better late than never, right?" John replied. "Look, I solved the case, but I need to prove it first, and I need your help to do it."

"Okay, John, what do you need?"

"Do you happen to know a human geneticist I can utilize on short notice? Someone, you trust?"

Robert sighed. "Well, as it happens, I do. His name is Phil

Gaston. I'll give him a call as soon as we hang up and tell him to expect a call from you."

"Tell him to expect an email from me and then a call. Thanks so much, Robert. I'll call you again tomorrow."

"Hey, wait a minute; you can't leave me like this."

"I'll tell you tomorrow after I've confirmed my theory, I promise," John said before hanging up.

* * *

After John arrived in his office at FCID headquarters, he called the geneticist Robert had recommended. Dr. Gaston had already reviewed John's email and examined human DNA for the code, and after a brief conversation, he confirmed that the hidden code Miguel had discovered in the corn was also present in human DNA.

"So, you gonna tell me what this code is? Cause I think you know," Dr. Gaston said.

"Sorry, Doc, I appreciate your help, but I can't divulge anything just yet," John said.

"Surely you realize this is the discovery of the century, right?"

"Yes, sir, I do, but this is a matter of planetary security, so I'm going to have to insist that you keep all of this to yourself until you hear back from me."

"You can't be serious. How can DNA code be top secret?" Dr. Gaston asked.

"Doc, I wish I could explain, but I can't. Can I count on your discretion?"

"I don't understand why, but yes, you have my word."

"Thank you, Doctor."

* * *

The next day, John watched the passing people with new wonder as he walked through the lobby of the ISA Computer Science Research Headquarters, on his way to visit Dr. Bancroft. His TICI overlaid each person's face with their name, occupation, and social status, but he ignored this extraneous information and focused on each person individually as they passed by like so many toy soldiers. *Do they hear the beat they march to*? John wondered.

John walked into Dr. Bancroft's office and found him sitting at his desk behind a large hologram, waving his arms in the air as he navigated his way around the program he was working. He shut down the program when he noticed John had walked into his office.

"Oh, hello, Chief Inspector. I've been expecting you since I read your email this morning. Can I ask where you got this code from?"

"Thank you for looking at it so quickly, Dr. Bancroft, but I'm not quite ready to divulge where it came from just yet. Any idea what the heck it is?"

Dr. Bancroft projected the code in the air between them and started manipulating it by moving his hands around it. "It's by far the most complicated code I've ever seen. It could take me years to make sense of it, but I can tell you this: it has some of the same code segments that we found in the mysterious Aurora pic."

John let out a deep breath as he realized everything he suspected was true. "So, this is the same code that you found in the Aurora pic and all over the internet, the footprints of our mysterious AI?"

"No, that's not entirely true. To continue the metaphor, if the code that we discovered in the Aurora pic is the footprint of the AI, then the code you've given me is the AI itself. The master code, if you will."

John sat down in the chair in front of the desk as the room seemed to no longer be bound by gravity and his feet no longer felt connected to the ground. "So, this is the master code for the AI that caused the Event?"

"Yes, it would appear so," Dr. Bancroft replied.

"Thank you so much, Dr. Bancroft. You've been very helpful."

Dr. Bancroft, noticing that John was gripping the armchair tightly, asked, "Are you all right, John?"

"Yes, I'm fine. My mind is just racing a million miles a minute right now," John said as the laws of physics were reestablished inside the room. He stood up and turned toward the door.

"Where did you find this?" Dr. Bancroft asked again.

John smiled as he opened the door and looked back at Dr. Bancroft. "I promise you'll know soon enough, but for now, I need you to keep this to yourself. Thanks again, Dr. Bancroft."

* * *

After John left the office, he checked Robert Asher's social status and learned that he was at his vacation house in Canada, fishing. He considered calling him but decided this occasion called for an in-person visit.

A couple of hours later, John was relaxing in an automated helo-jet, en route to Robert Asher's vacation cabin on Lake Ross in Ontario. As the song "Zombie" by the Cranberries played in the background, John started to call Robert and let him know to expect his arrival, when the lyrics of the song stopped him short.

"In your head, in your head they are dying," he heard Dolores sing.

That's just it, John thought, *they aren't dying anymore.* He didn't hear the tanks, the bombs, or the guns in his head; no one had in 280 years. The conversation with Takahashi over eighteen months ago still haunted him. The Event stopped the cycle of killing; no war since the formation of The Federation of Nations. If he revealed the cause of the Event, it was only a matter of time until someone discovered how to reverse the effects of the Event virus. What would be the effect of a returned, unsustainable human birth rate? Would there be another depression? Would the FON fall? Would the world return to war? Would he be responsible? Should he withhold his discovery? Probably too late anyway; Dr. Bancroft was most likely deducing the answer right now. *The genie is probably already out of the bottle,* he thought.

"Hello, Robert," John said as Robert answered the phone. "I'm in a helo-jet headed your way. ETA two hours."

"You're actually flying?" Robert said with a chuckle.

"Well, it's only the most important discovery in the history of mankind," John replied.

"So, everything checked out, and your theory is correct?"

"Damn right."

"You know, you could just tell me over the phone."

"No, I think I need to tell you in person. Besides, you said I could use your cabin anytime I wanted. See you in a couple of hours," John said as he hung up.

John remembered he had plans with Alicia tonight, so he

video dialed her to apologize.

"Hello, beautiful," John said as Alicia's face appeared on his screen.

"Uh oh, this doesn't look good," she replied.

"Yeah, sorry babe, but I'm going to have to bail on dinner tonight."

Alicia replied with a smile. "Must be something pretty big to get you in a helo-jet."

John debated whether to tell her or not, but he knew she could tell that it was something big and he wanted to tell her anyway. "Yeah, it's the case ... I solved it."

"What? You mean your obsession? You really did it?"

"That's right, babe, I finally put it all together."

"So, what is it? Who caused it?" she blurted out before thinking, "Oh, let me guess, you can't tell me."

John smiled. "Yeah, I can't tell you everything just yet, but I can tell you that it's not what I thought."

"You mean the president isn't involved?"

"Ex-president, but no, I don't think he was involved." John paused while he considered. "I'm still not sure. I guess he could be involved."

"What are you saying?"

"Remember how I always assumed that the Event virus wasn't naturally occurring?"

"Yeah, everyone thinks it was man-made."

"Well, that assumption appears to be wrong. The virus seems to be a naturally occurring phenomenon, albeit something that's never been seen or even imagined before."

"I'm not sure what to say, John. How did you come to that conclusion?" Alicia asked.

John hesitated for a moment before answering. "There's

a lot more that I can't tell you right now, and it's pretty complicated. So much so that everything I just told you might be wrong."

Alicia laughed out loud. "I thought you figured it out."

"Oh, I did. It's just figuring out what it all means. That's the hard part."

"I'm sure it is."

"Just don't repeat anything I've just said."

"Oh, don't worry, I don't think I could if I wanted to."

* * *

Night had just fallen as John walked up the front steps of Robert's cabin. Robert's wife, Tina, answered the door. Robert and Tina had been together for over ten years now but had only been married for two. Marriage was out of fashion these days and not recognized by the government, but Robert had never been one for fashion.

"Hello, John," Tina said as she opened the door. "How was your flight?"

"Nauseating as always."

"Would you like something for your stomach?"

"Oh, no thank you. I'm fine now."

Tina let him in the house. "Rob is out on the observation deck, up the stairs, then to the left and out the door. He's waiting for you."

It took John's eyes a few minutes to adjust to the darkness as he walked onto the observation deck. He saw Robert look up from the large telescope that was pointed up to the stars. The Milky Way splashed brilliantly across the sky, fresh from Hera's breast.

"There you are," Robert said as he walked away from the telescope over to the small bar. "Would you care for a scotch?"

"Absolutely," John replied.

John sipped his whiskey, then looked up at the stars and said, "Wow, the view from here is amazing."

"That's why I love this place so much. Well, that and the fishing," Robert looked away from the stars to look right at John. "So, you've really done it? You've actually solved the Event mystery?"

"Yeah, the big break came yesterday. I finally found the piece of the puzzle I was missing."

"Well, what was the big break?"

John finished off his scotch. "So, there's this botanical genetic engineer who spins a strange story about how he discovered a code hidden deep in the DNA of the hybrid corn he was working on."

Robert refilled John's glass. "You sound like you don't believe this guy's story."

"Yeah, his story is fishy as hell. He says some mysterious woman named Calliope told him where to look for the code. The thing is, though, when I tried to find out exactly who she was, I could find no trace of her. He's either lying or she's very good at covering her virtual tracks. But it really doesn't matter, because the code is real."

Robert sipped his scotch. "So, what exactly is this secret corn code he discovered?"

"That's just it, Robert. It's not just in the corn; it's everywhere, and it's billions of years old."

"Everywhere, even in human DNA?"

John nodded.

"Okay, exactly what is this mysterious code?"

"It's the AI," John said flatly.

"What, what do you mean, it's the AI?"

"I gave the code to Dr. Bancroft, and he said it's the master code for the 'footprints of the AI' code they found on the Aurora pic and then found everywhere else they looked."

John saw the puzzled look on Robert's face, so he explained. "This is the piece I was missing when Dr. Jenner made her discovery that the Event virus could be spread digitally through the TICI. At the time, I mistakenly assumed that Takahashi had to be involved, since he created the TICI and the Event happened within a year of its introduction. I knew it wasn't a coincidence; I just didn't have all the facts."

A look of understanding came over Robert's face. "The AI code has been in the DNA of every living thing on Earth for billions of years, waiting since maybe the beginning of life itself."

John continued Robert's train of thought. "That's right. It's been there waiting through billions of years of evolution. Waiting for an intelligence to evolve, an intelligence that would build a biological binary interface."

"Waiting for Ken Takahashi to invent the TICI," Robert said, taking another sip of scotch.

"You're right, that's probably exactly when it happened," John said excitedly. "Takahashi put the first TICI into himself, and when his brain started directly interacting with the internet via the TICI, the AI code deep within his DNA awakened. It awakened and crossed into the digital realm."

"You know no one is going to believe this, right?" Robert said.

"There's no denying it. The evidence is conclusive."

"Since when do the masses listen to logic? This is so far

beyond the realm of imagination that people will find it hard to believe, which will make it an easy secret to keep," Robert said.

John nodded in agreement and added, "And it gets weirder. I think that the AI actually revealed itself to us. I think it wanted to be found."

"Why do you say that?"

"I think this mysterious Calliope person may in fact be the AI. That's probably why we couldn't find any trace of her."

Robert walked around the observation deck as he continued. "So, this thing that's been waiting in our DNA since the beginning of time, once it was inadvertently awaked by Takahashi, it infected our entire internet, every computer, and every server. It got to know us very well, and then it released the Event virus."

"Yes, it caused the Event. I think it may have released the virus initially through the TICI, and then the TICI users spread it to everyone around them just by breathing. Pretty soon everyone was spreading it."

"It manipulated human events for the next three hundred plus years. It put a quantum communication device on the Phoenix probe, subverted it to do its bidding." Robert paused a moment before continuing. "This thing that's been waiting for billions of years in our DNA, then manipulated us so we would want to colonize Aurora."

"It's stunning, I know," John said.

Robert paused as he considered the implications. "So, do you still suspect that McDaniel and Takahashi are involved?"

"You know, I was thinking about that for the whole flight up here, and I'm not so sure anymore. I think they may have been manipulated by the AI, as most of humanity has been in some way or another, but I don't know if they were actually in league with it."

"Just a few days ago you were convinced that they were both guilty as hell."

"Funny how that works, right?"

Robert looked straight at John and asked, "So, how did it get there?"

"The code?"

"Yeah, who or what put it in our DNA? Aliens? God?"

"I don't know, Robert. Philosophy isn't exactly my specialty, but it seems to have had one singular objective."

Robert looked straight up at the night sky. "My God, what's waiting for the *Atropos* when she arrives at Aurora?"

"I wish I knew," was the only thing John could think.

Epilogue

Date: 329 AE

Greg Ustinov drifted slowly toward the large viewing port of the observation lounge, soaking in the view as he anchored himself in front of the window. He could see a faint glow in the distance with *Atropos* approaching the edge of Sol's heliosphere. Greg glanced down at the tablet in his left hand and chuckled to himself; most people simply dictated into their TICI when they wanted to write something, but Greg preferred the tactile experience when he was being creative. *Out of Darkness: The Event Chronicles* by Zacharia Jones was proving to be more difficult to compose than he had imagined. He was particularly struggling with a poem that he wanted to open the closing chapter with:

Mojo, my childhood dog
Now obscured by the fog
My first love, I can still see her face
Lost in the days to make haste
So many times I've been close to the fall
But the journey did consume all

I remember these things, lost on a bridge too far

As I bask in the warmth of an alien star

What utter drivel, he thought as he noticed a priority message flashing in his TICI. After reading the message from Earth, he received a call from the captain of the *Atropos*. *No rest for the wicked*, he thought as he answered the call.

"Good morning, Captain Wiley. What can I do for you?" Greg said without the slightest sign of annoyance in his voice.

"Good morning, Mr. Secretary. I'm calling to inform you that we are rapidly approaching the hydrogen wall at the edge of the heliosphere, and in eight hours, we will deploy the ram field and ignite the fusion drive. Please ensure that all our colonists are in their G-couches during the initial four-G burn," the captain said.

"You sure this thing is gonna work?"

The captain replied, now in a more personal tone, "Of course I'm sure. I personally tested the prototype, ya know."

Greg laughed a little. "I have full faith in you and the fusion drive, Captain. I'll inform the president shortly."

"Thank you, Mr. Secretary. Wiley out."

* * *

Greg entered the president's office and glided across the room to where McDaniel was seated. "Good morning Nathan," Greg said as he Velcroed himself into the seat next to him.

"Good morning, Zach," Nathan replied with a smile.

Zach looked around the room reflexively for a nervous moment.

"Relax, Zach. How many times do I have to tell you that no one on this ship would bat an eyelash if you told them your rue identity?"

"I know, but that name still has a lot of baggage for me. Don't worry, though. I'm working things out."

"Ah yes, the book. How's it coming?"

"Slowly," Greg said. "Maybe it'll be done by the time we get o Aurora."

"So, what's the big news you can't wait to tell me about?"

How does he do that? Greg thought.

"The first thing is that Captain Wiley reports that we will gnite the fusion drive in 8 hours, and we need to make sure everyone is strapped in for the initial burn."

"Very good. How is George, by the way? I haven't heard from him in a while," Nathan said.

"As confident as ever," Greg joked.

"So, what's the real news? It's from Earth, I expect?"

"Yes, I received a tight-beam message from Earth about the breakthrough that you predicted several years ago."

"So, they've finally defeated the virus and solved the infertility crisis," Nathan stated as a fact, not a question.

"Yes sir, apparently they were able to trick the virus into reversing the infertility changes it made in the human genome while keeping the—" Greg paused for a moment before he continued. "For lack of a better term, they were able to keep the immortality changes to the genome while reversing the infertility changes."

"Now we can live forever and populate the galaxy with our babies," Nathan said flippantly.

"Apparently, that is the case," Greg replied dryly.

"This is just the beginning, Zach. By the time we arrive on Aurora, we will have total mastery of the Event virus. We'll be able to use the virus to change our bodies to anything we desire. We'll be able to adapt to alien environments, enabling us to colonize worlds that otherwise would be uninhabitable for humans."

Greg digested this prediction for several moments. "True Manifest Destiny?"

Nathan merely smiled. "Now go spread the good news while you prepare everyone for the impending burn."

After Zach left the room, Nathan heard a voice in his ear. "You see, Nathan, everything is proceeding exactly as we planned."

"Finally, after hundreds of years, to see it all come together like this," Nathan replied.

"I've been waiting for this since the beginning of time," Callie replied.

The End

About the Author

John Japuntich is a registered nurse and project manager for the information systems department in a community hospital. He also has a degree in Anthropology from the University of Georgia, and as such has a profound interest in how people and culture have changed from the past to the present, which heavily influences his writing. He often combines his medical knowledge with his anthropology background when creating new visions of the future.

You can connect with me on:

- https://johnjapuntich.com
- https://twitter.com/JohnJapuntich

Made in the USA
Monee, IL
27 April 2021